MW00604004

Ollie's World

Linda Sealy Knowles

For Get Me Not – Winged Publication
(Where stories take flight)

ISBN: 978-1-956654-81-3

With Love

To my friend, Rick Ward, who enjoyed the Maxwell Saga and inspired me to write Ollie's World. I am eternal grateful for his encouragement.

A personal note

To my friends, readers and fans. . .

Many of you have requested that I continue writing about Jesse and Rae Maxwell, in the Maxwell Saga. In these stories, Miss Ollie came back into my life. Miss Ollie was a servant for my grandparents on their small farm in Limason, Alabama. The last time I visited with her, I was about twelve years old. When we visited my grandparents, I spent my time in the kitchen with her.

Ollie will always have a special place in my heart.

"Ollie Worlds" is a fun-filled story with many exciting events taking place with all the other characters in these stories. Miss Ollie tell stories about her life as a small child. You'll laugh and maybe shed a tear, but I feel you will enjoy this story.

As I sat at my computer writing, I could feel each character as if they were alive. I hope you will have the same effect as you read about them.

Other books by Linda Sealy Knowles

Maxwell Saga
Journey to heaven Knows Where Book 1
Hannah's Way Book 2
The Secret Book 3
Bud's Journey Home Book 4
Always Jess Book 5
  Ollie's World Book 6

****

Kathleen of Sweetwater
Sunshine Brides
Trapped by Love
Joy's Cowboy
Abby's new Life
The Gamble
A Stranger's Love
Anna, the Lawman's Problem
Forever Mine

Chapter 1

In the bright summer sun, Hope Maxwell, big with child, wobbled down the sandy, dirt lane that led to her sister, Rae and brother-in law's Jesse, ranch house, while her two children raced ahead. Jay waved at his friend, Boo, who was standing at the gate waiting to enter the yard. Bud Downey, husband of Rosie, a lifetime friend and neighbor of Will and Hope's had come over earlier and left Boo to play with the children, while he rode into town with Will.

"Morning Boo," Hope said as the children raced around the yard and hurried to the big shade tree in the middle of the well-groomed yard. Hope warned them not to stomp on Rae's pretty flowers surrounding the tree. Willa climbed like a monkey while Boo gave Jay a boost to a lower limb as he scooted up the large, old tree trunk.

Hope could hear laughter coming from the children as she entered the porch and flopped down in the comfortable, padded chair that Miss Ollie sat in all the time.

Just then Ollie walked out onto the porch with a cold pitcher of lemonade and poured both of them a glass. She sat down in a straight chair.

"Oh, Miss Ollie, I'm sorry. I sat in your chair," Hope attempted to push herself up.

"No, stay right where you is, child. I'm fine right here, and I can see the tops of those young'uns heads, too." Ollie passed Hope a glass of cold lemonade and a pan filled with freshly picked green butterbeans.

Hope reached for both and sighed. "I'm so hot. My belly is so big I can't hardly put this pot of butterbeans in my lap." She kicked off her sockless shoes. "I'm gonna sit right here barefoot with my pantaloons and skirt pulled up around my knees. If the men folk don't like it, they can just look the other way or go back to the barn."

Ollie giggled and shook her head. "My goodness child, you ain't wearing no shift or petticoat, and you're sitting out here practically naked. You're a mess for sure. Have you being having any pains? Is Dr. Tim right that you only have two more months?" She casted worried eyes at Hope, whom she called her baby, because she helped raise her from the age of three.

"Yes, I have a big pain every day and it's called Will. Lordy, that man is trying my patience, if I ever had any." Hope looked toward the door, expecting her tall, handsome husband to come looking for her any minute, when she remembered he had gone into town. "Thank goodness that man has got something to do for the next few hours. He guards me like a dog with a big bone."

"Child, you knows that man loves you better than himself." Ollie took a sip of her lemonade. "Shoot, this stuff needs more sugar."

Hope leaned back in the comfortable chair and fanned herself with a soft hanky. "Miss Ollie, as many years as I have lived here on this ranch and now next door, I know so little about you. Rae has told me bits and pieces about your life, but nothing that I really remember. You know I was just a little girl, about three when I came here with Rae. Oh, I have many memories of you taking care of me, making cookies, and rocking me to sleep. I loved you like you were my mama. Well, I don't mean that I don't love you now. It's just I remember how I followed Will everywhere and he tried many times to spank my bottom, but you and Hank wouldn't allow him to touch a hair on my head." She sighed. "Guess I've always loved that big bully as long as I remember."

Ollie nodded. "I can remember how much he disliked all the boys that came sniffing around the ranch wanting to court you. He was one jealous young man."

"Come on now, Miss Ollie, tell me how and when you came to live here on this ranch. I do remember Rae said something about you being just a young lady. How old were you and did you come as a slave?"

Screams and squeals came from the front yard. Willa, Jay and Boo were jumping up on Will's body as he tossed Jay on his back, while holding Willa in his arms, and Boo was riding on his long, booted foot.

Hope and Ollie pushed up from their chairs to watch the excitement. The three children always loved to grab a ride on Will's tall frame whenever he came around.

"Shoot fire, Ollie, I thought he was gone for a while. Wonder why he's back so soon?"

"Run along and play now," he said to the children while patting Willa on the bottom. "I've got to check on your mama." Will watched the children run back to their tree house then walked over to the porch. "How's my two favorite girls this morning?" Will asked, as he reached for Hope's glass of lemonade and drank it down in one big gulp.

"What are you doing back so soon? I thought you were going into town with Bud," Hope pasted on a forced smile.

"We were on our way when we met Mr. Downey and Tater leading two ponies that they had found in a big gully on the edge of their property. One of the ponies had a bad cut on its side, so Bud decided to take them back to his pa's place. I told him I could wait and go into town tomorrow, so here I am." He rattled the glass of ice.

"Give me that glass and I'll fill it up for you." Ollie reached for the pitcher when Hope held up her glass. "Please, Ollie, pour me a fresh glass as well. I'm so hot and thirsty." She glared at Will.

***

Will laughed, gave her a sassy grin, and walked into the kitchen. He lifted the lid on the big pot simmering on the stove and smelled deeply. Ollie was preparing a delicious beef soup for lunch. Two large cakes of baked cornbread sat on the table and a fresh blackberry cobbler covered with a soft white cloth that was stained around the edges with the juice of the berries.

Whistling, Will strolled back onto the porch with Ollie and his sweet wife. "You better shell those beans if they're going to be part of supper." He turned the pitcher up and poured himself another glass of lemonade while watching the daggers shoot toward him from Hope's eyes. Man, he could rile her with just one word lately. She acted like a cat with its tail caught under a rocking

3

chair. "How have you been feeling this morning, sweetheart? Can I do anything for you?"

"Yea, pray for snow," she responded sarcastically.

"Oh, honey, believe it or not, the babe will be here before you know it." Will gave her a sweet smile, but she didn't return it.

"I guess I better go out to the corral and see if I can help Hank and Jess with the new calves. A couple of them are having to be bottle fed for a few days." He stood and leaned over and kissed Hope on top of her head because she refused to lift her face so he could kiss her Rosie lips. Whistling the same tune, he strolled around the side of the house to the corral.

***

"Now, you listen to me child," Ollie scolded Hope as soon as Will was out of hearing range. "Will is a good husband to you and you are so mean to him. You have got to behave yourself and be the sweet wife he married. He can't control this hot weather and he can't help how you feel carrying that new baby. I know one thing, and you think about what I am saying." She looked side to side to make sure no one overheard her. "He didn't get you in this situation by himself."

Hope pressed the glass of cold lemonade on her forehead. "I know. I'm just so miserable, and I guess I want him to know it." Hope wiped the sweat from her neck and leaned back. "I'll be better, I promise, if you will tell me about your life." She grinned and pushed on Ollie's knee.

"Oh, all right." Ollie sighed and leaned back in her chair and thought for a moment. "Let me see . . . where to begin." Her fingers worked fast as she started shelling the beans. "I will start back as far as I can remember when I was a small child.

Chapter 2

"My folks were field hands on the Waverly Plantation--
that's about twenty miles north of here," Ollie said. "I was about
four, I think. My folks worked out in the hot fields picking cotton,
butterbeans, or corn from daylight to dark every day. I was too
little to work and too little to be left alone at our shack. Each day,
mama flopped me down at the end of whatever row she had to pick
or hoe.

"You think you're hot now? Well child, I can remember it was
awful hot with that sun bearing down. My mama cut a hole in a
piece of a box and made me a big hat. It was a little uncomfortable
on my tiny head, but at least it kept the sun from beating down on
me. One day as I played with my pet, a tiny, roly-poly bug, the
master of the plantation came driving by the fields with his wife
and little girl. Everyone kept working, but I stopped playing and
watched them. They were the prettiest-looking people I had ever
seen. The master got down and hailed one of the slaves to the end
of a row and spoke softly with him. The little girl jumped down off
the carriage and ran over to me.

Her mama called for her to come back and get in the carriage,
but the pretty little girl acted like she didn't hear her. She was
dressed so fine in a green dress with a white pinafore overlay. She
had long blond ringlets with two big hair bows holding her hair off
her face.

"What you got in your hand?" she asked me.

I quickly hid my hand behind my back and mumbled,
"Nothing, just my pet."

"I want to see it, now. Show me!" she demanded.

"I saw her mama getting down out of the carriage and begin
walking toward us. My mama was watching, standing as still as a

statue looking my way, very upset.I finally held out my hand and showed the bossy girl my pet. It had rolled into a tiny ball.

"Where is your pet? I don't see anything."

"Right here. It's rolled into a ball. You done scared it," I said.

"That isn't a pet. That's a nasty bug." Just as her mother reached us, the bossy girl slapped my palm, and I dropped my precious bug. It had fallen into the tall weeds growing all around my bare feet.

"Patsy, you heard me calling you. Get back to the carriage this minute." Her mama placed her delicate hand on her daughter's shoulder, but she jerked away.

"No! I want to play with this little girl. I want her to come home with us. My mama finally was able to get enough nerve to come to the end of the row in the field where I stood frozen. The girl screamed and her mama begged her to be quiet.

"I'm sorry," the master's wife said, looking at my mama. "Patsy is hard to handle sometimes. We must go now." She grabbed Patsy by the hand and practically dragged her toward the carriage until the master witnessed the ugly scene his child was making. He hurried over and picked her up and shook her good to make her stop screaming. Then he whispered something in her ear. They drove away, heading to the big house on the other side of the field.

"Mama, I didn't do nothing. She wanted my bug, and she slapped my hand and now I don't have it. I didn't say anything to the Master's woman, I promise you."

"I know child. I've got to get back to work. You just sit and we'll have lunch in about an hour. I'll take you to the outhouse then."

"Good Lord," Hope said. "You had to sit out in the heat all day, every day, with no toys or anything?"

"Toys? Child, I had nothing, but I did have my folks in the fields. Anyway, the next day, the master came driving out to the fields and stopped at the end of the row where I sat playing with a few sticks.

"Which one of those darkies is your mama?" He actually spoke to me. I was so shocked I just pointed at my mama who had stopped hoeing and started stepping over the rows coming toward me. By the time she reached the end of the row, she was trembling.

6

"Is this child yours?" he asked.

"Yes sir, Master." Mama looked down, almost in tears. She grabbed me and pulled me into her skirt front.

"My little girl, Patsy, wants her—' He was looking down at me,' --to come and play with her at the big house. I would like for her to come and stay at the house for a few days, day and night, and see if they can get along. My child needs a companion, and she wants your little girl to be her friend. Your child will be better off at the big house than sitting out here in this heat. What do you say?"

"Whatever you want, sir." My mama knew she had to do whatever the master wanted. At least he was asking, instead of demanding.

"Good, pack her belongings and bring her to the house after you complete your work today."

"Sir, she ain't got no more than what she has on her body." Her mama held her head down, embarrassed that she couldn't care better for her child.

"Before you bring her, stop at the commissary and pick her out three complete outfits-- dresses, shoes, underthings, and gowns. I will take care of the expense if your child gets along with mine. If not, we'll keep her new things when we send her back to you."

"Well, honey child, you can't imagine how happy my parents were. They was so proud that they had a child who was going to stay a few days in the big house. Later that day, when mama took me to the big house, all bathed and dressed in my new duds, she warned me that I better behave or she would beat me."

"I guess she was happy that you were finally going to get a better life than she had," Hope said.

"Shucks," Ollie commented, "I better call the young'uns in for lunch because the men folk are washing up at the back door.

***

Will entered the dining room with a clean Willa, Jay and Boo. They hurried and took their seats at the table and waited quietly. Early on they had learned that if they misbehaved at the table, Ollie would get her wooden spoon after them.

Jess, Hank, and John came into the dining room with clean faces, hands and wet hair. They had all stopped at the back door and washed up before coming to the table. They removed their work boots, too.

"All you fellows take your places and one of you bless this hot meal before you dig in," Ollie demanded since Jesse and Rae were out of town and the blessing was one of Jesse's responsibilities.

"I want too," cried Willa. "May I, Daddy?"

A big sigh of relief was heard all around the table as Will grinned at the excited face of his lovely little girl. "Of course, Sweet Pea. Go right ahead."

Willa waited for a second to make sure all heads were bowed and eyes closed. "God, bless this good food, bless Miss Ollie, my mama and Hanky. Bless Daddy, and my dumb brother. Amen." Several snickers were heard from some of the men.

"Willa, dear, you did a good job except for the last part. You had better work on your blessings before you ask to say it again." Hope glanced at her precious little girl with an admonishing gaze.

"Well, he's dumb," she said, as Jay reached to sock her, but he saw Miss Ollie watching and probably decided he would get her later.

"Jess," Ollie asked. "Where is Mary Beth today? Has she gone into town?"

"Actually, Dr. Tim, had to go out of town for a day or two, so she's gone to help Hannah at the office. She is going to stay with her until her pa comes home."

"Well, you just come here for your meals. One more won't matter," Ollie said, as she slipped onto the bench and filled herself a bowl of soup.

"Boo, how's Rosie and Justice doing? I haven't seen them since Sunday afternoon. Is Justice doing well?" Ollie asked as she tasted her food.

"Yes, ma'am. She said she was coming to see you today," Boo blew on his soup. "I guess she is waiting until it gets cooler before she comes over."

"I'll sure be glad when Papa Jesse and Rae get home. I know Rae is having a grand time shopping for fancy dresses while papa is selecting a few good horses. The train from Dallas should be arriving in about three days. Maybe they will be on it," Hope said.

"Miss Rae didn't know how long they were going to be away. It doesn't seem possible that they could be married twenty-five years. Sure don't. You was just a little tyke when Jesse brought you and Rae to stay here for a few days. You were the prettiest little girl I had ever laid my eyes on." Ollie's eyes held a faraway gleam.

"Ollie, I can't remember that day, but I remember many wonderful times helping you cook, and when we made jars of blackberry jam." Hope giggled as she remembered picking the berries with Ollie and a snake crawling between Ollie's legs. She screamed and kicked the snake and then peed on herself.

"All right now. I know you're remembering that snake that nearly caused me to die a natural death out in those briars. I threatened to whip you good if you told anyone that I embarrassed myself after kicking that snake and then beating it to death with my long stick." Both of them laughed until tears shined in Hope's eyes.

***

"Come child and help me place those two dozen pork chops in this big pan. I am going to bake them now so the kitchen will be cooled off for supper. I have already washed the butter beans and I will put them on to cook."

"You want me to peel the taters and get them ready to cook. We still have two fresh loaves of bread for supper. I told Will to stop at Rebecca's bakery and get one of her pound cakes, if she has one. If not, get any kind of cake for dessert tonight. We still have a bowl of fresh strawberries."

"Willa, you want to help mama wash the potatoes when I peel them?" Hope asked, as her six-year-old daughter came into the house.

"Yes ma'am. Can I wear an apron?"

"Sure thing, sweetie pie. All cooks wear aprons, except your mama. She says it's too hot."

Ollie wrapped an apron around Willa's tiny waist and then took a white tablecloth and covered the soup, leftover cornbread and cobbler left from lunch.

"Now Ollie, you sit down right here, drink you tea and rest while we peel these taters. Please start on your story again. You left off when that little girl Patsy was going to have a birthday party.

Chapter 3

"All right, but it is hard to watch others work." Sighing, she sat down and put a spoon full of sugar in her tea. After taking a sip, she said, "By now, I had lived in the big house with Patsy for nearly two years. We were both six years old. Her parents decided to give her a big party to celebrate. All the master's White friends, their wives and young children, were invited. No one would dare miss the party for the master's child, since he was the biggest land and slave owner in Mississippi. He was an important man and no one wanted to get on his wrong side."

Ollie took another sip of tea. "Patsy had many presents and all the young'uns sat around the fine dining table. The birthday cake was the prettiest thing I had ever seen. Patsy's mama lit the six candles and stood Patsy in her chair. The children sang Happy Birthday while Patsy blew out the candles. One of the house maids giggled near the curtain where I stood, out of sight, and said that the brat probably spit on the cake." The other housemaids laughed.

"It was my birthday, too. I was six years old. Mama told me that morning, before she left for the fields. Funny, how me and Patsy shared the same day of birth. Of course, I wasn't invited to the party. Patsy wanted me to come. She tugged on my arm trying to make me come into the dining room, but her mama said no and made her turn me loose.

One of the house servants done told me that I was a darkie and darkies didn't get invited to White folk's parties. So, I hid behind the heavy drape in the dining room and watched the big celebration. I couldn't stop the tears from sliding down my face. Margaret, the oldest, house servant, pinched my arm and said for me to be thankful for what God had given me, instead of bawling for cake and presents."

"When she saw more tears falling, she continued, 'Child, God done give you a nice roof over your head, clothes and shoes to cover your body, a full belly every night and a clean room to sleep with many people to watch over and protect you. You are a blessed child, and don't you forget it. Now dry off those tears and be happy for that spoiled child who you're forced to take care of.'

"I sho tried to be good and thankful, but it was hard to watch Patsy open up a lovely doll that had long, blond pigtails. It was the prettiest baby doll I had ever seen. Patsy took the doll and tossed it on the floor as she grabbed another present.

Well, after that day, I never shed another tear until years later. One night Patsy's mama told her to pick up her toys before she went to bed. Of course, Patsy didn't do it so when her mama came into the room, she was furious. The next thing I knew she blistered my behind. She screamed it was my fault that Patsy misbehaved. From that night, I did whatever Patsy's mama told her to do. I helped Patsy pick up her toys or get her undressed for a bath. Many nights Patsy and I wrestled until I got her undressed. I wasn't going to let her mama whip me again because she was an unruly child. She climbed in bed like a little angel, and I laid down on my palette beside her bed."

Hope sat up in the comfortable chair, stopped peeling the taters and stared open-mouthed at Ollie. "You mean to tell me that Patsy's mama beat you because her own child misbehaved? How cruel was that!" Hope faced flamed red. "You didn't have your own bed in the little girls' room? You slept on the floor? Mercy, I can't believe how mean a person could be to a child."

"Sleeping on the floor wasn't new to me, honey child. I slept on the floor in front of the potbelly stove when I lived in the shack with my folks."

"You sure have opened my eyes to appreciate the small things in my life." Hope shook her head and gave Ollie a sad smile.

"Did you sleep on the floor when you were a little girl mama?" Willa asked.

"No, of course not, sweetie. Now listen to Miss Ollie. She's telling us about her life as a little girl."

"You know the best thing I loved about caring for Patsy was getting a chance to learn. You see, her mama hired a tutor to come out almost every day to teach her to cipher and read. Patsy hated learning. She gave the young, hawk-faced man fits. The tutor had gotten so upset with her that he finally made her recite sentences over and over until she memorized the words. Then when her mama came in the classroom to get a report, he would have Patsy read the sentences out loud to her.

One day the teacher saw that I was learning to read. He'd flash a word for Patsy to say, but she couldn't. She just defied him by looking out the window. I would mouth the word correctly and he saw me. One day, when Patsy was in the water closet, he told me to never let any White person know that I could read or cipher numbers. He said he would get in trouble because he wasn't paid to teach the slaves' children. White people didn't want an "uppity" Negro around them.

'I won't tell no-body.' I made the sign of the cross over my chest, just like I had seen other servants do many times. The tutor laughed and patted my head as we waited for Patsy to return to the classroom.

"One morning, Patsy and I was woke up by a house servant who was in our bedroom. She was packing all of Patsy's clothes and playthings. I was told to get my belongings together and take them down to the servant's quarters. 'Violet will show you where to put your things.'

Patsy and I had no idea what was going on. She told me that they were probably going on a trip with Papa. Later, I asked about Patsy.

'Child, Patsy is going away with her mama and she will not be coming back. Her folks are taking her to an all-girls schools up north.' I remember crying for the loss of my little friend. Patsy was going to hate that new school. Her mama would soon learn that the tutor didn't teach her little girl anything."

"But, Ollie, how old was this Patsy?" Hope wiped her hands on a tea towel.

"I reckon she was about seven years old. I never got to say good-bye to her. But, later I was told that I wouldn't have to go and work in the fields, like my folks, but I would continue to live and work in the big house. I was going to be a kitchen servant. Oh, I was thrilled, but I didn't show my excitement. I knew that every day I would have plenty to eat."

"Is this where you learned to cook and bake?" Hope asked.

"Sure was. This one old woman was having trouble with her hands rolling dough and pinching biscuits, so she taught me to do it. Later, she taught me to make pie crust and dumplings. I stood on a small stool while the old woman hummed, and I rolled and pounded out the dough. I loved working in the kitchen, and I didn't mind washing dishes."

"Goodness, Ollie. Look at our little helper. She has fallen asleep at the table. She's too heavy for either one of us to move her. I'll go to the back and get John's attention." John worked on the ranch part-time and on his flower farm with his wife Katie, who was Rae's aunt.

In a few minutes, John carried Willa to the front bedroom and pushed the curtains back so a breeze could flow in the window. "She looks just like an angel," John said.

"Thanks, John, and tell Aunt Katie hello." Hope and Ollie watched him walked back to the corral to saddle up his horse.

Hank came up the back walk and removed his boots on the porch. "Howdy ladies, how about a big glass of something cold? It's too blasted hot to stand out in the sun and walk around and around with those new colts." He had worked for Jesse's and Will's papa while he was alive and stayed on to help Ollie raise the two boys.

Chapter 4

After Will watched Jess move all the colts back in the corral, he told Hope that he was going to their house and work on the new baby's room. He was building a new cradle, even though they still had the other one. Will wanted the new baby to have its own cradle. He would see them at supper.

Later Ollie, Hope, Willa and Jay were sitting at the kitchen table having a light snack before the supper hour. The barking of Jay's dog was getting on Ollie's nerves. Using her wooden spoon, she hit the table. "Jay, give that dog a treat to hush him up."

Jay slid from his chair and walked to the front door. Two Pawnee Indians entered the back door, just staring, looking all around. The two men were dressed in brown buckskin shirts with beading around the neck and buckskin pants that covered the top of their soft moccasins. They wore a brown, beaded hairband to hold their black hair out of their faces. Their skin was bronze with a tint of sunburn.

"We have uninvited company," Ollie said, very calmly. "Jay, run and find the men." Whirling to Hope, who had turned white as death, Ollie said, "Don't show fear." Hope nodded, while pulling Willa as close to her body as she could.

One of the Indians stepped over to Willa and picked up one of her long blond pigtails. She tried to wiggle further away from him. He took his knife from his scabbard and twisted the long pigtail in his hand. He was ready to cut it, but Hope snatched the hair from his hand and moved Willa away from the man. He mumbled something to his friend and both men laughed.

The other Indian turned to the table and lifted the tablecloth. He smiled and poked his dirty finger into the big bowl of soup. He sucked his finger and moaned, "Good."

Ollie was shocked at the dirty Indian's actions. She held her big wooden spoon and before she knew it, she hit the man on the knuckles. The Indian howled and shook his hand. She pointed at the chairs and said, "Sit."

The two men glared at each other. Looking toward the door, both men eased down into the chairs and watched Ollie's every move. She filled two bowls of cold soup and placed them in front of them.

One man picked up the bowl and slurped it down before his companion even got his. He held up his bowl for more. Ollie quickly passed him a glass of cold tea and he drank it down in one big swallow. He let out a big burp and grinned big at Ollie. "More," he said in perfect English.

Ollie poured him another glass of tea and reached for his bowl. She refilled the soup bowl and passed him a plate of cornbread. He pulled several pieces off the plate in front of him and said something in Pawnee to his partner. After getting their fill of food, one of the Indians said, "Come," and rose from the table.

***

"Where boy, Jesse." The two Indians walked to the door and stepped out onto the back porch when they saw Hank and Jess hurrying from the barn with their rifles.

The two Indians stood and watched the men approach. They stepped down from the porch and held up their right hands in a sign of friendship.

Jess raced up to the two men and laughed, while holding his hand up in a show of friendship.

"Where's your leader, Jesse? Come to talk. Need meat for my people."

"Spotted Horse, meet my friend, Hank. Who's this man?" Jess had remembered meeting the Indian when he was a young man on the range with Jesse.

"Little Owl. He's wise Indian who needed to meet my White friends."

Jesse and Hank nodded toward Little Owl and invited them back inside the house.

"No," Spotted horse rubbed his stomach. "Belly full. I want black woman to live in my teepee. Great cook."

Jess tried to hold back a grin, but he couldn't contain his

laughter as he replied, "Miss Ollie belongs here with us. I can't allow you to have her, but I know that if Jesse, my pa, was here, he would give you almost anything else you wanted."

"Beef. We need meat. Buffalo gone far away. We will hunt them later, but need food now. My women and children are hungry."

"I understand. Hank and I will ride out on the range with you to cut out a dozen steer. Do you want a milk cow or two?"

"Good, children drink milk," Spotted Horse smiled.

"Let me go and tell Miss Ollie where we're going. Go with Hank while he saddles up our horses," Jess said.

Hope hugged Jess and thanked him for coming so fast. "Where's Jay?" she asked.

"Here I am, mama. I did great, didn't I, Uncle Jess? I ran as fast as I could and told him that Indians were in the house."

"You sure did boy. He nearly scared me and Hank to death," Jess commented, with a little laugh.

"Hope, please don't be afraid. These Indians are friends of Pa. They want some beef to feed their people while they hunt the buffalo. Hank and I are going into the north pasture and cut out a dozen or so cattle for them. Do we have extra flour and sugar that we can give them?" Jess asked Hope.

"I'm sure we do, and if not, we can go into town and replace what we give them. There should be a barrel of sugar in the cellar and flour is in the pantry. Come and I will show you."

"Ollie, Jess wants to give the Indians flour and sugar. Is this all right with you?" Hope asked as she waddled toward the pantry.

"Of course. Flour is in the pantry and sugar is down in the cellar. Actually, the flour is still in the bag and the sugar may be, too. I haven't been in the cellar for a while. Hank will know for sure."

"We haven't had lunch but we'll be back before supper," Jess said.

"Mama, can I go with Uncle Jess? Please!?" Jay pleaded, while Hope looked skeptical.

"Let him go, Hope. He can ride in front of me."

"Jay, you mind Uncle Jess and behave around the cattle," Hope said.

Jess, Hank and the two Indians rode about mile onto the open range and cut out a dozen steer and two milk cows. As the two men were preparing to depart with the gifts of food, the older Indian rode real close to Jess and said,

"You know I am big chief of my people. I make black woman my wife. She cook in my teepee just for me. I bring you many furs this spring for her."

Hank overheard the Indian trying to bargain for Ollie. "Sorry, Chief, black woman is not for sale. She is already somebody else's woman. You take the beef, sugar and flour and be on your way."

Watching the men herd their new cattle down the valley, Jay turned to Hank. "Who does Miss Ollie belong to?"

"Little ears have big mouths," replied Jess to Hank and both men laughed.

***

By late afternoon, Jess, Hank and Jay had returned from the open range.

Jay was nearly asleep in Jess's arms when they arrived back at the ranch. As

the men washed up, Hank told John all about their adventure with the two Indians.

"Hey Jess," John said, as he reached for a slice of cornbread. "I forgot to tell you that the dry goods store has received a big shipment for you. The proprietor said something about a mattress." John poked Hank into his side, grinning big. Jess had said that he and Mary Beth had been sleeping on the hard floor since they moved into their new home up on the hillside next to Will and Hope.

"Great, I'd like to drive into town early in the morning and get it. Will, can you go and give me a hand? I'm sure that mattress will be pretty heavy. Since we are taking the wagon, we can get purchase anything else that Ollie might need."

"Hope, do you mind if I go into town with Jess in the morning? You gonna be all right if I'm away for a few hours?"

"I'll be just fine. Ollie and I will make a list of things we could use in the kitchen." Hope was pleased to know that Will would be out from under her petticoat. Every time she moved, he asked how she felt or could he help her.

After Ollie filled out a list of items, including the replacement of sugar and flour, she sat down in the rocker on the front porch and waved as John and Jess left to go home.

Hank joined her, plopping down on the porch steps while he watched Will and Hope stroll up the road to their house.

The day had been long and everyone was ready to settle down for the night. "I sure hope Jesse and Miss Rae are having a good time, but I sure do miss them," Ollie said, as she swatted mosquitos.

Chapter 5

Early the next morning, Jess and Will drove the flat-board wagon to town to pick up the new mattress that Jess had ordered several weeks ago. While Will shopped in the dry goods store, Jess headed a block down the road to see his lovely wife, Mary Beth. She was working at the medical office of her father, Doctor Tim O'Riley.

The doorbell jiggled as Jess pushed opened the office door. A young girl peeked around the corner and called Mary Beth. "Your handsome husband is in the waiting room."

Mary Beth patted her hair and pinched her cheeks as she rushed to the front room to greet the love of her life. "Morning, handsome," Mary Beth greeted him with teasing smile.

"Morning doll. When do you think your pa will be back? I sure miss you," Jess cuddled Mary Beth close.

"We're expecting him tomorrow, if not later this evening on the stagecoach. The office has been so busy. I am pleased that you came in this morning. I have wonderful news-- maybe, if you agree." She reached in her apron pocket and fingered the letter.

"Tell me. I am sure I'll agree, if it has something to do with you. I only want to make you happy." Jess pulled her into an examination room and, using his foot, closed the door. He kissed her with all the passion that had been built up. Laughing, Mary Beth said, "Oh my."

"Now, what is this wonderful news that you have received?" Jess asked, while lifting her onto the examination table.

"Well, you know how I have always been disappointed that I was expelled from nursing school."

"Of course, I remember. It was because of me taking you to your room at the ladies' dormitory. That witch of a watchdog made it seem like I was living with you."

"All that wasn't true, but nevertheless, I couldn't continue in their school. Well, after all this time, they have decided that I can continue with my classes. All I have to do is write to them and give them a time when I would like to return." She held the letter out in front of her. "I believe that papa agreed to send them more money for something they need at the school, but I don't care why they changed their minds. I want to be a nurse, and if I can get back into the school, then I want to go." She stared into his confused face. "I mean, Jess, if you agree that I can go back to Ohio." Mary Beth sighed. "I know we will be apart, but with the train coming so close to home, I can travel back and forth, and you can come see me. What do you think about all this?"

"Mary Beth, you know that I only want you to be happy, but we've only been married a few months. We haven't even furnished the house properly." He helped her down from the table and opened the door. "We need to wait until your pa returns to make a final decision. I will not stand in your way if you want tto continue your education, but it will be hard to live without you for a year. We really need to talk about this decision some more."

Hannah called to Mary Beth to come and help her with a patient who needed to have his collar bone snapped back into place. "Coming mama," she said as she walked Jess to the front of the office. "I will see you early this evening," she said as she stood on her tiptoes and kissed him bye.

Jess walked slowly to the store to meet Will and load up the new mattress. He had been so happy to have received it, but now, he didn't like the idea of sleeping on it all alone."

"Why the long face, Jess?" Will asked as Jess walked into the store.

"Mary Beth received word from the Ohio University of Nursing that she can return and continue her schooling. She is so excited and wants to finish her classes so she can become a true nurse. All this means is she will be away from home for a year."

"How do you feel about that?" Will asked.

"I want Mary Beth to be happy, but we just got married a few months ago. I don't know how I feel, but I'm sure we can work something out."

***

Hope and the children were already bored once they had helped with all the chores around the house. Will had hired Mary Lou, a church friend of Ollie's, to come twice a week to clean, wash and iron for them. Hope declared that she could do everything, but he wouldn't hear of her doing all that work while carrying their third child. He enjoyed spoiling his young beautiful wife and he wouldn't listen to any of her nonsense.

"Come on kids. Let's go down and help Miss Ollie cook lunch. You know she's getting on up in age and can use a lot of help since Rae and Jesse are out of town."

"Mommy, can I make a pie? I like playing with the dough," Willa asked.

"If Miss Ollie hasn't already made one, I am sure she will let you help her."

Hope strolled down the sandy road while Willa and Jay raced up ahead. She stopped to pick a few wildflowers for a bouquet. She stood and her head whirled. She reached for something to catch herself, but there was only air around her. Slowly she went to the ground, and everything went black.

"Where's your mama, Willa? Ain't she coming with you two?"

"Yes, ma'am, she's right behind us."

***

Ollie walked to the front porch while Willa and Jay raced around in the kitchen attempting to get the first cookie off the tray sitting on the counter.

Ollie looked down the sandy road. "Jay, go to the barn and get Hank! Your Mama is lying in the road."

Ollie wobbled off the porch, opened the fence gate and rushed as fast as her old legs would carry her to her precious baby girl. "Oh Lord, please take care of my baby, and her baby." She stumbled in the sand as she headed toward Hope. Hank and Jeremiah, Ollie's black friend, rushed ahead of her. Hank bent down and lifted Hope's head in his lap. "Hope," he called and patted her Rosie cheeks. She rolled her head and opened her eyes, giving Hank a big smile.

"Mercy me, I don't know what happen." She reached and touched Hank's face. "Thank you, sweet friend. I just need help to stand up."

"Hell fire, mama. You scared the daylights out of me,"

proclaimed Jay.

"Young man, you better watch that mouth of yours. Don't you know that talking ugly *makes you ugly?* Besides, your britches will set on fire when your papa hears that you have been cussing again, like some others around here." Ollie glared at Hank.

Hank and Jeremiah lifted Hope to her feet. Jeremiah asked if she could walk or did she need them to carry her.

"You two old goats don't need to be picking up my baby girl. Just hold her tight. One of you needs to go get Doctor Tim and tell him what happened to this child."

"I'll go," Jeremiah said, after he helped Hope get settled in a rocker on the front porch.

"Don't you go getting lost in town? You hurry back here quick as you can!" Ollie wiped a wet rag on Hope's face, and Willa gave her a big glass of lemonade.

"Oh, thank you. This is just what I needed." She took a swallow of the cool drink and looked at everyone. "I'm sorry I scared ya'll. I was picking flowers and got dizzy, I guess. Next thing I knew, I was on the ground."

"Hank, help me walk Hope into the first bedroom where she can stretch out and rest comfortably until my boy, Tim, gets here." Ollie motioned for Hank to take ahold of Hope's right arm while she got the other one.

"Look you two, I can walk by myself."

"You might can, but you ain't. Hush and walk slowly and let me brush that sand off your clothes and out of your hair. Lordy mercy, child, you're just a mess."

"I hope if Jeremiah meets up with Will and Jess, he don't scare them. You both can see that I'm fine." Hope laid down, and placed her hands on her stomach

"We can see that, but that husband of yours will be crazy until he sets eyes upon you," Hank said, and then asked Ollie if he could help her anymore with Hope.

She led him to the bedroom door and said everything was under control now that Hope was lying down. I'll clean her up and then finish lunch. I'll send Jay after you when it's ready.

***

On the way back to the ranch, Jess was quiet. All he could think about was his new bride leaving him to go back to nursing school. Will had tried everything to get him out of his grim mood, but nothing worked so he just sat back on the wagon bench and looked at the scenery. Suddenly, Jess straightened. "Isn't that Jeremiah riding toward us? He's riding that old mule of his pretty hard." He pulled his team to a stop and waited for Jeremiah to reach them.

"Hey old man, where's the fire?" Will asked laughing.

"I'm heading to the town for Dr. Tim. Listen Will. Hope took a tumble while walking to the house. She says she's fine, but Ollie wants Dr. Tim to look her over."

"You sure she is all right?"

Before Jeremiah could answer, Will said for Jesse to get this wagon moving. "Hurry back with Tim!" Will called to Jeremiah.

As the team and wagon flew down the road toward the ranch, Jess told Will that Doctor Tim wasn't in town. He is coming home on the train today."

"Oh Lord," Will said, nearly standing in the wagon. His guts were churning, and he was scared to death for his precious wife. "Hurry Jess," Will pleaded.

Finally, the ranch house came into view. Will didn't even let the wagon stop before he jumped down and raced into the house. Ollie was standing in the front room with a big glass of lemonade in her hand.

"Where's Hope?" He yelled and raced passed Ollie and entered the front bedroom.

Hope's eyes opened when he barreled into the room. "Here I am Will. I'm fine, so please calm down." She held her arms out to him.

Will slid down on his knees and wrapped his arms around his baby. He kissed her neck and pulled her closer into his hard chest. "Are you hurt anywhere? Do you think the baby is all right? How did you fall?" Will fired one question after another, not giving Hope a chance to answer.

"I am fine, really Will. I was walking down the road and I stopped to pick a few wildflowers and next thing I knew, I was on the ground. Everything went black for a few minutes. Ollie and Hank came and picked me up and brought me to the house.

Jess and I met Jeremiah going to town for Dr. Tim, but Jess says that he is out of town until this afternoon. Can you feel the baby?"

Before Hope knew it, Will push her back down on the bed and laid his head on her stomach. "What are you doing? Get off me," Hope complained.

"Hush, I'm listening for the baby's heartbeat and I can hear it," Will said softly.

"Oh, my dear husband. I told you the baby is fine. I didn't fall hard. I just went slowly to the ground. Ollie has already bathed me and gotten all the sand off my body and out of my hair. I did look pretty awful."

"You aren't to get out of the bed until Doctor Tim checks you over. I feel like I need a drink."

"Here, my boy, have this glass of lemonade. I will go and get Hope some more." Ollie handed Will the glass, turned and left the two alone.

Hank came into the house. "I heard Will and Jess. Guess Will is upset. I told Jess that Hope is fine so he drove the wagon on to his house. He got a nice, new mattress. I'm going to walk up to his house and help him get it in and on the bed. It's hard for one man to handle alone."

"Hurry back and we'll eat. I'm sure the young'uns are hungry, and I know Will can eat. He's always hungry," Ollie laughed.

"I'll bring Jess back. Mary Beth usually has something to eat before she comes home."

"What you mean? Don't she cook supper when she gets home?" Ollie asked with a puzzled look.

"Don't think that's the way of things, but it ain't none of our business what those two young people do about eating. Don't you start asking any questions?"

"Now you listen to me, you old goat. I'll ask anything I want. Don't you start telling me what I can or can't do? I get enough lecturing from Jeremiah."

Hank walked out the side door mumbling a few remarks under his breath about a hardheaded old woman.

Later, Hank and Jess came into the ranch house with their hair combed and faces washed ready to eat. Neither of the men shut the side door.

"Hey you two. Don't act like you were raised in a barn. One of you close the door," Ollie said. She had prepared a small tray for

Hope and Will was eating a plate of food beside her bed. The children were sitting at the table waiting for Hank and Jess. Jay kept twisting and attempting to reach for a hot biscuit.

"Quit wiggling like a worm in hot ashes, and let the boys sit and ask a blessing over this food, "Ollie said to Jay, while Jess tried not to laugh.

"Say a few words, Jess, so we can eat. I'm starved, "Hank demanded.

Chapter 6

Mary Beth parked her carriage next to the Union Pacific's platform as it released a cloud of steam, and grinded down to a slow stop. The conductor was the first off with Doctor Tim following close behind. "See you next time, Doc," called the old man.

"Pa!" Mary Beth waved and yelled as she stood in her black carriage.

"What a surprise? Thanks for coming to meet me," Dr. Tim said.

'Oh, Pa, Jeremiah came into town looking for you. Hope fell and Ollie sent him to get you. Ollie and Hank are with her now."

"All right, calm down. Can I use your carriage? I will go straight out to the ranch now."

"I will go with you. I'm ready to go home, now that you're back. Mama can handle the last of our patients this afternoon."

"Hang on," Doctor Tim said, "I'll drive."

An hour later, they raced into the front yard of the Maxwell's ranch, the two horses dripping white form. Jess and Hank rushed out of the house and greeted Mary Beth and Doctor Tim. Jess walked around the carriage and helped his sweet wife to the ground. He leaned over and kissed her on the cheek.

"I'm surprised to see you tonight, but sure glad you're home." He bent down and whispered in her ear, "We have a brand-new mattress to break in."

"Oh you," she said, grinning, as she shoved him backwards.

"Let's go in." I'm sure Ollie has some supper leftovers to feed you and the doc."

Will rushed into the living room and greeted Doctor Tim. "Oh, I am so glad you are here. Hope is dozing, but I know she will be happy to see you."

Doctor Tim walked into the bedroom and opened his black bag. Hope opened her eyes and smiled. "Oh, Doctor Tim, you didn't have to rush out here this evening. I'm fine," Hope said.

"Now, you just lie still and don't fret about me. I would have never been able to rest until I knew you were fine. I am going to listen to the baby's heartbeat. Lie still."

Tim moved his stethoscope around and around on Hope's seven-month pregnant belly. He was grinning while he shook his head. "Hope, your baby has a strong heartbeat. Do you have any idea why you fell?"

"I was walking here from my house and stopped to pick some wildflowers. I got a little dizzy and everything went black. I remember going slowly to the ground."

"All right, I'm glad to hear that you bent down. Your head wasn't hurting you?"

"No, I was feeling good this morning. The flowers were too pretty to resist, so I bent over and picked a bundle. When I stood, everything was spinning around and down I went."

"Well, you are fine, but I would like for you to continue to stay here in bed for the night. If you feel all right, you can go home in the morning." Doctor Tim stood and wasn't able to hold in something that he had just discovered.

"Will, Hope, I have something wonderful to tell you." He looked at the young couple. "While examining the baby, I heard two heartbeats, not just one."

"What!" Will sat down in the chair beside the bed.

"Two heartbeats? You mean I'm going to have twins." Hope stared at Ollie who stood at the foot of her bed. Ollie's hand covered her mouth.

"Yep, that is exactly what I am saying. This is the reason you are so much bigger than you were with Jay and Willa. I don't know why I haven't heard the second heartbeat before, but I heard both of them just a few minutes ago. Will, would you like to listen to the heart beats?"

"Can I? Yes, please," he said quickly.

"Lie back Hope and here, Will. Place the ends of the stethoscope in your ears and I will move the instrument around."

Will's face turned red, sporting a big grin, and he smiled. "I hear them. Two strong beats." Leaning over Hope, he gave her a big kiss. "A miracle," he whispered.

***

Hope patted the bed next to her. "Ollie, please come and sit beside me. Now that Will and the kids have gone home. I am too excited to sleep after learning that I am carrying two babies, not just one."

"Boy, Rae is going to be so surprised to learn that her little sister is going to have twins. We are all going to be very busy with two little ones. I hope I can rock both of them at one time," she laughed, as she moved a rocking chair next to the bed.

"I am happy, I think. Guess I will have to be once I get used to the idea. Maybe I will have a boy and girl. That would be nice. Jay could have a little brother and Willa could have a little sister. Oh well, God will grant me whatever he wants me to have."

"That's right honey. Only God will decide what you gonna have. Do you remember hearing that I had a baby boy when I was only a child myself?"

"I seemed to remember something about that. But I want you to tell me what happened to you after Patsy and her mama left the plantation. You said that Patsy was going to be sent to an all-girls school up north."

"That's right, they did. I never saw Patsy again except when she returned about five or six years ago. "You remember when Will took me to Waverly to see her. Doctor Tim had been called out there to doctor her. He told me about her and Will and I arrived just in time to sit with her for a few hours before she passed away. That was a very happy and sad time for me," Ollie comment softly.

But Ollie, after her mama and Patsy left the plantation, what happened to you?"

"After Patsy left, I was sure I would be sent out to work in the fields with my folks, but the master's foreman said I was to continue to work in the big house and help out in the kitchen. Boy, I was one happy little girl. I liked being in the warm kitchen and helping the old cook roll out dough. Her hands were almost cripple, and she had a hard time working the dough. She taught me to pound the dough, set it to rise and cut it into dumplings or roll out crust for pies. She was a wonderful cook; only the kitchen cooks knew that I did most of the work with the dough. I never bragged on myself."

"So, that's how you can bake such wonderful pies and dumplings," laughed Hope.

"Sure is. But I learned a lot of other things too. I learned all the gossip about all the other black folks. I learned right quick like to keep a civil tongue in my mouth. The older women could spout gossip and lies about others on the plantation, but I better never repeat anything I heard

One time I was overheard repeating some gossip about a young gal who was going to be sold because she was with child and man, oh man, I got the daylights scared out of me. One of the cooks said that I had better give my heart to Jesus because my butt belonged to her. I just knew I was dead meat, but the old cook saved me.

She called the woman off me, saying, "I'll take care of her. She works for me and I need her now." Lordy, I was happier than a pig in slop."

"Oh Ollie, you're so funny," Hope said. "What else did you have to do in the big house?"

"Well, I was up at 4:30 a.m. every morning, in the kitchen. I had to put wood in the stoves, and place buckets of water on the stove to heat. I got down the plates and silverware and stacked them on tables in the long hallway. The single field workers would come in and help themselves to the food that we cooked and placed on the tables.

"I rolled out biscuit dough, cut the pork into bacon slices, and broke dozens of eggs into a big bowl to scramble. Another cook fried the bacon and cooked the eggs. Sometimes, especially in the winter, we served big pots of oatmeal instead of bacon and eggs. After the breakfast was over, two other girls and me, washed and dried all the dishes, cleaned the counters, mopped the floor and then started peeling raw vegetables for lunch. I really didn't have time to work anywhere else in the house. With the Master's wife gone, there wasn't any more parties held at the plantation. I hardly ever seen the master, only the head foreman. He was angry all the time, so I kept out of his way."

"Gracious, Miss Ollie. You were only about eight or nine." Hope shook her head. "Golly, I never dreamed I had it so easy around here," she said as she pushed the quilt down off her big belly. "Did you ever get to go and visit with your folks? I know you said that they worked as field hands."

Ollie moved to the rocker. "Almost every evening, I took bowls of leftovers to them. See, if you were married, you had to provide your own food. The old cook, well, she knew what I was doing and sometimes she would add an extra biscuit or several cookies in my container for my folks. She was a gruff old woman but had a heart of gold. Once I said to her that they might get caught stealing food from the kitchen.

She responded by saying, "let sleeping dogs lie." So I kept giving them food every evening.

"I bet your mama and papa were happy that you loved them enough to risk getting put out of the big house or off the plantation."

"My mama was a woman of few words. She never said thank you or how are you doing? She just took the food, sat down with papa and ate. I would try to talk with them but they were so tired, they didn't respond. One night I was there, and I noticed my mama's knitted shawl. The days were still warm, but the nights were getting cold. The shawl was the only wrap she had to wear to work in. It had big holes in it and threads were dangling down about to come loose. I asked her if I could take it with me to the big house and repair it. She was reluctant at first, then she tossed it to me.

Sissy, a young black upstairs maid knitted all the time. I asked her if she would repair the holes and do something with the loose threads. She did, and it looked like a new one. I was so proud of it. I rushed it back to mama with a big container of food. She took the shawl, wrapped it around her small frame and sat down to eat. No thank you, no nothing, but I was so proud for her. I gave the maid extra pieces of cake or more cookies for a long time as a way of thanks for the work on my mama's shawl.

"Oh Ollie, your mama was pleased, and you know it. She just didn't know how to say, thank you." Hope patted Ollie on her knees as she sat in the rocker.

"Yes, your right." Ollie said, wiping a few tears away.

"Go on," Hope said, "I love hearing about your life."

Chapter 7

As time when on, I was a very pretty, young girl at the age of fourteen. Words spread that the master was thinking about selling his slaves and the plantation. He wanted the yard around the house to look grand. So it was said that he sold several older slaves and bought a young black boy. He wasn't real dark like so many of the field hands. He had dark, tight wavy hair and beautiful white teeth. It was rumored that the master bid for the new boy off the slave block in Natchez, Mississippi. But that was just gossip. Anyway, he began to come into the kitchen several times a day. The old cook said that he had eyes for me."

"Well, if he wants me to notice him, he better have a chivalrous manner," Ollie said.

"What in the world is that—chivalrous manner? Does he have to have money?" the old woman questioned.

"No, it means that he better be courteous, behave himself toward me. I can read and I know how a man should treat a woman—one that he likes anyway."

"Well, sister, I ain't sure he has any of that in his bones, but he sure likes looking at you," she said as she chuckled and walked into the big pantry.

"I looked over at the door and he was motioning for me to meet him in the woods behind the plantation house. He nearly scared me to death. Standing in the doorway mouthing and making motions at me. Then he turned and walked outside. I rushed to the door and looked out. He was bent over in the flower bed next to the steps. I felt my face glowing from heat.

"Well, pretty girl, are you going to meet me or not?' I quickly said yes, and rushed back in to the kitchen.

Later that night, after delivering food to my folks, I whipped around and strolled out to the woods where he had said to meet him. Lordy, my heart was nearly jumping out of my chest. I felt like a shameless flirt. I didn't even know this young man's name and there I stood pressed up against a tree, allowing him to kiss me on the neck and his hands moving all over my body.

Suddenly, I remembered one of the old cooks saying, 'why should a man buy a cow when he can get the milk free?' I shoved the boy away from me and ran as fast as I could up the back steps to the big house. Racing up the back stairs to my room, I jumped in bed, clothes and all." Ollie sat in the rocking chair fanning herself as if she was reliving her first love experience.

Hope laughed and laughed. "Ollie I could feel that young man's breathe on your body."

"Me too," Ollie grinned. "Now you hushed child if you want me to continue."

"I promise not to say anything else," Hope said and smiled.

"Oh, I kept meeting that young man. We were in love. One night he told me I was *hotter than a pistol.* Well, that night I gave in to his love demands. After a month or so, I knew we had to get married.

He loved me, so we met with my folks and told them we were in love and wanted to jump the broom. I was young and stupid. I even told my folks we were going to have a baby. My papa went wild. He hit my young man and tried to strangle him. I was able to pull papa off my lover's body and he raced out of the shack.

My papa turned on me and beat me so bad, I was sure I was going to die. He said he would beat the baby out of my body. "I tried to teach you to value your virginity, but no, you had to spread your legs to the first young man that looked your way." He stormed out the door and mama left me lying on the floor. She went to their bed, climbed in it and went to sleep.

The next several days, I laid in my bed in the big house. The other cooks covered for me and never said an ugly or unkind word. Later, I learned that the master had sent my man away, never to be seen or heard from since. Several months later, I began to have a big belly, but the cooks and maids in the big house were good to me. I stopped taking food to my folks, which made me feel guilty. The old cook said they deserved to starve as far as she was concerned. "Good parents love their children, no matter what, as long as they don't hurt others. You may have disappointed them, but you didn't murder no body."

"The master saw me one time, but he looked right through me. He never said a word to me. A few months past and I went into labor. The maids took me upstairs and one of them got the old midwife to help bring my beautiful baby boy into the world. For the first time in my life, I felt love. Holding my babe in my arms and smelling the sweetness of his body brought me the greatest joy.

Several months passed and I loved playing with my boy. The cooks let me keep him in the kitchen while I worked in the morning. Thank goodness I was a good worker and great pie maker. Several of the slaves were dropping like flies in the fields from a high fever. Afterwards, the doctor declared the typhoid fever was spreading like wildfire over the plantation. My folks were some of the first to get it and I did all I could to help them. With no medicine to give them, there wasn't much anyone could do, but give them water and try to keep them cool. Soon, my folks were dead, and my baby got it. Lord, I thought I was going to die. I rocked him and cried while I felt the life slipping out of his little body. Some of the older men helped me to bury him next to my folks.

For more than a year, I was like a creature that I heard tell comes back from the dead—a zombie. The older house-help was good to me. They fed me and gave me simple tasks to perform. My old friend told me that God has a reason for everything he does, and my baby was in a better place. "Get back to living girl. You're young and many good and bad things will happen in your life. You are strong and you can handle everything that slaps you in the face, with God's help.' After that, I pulled myself up by my bootstraps and tried to live each day that was pleasing to our Lord."

Later, the foreman called all the field hands, cooks and house maids to gather at the steps of the big house. "Can any one of you read?" he yelled to the White men standing around. "The master said for me to read this notice, but I'm afraid I need some help." None of the men stepped forward so I raised my hand. "I can read.

"Murmurs spread through the crowd of people while I walked up the steps. How does she know how to read?' and 'She thinks she's an uppity black. Those were two phrase I heard. I stared to shake and thought I should have kept my big mouth shut."

The old foreman passed the letter to me and said for me to read it aloud. I glanced down at the letter and read the bad news to all the slaves. "Today, because of the Typhoid fever, everything on this plantation must be burned to the ground. All the fields, even the cotton and corn, the shanties, personal items-- except what's on your backs, will be burned. Nothing will be left standing but the Waverly Plantation House." All the men will begin burning this very day. The women will stand guard with the children and make sure the big house doesn't burn."

"I turned and gave the note back to the foreman and he waved his hand and said for the men to get started. The men built a bonfire and lit the torches. By dark, there wasn't a green vine in those fields or a shack standing. Black smoke could be seen for miles. All the men and women just wandered around, kicking at the black dirt. Some of the young men were crying and the older men just laid with their heads in their woman's lap. A sad, sad day for sure."

"Where did everyone sleep and what did they eat?" Hope asked.

A few women had kept some of their food supplies and made big pots of soup. Many went hungry. After two long, days the master returned with two big wagons and drivers to gather some of his things out of the big house. The men went into the house and waved at several of the big slaves to come and help load furniture and other personal items onto the wagons. Finally, the master called everyone together and said that he was going to sell the plantation house and land. "I can't replant the fields, put clothes on your backs or feed everyone."

He lined us up for the last time, and his foreman passed out the Freedom Papers. Everyone was free to leave and go and make a new home somewhere else."

"I guess that made everyone happy. Now they didn't have to be slaves any longer. Right?" Hope said.

"That true, but where would they go, with only the clothes on their backs and no money. Many of them were born on the plantation, just like me. I had never been more than ten miles from Waverly. One time I got to ride into town with Patsy because she had thrown a hissy fit, but I didn't get to get down from the carriage."

Ollie wiped her eyes. "I can still remember those young Black bucks, running and jumping around in the sandy dirt in their bare feet. Many of them heading down the long road to a new life, so they hoped. There was so much fear in the air, as many of the women cuddled together, crying and praying for answers. What did freedom mean to them or even me?

I had mixed feelings about what to do. Should I leave or stay and dig in the burnt fields for something to eat. The anticipation of what laid beyond the gate of freedom was just too great. My blood was bubbling with excitement and fear.

"I guess you were afraid, with being totally alone except for a few friends. They were in the same shape as you were." Hope snapped a few more beans.

"Yep, I was. I stood with my mother's shawl wrapped around my shoulders, wishing that she was standing beside me. As I watched the women crying and praying and the young men racing down the road, the master directed his horse over to me. "Ollie," he yelled down at me. "How did you learn to read? Did that tutor teach you?"

I could tell the master was angry and I did not want to lie. I remembered the promise I had given the tutor, I said, "No sir. Patsy taught me."

Responding with a wicked laugh, he said, "That's odd, especially when my brat can't even read herself." He kicked his horse in it sides and rode closer to me. He reached down and snatched the shawl from around my shoulders. "Everything has to be burned," he said.

"I wanted to plead with him to give my mother's shawl back, but I was afraid of what he might do to me, I walked to the big house and sat on the steps and cried. Later that day, we all stood near the antebellum house with the large four columns and watched the Master and the wagons drive away, never to be seen again."

Hope fluffed up her pillow and adjusted her body on the bed. "What happened to the house? Did some of the people get brave enough to go inside since the master and all of his men were gone?"

"Late that same day, a storm came with buckets of hard rain, lightning and hail. One of the older men walked up on the back porch carrying an axe. In a few minutes the front doors of the house were opened and he waved at everyone. 'Come, we will use the house as our own. At least until we are run off.' Well, ladies, children, old women and men entered the big parlor. It was the first time most of them had been inside. One old lady said, she felt like she had died and gone to heaven. I went inside and instructed one of the older ladies to assign rooms to the families. There were six bedrooms upstairs and many small rooms downstairs."

"How long did the slaves get to live in the house before it was sold?" Hope asked.

"Well, I was long gone for many years. Many of the old people were still living in the house when Runner sent for me. Runner, one of my dearest friends, told me that whenever buyers came to look over the house and property, they would scare them off. Some of the men would get in the attic and make haunting sounds. They would rattle chains or slam a board on the floor, open and close doors. She said the people would run over each other attempting to get to their carriages. As for as I know, the house never sold."

Ollie laughed and when she didn't hear a sound coming from Hope, she noticed that she'd talked her to sleep.

Chapter 8

Ollie covered a yawn with her hand and glanced down at the sleeping beauty with her long, blond hair spread over the pillow. Hope was a young woman of twenty-five who still looked eighteen. Ollie remembered the evening nearly twenty-two years ago when Jesse brought Rae and Hope to the ranch to stay a few weeks with them. Hope was a sweet child who could get into so much mischief in a blink of an eye.

Hope loved Will and followed his every step during the day while he worked around the house, in the barn or caring for the animals. He pretended he didn't like her trailing after him until she got hurt and cried. All she had to do was lie her head on his shoulder and say, "I luv you, Will," and he melted.

Will soon became her caretaker and protector for years. Being twelve years older than her, he tried to date young ladies in town. Hope never liked any of the young girls he brought out to the ranch and Will found fault with every wild buck who tried to capture Hope's attention. Theirs was a love match from the beginning, thought Ollie.

She sat down in the rocker. I need to go to bed and not worry about this child, Worrying was like this old rocking chair. It just gave her something to do but got her nowhere. She leaned her head back and stared up at the ceiling. "Lord, please wrap your arms around this here child and protect her and the babies that she is carrying under her breasts. Amen."

Early the next morning Ollie opened the front door and found Jess sitting in her old rocker. "What you doing sitting out here. Why didn't you just come in and put on the coffee?"

"Sorry, Miss Ollie. I guess I wasn't thinking. I just needed to go for a walk this morning and do some thinking. I will put the coffee on if you really want me too. Not sure it will be as good as yours," he said with a sweet grin.

"Oh, go on with you; just sit and talk to me. What's got you so upset that you crawled out of your bed and walked down here, leaving your bride asleep?"

"I needed to get by myself and think. Mary Beth is still my bride, but she doesn't think that way. She says being married three months is a long time," he said with a sharp tone of voice.

"Now Jess, three months is not a long time, but don't twist my words so they take your side in your spat. Tell me what's wrong and maybe I can help you."

"Mary Beth has the opportunity to go back to nursing school in Ohio. She wants to become a real nurse so she be a real help to her papa."

"And you don't want her to leave you?"

"Right, and I feel guilty and ashamed. You remember, I'm the reason she got expelled from school. I had walked her to her room in the ladies dormitory and one of the teachers saw us. That was certainly a mess."

"We all know Doctor Tim tried to make them listen to reason."

"He did everything, but the school has their rules," Jess said, hanging his head down between his knees. "I told Mary Beth I want her to be happy. But I'm not happy. We just got married, for goodness sake." He took the coffee that Ollie offered him as they walked into the kitchen.

Sipping the coffee, Jess said, "I knew your coffee would be better than mine."

"Has she talked her plans over with Doctor Tim and Miss Hannah?" Ollie asked.

"Not yet. You know Doctor Tim just got home yesterday and he came straight out here. She'll go into town and talk with him about it. I am sure he will tell her to discuss it with me. He's a nice man and he will leave the decision up to us."

The front door banged open, and Mary Beth stood illuminated with the morning sunlight behind her small frame. Her flannel robe was not tied closed, and her pretty slippers were wet, covered in sand. Her hair was tied back into a long, blond rope and her blue eyes were blazing red. With her hands on her hips, she screamed, "You had to run to Miss Ollie and cry on her shoulder, didn't you?

You couldn't wait and talk over our decision with just me. No, you had to get everyone else involved so they could take sides against me. Well, let me tell you something, *little* Jess, if I decide to go back to nursing school, I will go." Mary Beth turned on her heels and rushed out the front door.

Jess bolted to his feet and started to the door. Suddenly, he stopped. "I'm sorry Miss Ollie. I know she didn't mean to be so ugly in front of you. I've got to go." The door slammed shut behind him.

Hope stood in the doorway of the guest bedroom with her mouth open. "What in the world? The noise is enough to wake the dead."

"It seems the new wedded couple is having their first big disagreement and Jess came to talk about it. Mary Beth wasn't happy." Ollie shook her head. "Jess has gotta learn if he finds himself in a hole, he needs to quit digging."

"Mary Beth will come around and I am sure Jess will agree to anything to make her happy." Hope turned and walked into the water closet.

***

As Jess headed up the hillside to the ranch house that Doctor Tim had built for them, his temper began to cool down. Mary Beth was right, he thought. I *shouldn't have talked to Miss Ollie, but heaven help me, old habits are hard to break.* Miss Ollie had always been there for him whenever he had a problem to solve. She always listened and gave good advice. Mostly, to follow his heart. *Well, my head says to tell Mary Beth no, she can't go away to Ohio, but my heart wants to make her happy, If becoming a nurse will make her happy, I have to live alone for the next year.*

Walking up on the big front porch, he saw Mary Beth sitting in their double swing. She jumped and hurried into his arms, "Oh Jess, I am so ashamed. I hope Miss Ollie will forgive me."

"Oh, honey, she will, and I am so sorry. I was feeling sorry for myself, knowing that you were going to be leaving me alone for a year. But, I want you to be happy and I agree that you should go to nursing school. We won't ask your folks, we'll tell them of our decision I know they will agree."

***

"Good morning, Ollie. Did I just see Mary Beth running

39

through the fields like a house on fire and Jess walking behind her heading to their house?" Jeremiah said, as he stood on the back porch.

"I reckon you did. Those young'uns are having their first big spat, but I'm sure they will work it out. Come on in and take your place at the table and I'll pour you a big cup of hot coffee."

Thanks, I could use something hot."

You don't look like you're feeling too good. Are you all right?"

"I feel like I've been chewed up and spit out, and I ain't done a darn thing."

Ollie set a cup of coffee in front of her dear devoted friend of many years and placed her cool hand on his forehead. "You've got a fever. Have you been coughing?"

"Oh, go on with you. I'm just hot from riding over here on my old mule. I should've hitched up the carriage and drove over. It's going to be hotter than blazes today."

"Tell me about it, Jeremiah," Hope said walking from the bedroom. She sat down across from him at the kitchen table.

"Girlie, what are you doing here so early? Where's Will and the kids?"

"Oh, I had a weak spell as I was walking here yesterday, and I had to lie in bed all day and night. Doctor Tim came and examined me. Guess what?"

"Sorry, Sweetheart," Jeremiah said using Hope's nickname that Hank tagged on her years ago. "I'm not up to a guessing game this morning."

"Oh, I'm sorry you feel bad, so I will tell you. I'm going to have twins!"

"Lordy gal, you've made me proud as punch. Will must be on cloud nine for sure."

"I think so, but it does take some getting used to. Two babies will be a hand full. I was thankful I had Rae and Miss Ollie to help me with my other two, and they were just one at a time." Hope smiled and gave a little chuckle.

"I think I hear that proud papa and your two little ones coming in the yard now. Let me get the biscuits out of the oven. That little Jay has an appetite like a grown man."

"Well, good morning, Jeremiah," Will said as he entered the

front door, allowing Jay and Willa to rush past him to the table. Willa ran to Jeremiah and gave him a hug while Jay pulled a chair out next to him. Jeremiah tousled Jay's hair and both smiled warmly at each other.

"Good morning, sweet wife," Will said as he lent down and kissed Hope. "How are you feeling this morning?"

Hope took his hand as he pulled out a chair and sat next to her. "I'm actually very well rested and feel good. I am starved, but waiting on the scrambled eggs to go with the ham that Ollie has fried."

"Can I help you this morning, Miss Ollie?" Will asked. "I'll pour my own coffee. Can I get you a refill, Jeremiah?"

"No, thank you, I'm fine."

"No he ain't fine either. He has a fever. Will, I want you to take him to town to see Doctor Tim?" Ollie placed the platter of biscuits and scrambled eggs on the table as she looked at both men, brooking no argument.

"Sure thing. Let me eat this delicious breakfast and I will hitch up the carriage."

"I don't need to go see Tim. I'm just hot. And besides, how many times do I have to tell you to stop treating me like I'm a little boy," Jeremiah said.

Will and Hope tried to hide their amusement as the two old love birds fussed.

"I need to go into town and get a list of supplies so you just tag along with me and we'll stop in and let him look you over. It will make Miss Ollie and Aunt Katie feel better."

"Can I go with you, papa?" Jay asked with his mouth full of eggs.

"Don't talk with your mouth full, you pig," Willa said.

"Willa, I will do the scolding, please." Hope said, giving her an 'I told you so glare.'

"Sure, you can go, after you go and tell Hank to come in for breakfast." Will told Hope to stay seated while he placed a few more plates on the table. Ollie thanked him and pushed him back to the kitchen table.

Chapter 9

Will allowed Jay to sit close beside him and handle the horse's reins. Jeremiah was almost asleep leaning against the padded leather seat. Will tapped Jay on the arm and placed his fingers over his lips, signaling for him not to talk loud. "I do believe that Jeremiah has a fever. He would never doze off like that if there wasn't something wrong," Will said, softly to his son.

Even with the pretty weather, the drive into town seemed to take forever. Bluebonnets bloomed next to a large field of butterbeans. "We'll have to stop and pick your mama some of those flowers on our way home. She loves wildflowers," Will whispered to Jay.

***

As the carriage stopped in front of Doctor Tim's office, Claire was coming out the front door with Hannah. "Hello, Uncle Will and Jay," Claire said. "Jay, did I see you driving Uncle Will and Jeremiah?"

"Sure did. Papa says I am growing like a weed, and I should be doing men things more often."

"My goodness," Claire tried to hide her smile. "When you come to school this fall, you';; have to introduce yourself when you come into class because I won't recognize you. Say hello to my mama and tell her I will be out there in a day or two."

"Hello to my favorite young men, this morning, "Hannah said.

"Jeremiah was taking a nap while I drove to town," Jay boasted.

"It was the safest way to travel," Jeremiah said, trying to appear that he wasn't napping because he was sick.

Will nodded. "Hannah, Jeremiah is not feeling on top of the world this morning, so he would like for you or Doctor Tim to look him over. Jay and I have a few supplies to get, so we will leave him in your capable hands."

"Come on inside, Jeremiah. Let's walk to the back and have Tim look you over."

***

Hope walked into the kitchen. "You know, I fell asleep last night just as you was going to tell me about you leaving Waverly. Give me a pot of those green beans, and I will snap them while you peel potatoes and continue with your story."

"Let go set on the porch and feel that morning breeze on our faces. Come on Willa. You can pull the green leaves off this here bowl of strawberries."

"Can I eat one or two, while I cleaning them?"

"Sure thing. Ain't no fun if you can't eat some," Ollie laughed as she placed the bowl on the table beside Willa. "Now, where was I last night?"

"You were all alone and trying to decide what to do. I remember that much before I dozed off."

That's right. I was trying to decide if I should stay or leave like so many of the others. I had no place to go, but I had no reason to stay. So, I started walking slowly right down the middle of the rode that led to the town of Limason. The sun was hot on my bare head, but the sandy road was hotter on my bare feet.

"You didn't have any shoes?" Willa asked.

"No child, all I had was the clothes on my back. I got tired of walking so I sat down on a log next to the road and watched the white clouds float overhead. It was a pretty day for traveling. Out of nowhere, a big white man sitting high on a large flatbed-wagon bench pulled to a stop directly in front of me. I was scared, so I acted like I didn't see him."

"He called to me, "Girl, you from Waverly?' I pretended to be deaf and dumb because he was a large man. There was a boy standing in the back."

'Girl, I'm not going to hurt you. Do you have a place to go?'

'No!" I shook my head without looking at him.

'Can you clean and cook? I need a gal to help me care for my son. He's ten and my wife just passed. My son needs someone to help prepare meals and wash. I don't like leaving him alone while I work the fields.' I didn't even look at him. Just kept my head

43

down."

"Look, gal, I don't have all day. Now can you cook, clean and wash?"

Realizing that I might have a place to start a new life, I raised my head and looked him in the eyes and said, 'Yes, sir. I cook, clean, wash, read and write, and I have all my teeth. Is that all you need to know about me?'

Eyes wide, Mr. Maxwell and his son busted out laughing. 'I believe you'll do. If you come home with us, I promise never to harm you and you'll have your own room inside my sod house, for now, but soon it will be bigger. Grab your stuff and jump in the back."

I stood, looked down at my bare feet. 'I don't have anything. The master made us burn everything except the clothes on our backs because of the fever."

'Well--Mr. Maxwell, shook his head, 'we'll soon fix that."

"Ollie, you got in a wagon with a total stranger, and you have been here on this ranch ever since?" Hope asked, wiping her eyes. "I can't believe you didn't have anything-- no shoes or clothes."

"You might say that was the luckiest day of my life, Mr. Maxwell, Jesse's grandpa was true to his word. He was always kind and gave me everything I needed. It is still that way here with his grandsons."

***

Doctor Tim told Jeremiah that he could button up his shirt as he placed his instruments back on the counter. He walked into the other room and whispered to Hannah, "Jeremiah's chest is filled with mucus. He has a bad cold, and it has settled in his lungs. Come with me as I give him the news."

"How do you feel Jeremiah?" Hannah asked, as she took his hand.

"Tell your husband to tell me straight out. No pussyfooting around. I know something isn't right and I don't want any coddling."

"Jeremiah, your lungs are filled with mucus. Your breathing is extremely blocked because of it. I am going to need for you to go to bed and I'll placed a tent of hot steam over the top part of your body. We have to break up the mucus and hope you can cough most of it up. If we don't, I am afraid that you may develop pneumonia and that wouldn't be good."

Jeremiah didn't say a word, so Doctor Tim asked him. "Do you want to stay here or would you like to go to John and Katie's home? Either way, I can take care of you. I just want you to be comfortable."

"No, I don't want to do neither. I want Ollie to take care of me. She'd be upset if I went anywhere else."

"I'm sure you're right," Doctor Tim replied. "Why don't you lie down while we wait for Will and Jay to return? I will prepare all the things I need to take to Jesse's place while we wait."

***

After a couple of hours, Doctor Tim, Hannah, Jeremiah, Will and Jay drove into the front yard of Jesse's ranch house.

Hope stood in the doorway. "Miss Ollie, something wrong. Jeremiah is with Doctor Tim and Miss Hannah."

"Goodness girl, get out of the doorway. Let them get inside. Willa, pick up your dolls off the floor." Ollie rushed to the front window to watch everyone move into the house.

"Ollie," Hannah smiled, as she gave her a tight hug. "Jeremiah is going to need some nursing for a few days, and he wants your gentle care."

"Lordy, what's wrong with my old friend?" Ollie twisted her hands in her apron.

"Don't fret, Ollie. I'm fine," Jeremiah said.

"You ain't fine and don't start telling me what to think. Come, I will let you use the front bedroom so I can hear you if you call me."

Doctor Tim carried the tent equipment into the front room and asked Ollie to bring him several tea kettles of steaming hot water. "Jeremiah's lungs need steam to help him breathe easier. I have used this method before, and it does work for most of my patients."

Will went into the bedroom and assisted Jeremiah with one of Jesse's night shirts. "Don't you think you should ask Jesse if I can use his clothes?" Jeremiah said.

"I would, but you remember that he and Rae won't be home for a few days. They are still on their honeymoon."

Jeremiah laughed. "That's right. They never had one when they got married years ago."

"Lie down, Jeremiah, so I can prepare the tent over your body.

45

After you rest for a while, I know Ollie will bring you something good to eat. I know you don't have an appetite, but I need for you to eat. It's important that you keep up your strength."

A few hours passed while Jeremiah slept. Ollie and Hope continued to pour hot water into the tent containers and his breathing seemed to get easier. Several times he sat up coughing until he was exhausted.

"Now Hope, I don't need for Will coming in here fussing about you taken care of Jeremiah. You go and get ready for bed. You'll sleep in Jesse and Rae's bedroom. You can visit with Will while I put supper on the table. I am going to slice ham. I've already made hot biscuits, baked sweet potatoes and green beans with little red potatoes. Everyone will be coming in to eat soon. Will and the kids will go home after supper, if he is sure you are getting rest. Hank will help me take care of Jeremiah and his personal needs."

***

A couple hours later, after Ollie had fed supper to Jeremiah and Hank had help him to the water closet, he slid back under the steam tent and went fast asleep. Will and the kids walked back to their house, after visiting with Hope, while Hank settled in the bunkhouse. The house was so quiet the frogs and crickets could be heard from the two open windows.

Ollie sat in a large rocking chair, knitting a blue and yellow baby blanket, when Hope walked in. "Oh, my goodness, Hope, you scared me to death. I thought you were sleeping."

"I am wide awake. I thought I would come in here and lie on Clair's other twin bed while you tell me more about what happened to you after you moved in with Mr. Maxwell and his son, Jake."

"All right, but you have to lie still and rest. We have had a long day, and I am so worried about my Jeremiah." Ollie pulled more thread out of her bag. "Now where was I? Oh, I remember now." Ollie looked up at the ceiling and began her story again.

"After I got use to the sod house, cooking, washing, and helping with the summer garden, Jake and I got to be great friends. Mr. Maxwell, was gone from the house all day, so Jake helped me build the fire under the big black pot so I could wash clothes, and he helped hoe and plant beds of bluebonnets around the house.

On Sundays, Mr. Maxwell would drop me off at the Black

church while he and Jake drove into Limason to attend the services at the First Baptist Church. They picked me up on their way home. Many times I got a ride home before they drove back my way.

Jake loved to tease me about catching a fellow at church. I told him one day as we ate dinner that I didn't want no young man. "I have it made here with you and your pa. I got everything I need and a lot of things I want. Those poor young men that live around here share a shack with a dozen people and they work from morning to dark to make ends meet. They may want me because I wear pretty dresses and shoes and I put money in the offering plate when it's passed by me each Sunday."

"What did Jake say to that?" Hope laughed and fluffed her pillow.

"He thought it was funny that I didn't want to marry. Jake asked his papa if he wanted a wife and he answered quickly. 'I don't have time to find a wife, must less have time to win over her parents and other relatives.' He held up his cup for more coffee as I brought the coffee pot over to the table.

"You see, Jake, when you try to court a southern gal, you ain't never good enough for the girl's pa. It takes a lot of time to convince him that you will take care of his daughter and then you've got to win over the brothers, sisters and the other relatives. Later, after courting for a while, if you decide that she isn't the one you want to settle down with, then be prepared for her entire family to hunt you down medieval style. Nothing will satisfy them until they have broken both your arms and legs."

Ollie threw back her head and laughed. "To tell you the truth, Miss Hope, I don't know who was more surprised with Mr. Maxwell's feeling about remarrying—me or Jake. She continued to rock with her hands folded. "I watched Jake grow to a nice young man. He went to church every Sunday and to many of the Saturday night barn-parties. He stumbled through years of puppy love and awkward dating. One gal who got her eye on Jake was something else. I saw her in town and heard that she wore less than a napkin's worth of clothes since her old man died. I steered Jake away from that one," Ollie laughed. "Many young gals wanted to date, but Jake wanted to do the chasing. He loved a challenge. When he was about twenty, he met Missy Watson.

"She was prettier than a basket of peaches," Jake said. "Lordy, that boy was head over heels in love. They made eye contact with each other in church, and after three seconds, they both knew they wanted to be together. He called on her, and on their first date, he took her fishing. Even though Missy hated fishing, being a true southern gal, she pretended to enjoy it."

"So, I am guessing he didn't take her fishing after they married?" Hope quizzed.

"Your right, but it wasn't long before the young couple married, and in just a few months Jesse was on his way. As far as I could tell, the couple was very happy except, for one thing. Missy placed her pa on a pedestal, and he was an authority on every subject. She felt Jake should question him about everything he wanted to do on the ranch, even though Mr. Maxwell was still alive and lived here. Over the first few months, Jake had to learn to be his own man."

"Will says that he hardly remembers his mama."

"Well, he was only four years old and Jesse was twelve when Missy passed." Ollie smiled down at the pattern on the blanket. "Lordy gal, Missy loved her husband and boys, but she didn't do too much around the house or ranch. She knitted and took long walks. She was good to me so, I worked hard and kept the house and boys clean. I thought Jake was going to die when she left this earth."

"What did she die from?"

"I don't know if they had a name for it, but she never got her strength back after having Will. The doctor was here for two days while she was giving birth. He said she had a complications, and she was going to have to stay in the bed for a month, not just two weeks. She had bled a lot, and that made her weak. After a few days, she finally let me bring Will in, and she tried to breastfeed him, but I had been bottle-feeding him, so he didn't want her milk."

"So, what did you do to help dry up her milk?" Hope asked, looking over at Ollie.

"I tied long diapers around her breast, making a binder as tight as I could. I poured hot water over her body while I bathed her daily. It wasn't long before the milk was gone." Ollie looked off into space. "Will was growing, opening his eyes, looking all around, but Missy wouldn't have anything to do with him. She was a jumble of emotions. One minute, she was crying, calling for Mr. Jake, and then she would scream at him to get away from her. It was a very hard time for all of us. We didn't know what to do to please her."

"What did the doctor say about her behavior?" Hope asked as Ollie pulled more yarn out of her bag.

"He didn't know. She wouldn't answer any of his questions. Just stared at him like he was a stranger."

What did Jesse's and Will's pa do?"

"Do? He didn't know what to do. He was almost as bad as her, and sad and scared for his lovely wife. He was having trouble sleeping and didn't eat. The man was just overwhelmed with worry about the care for Missy. But as days went by, she got a little better. She was physically never the same. Jake had to move into the room with the boys. Realizing she wasn't going to get well, at least any time soon, he hired some men to come and help build the big bedroom with a fireplace. He told her that he had built her a new room, but she wouldn't have it. Jake moved into the room and remained there."

"Missy was weak as a kitten, but she crawled out of bed each morning and moved around slowly. She never complained about the mess the boys made or their loud noise. After breakfast, she would give me a list of what she wanted me to do. Of course, I already knew what my chores were for the day, but I listened to her. After lunch, she and I knitted for many hours.

Several times a week she would have a ladies visit from town. She sat in the rocker on the front porch with her company and listened to them gossip. They enjoyed my tea and cake, while Missy just sat and listened to them chat without interrupting them."

"Did she ever go to church or shopping in town?" Hope asked.

"Once in a while, she would think she was strong enough to travel to town, but she would only allow Jesse to help her. Poor Jake, he just stood back and watched her smile and cuddle close to her older son. I would stay home from church and keep Will. She refused to take Will from the house. Said she was afraid he would get sick."

Hope yawned, and Ollie said it was time for her to return to her bed. She was going to dress in her gown and robe and sleep in the bed next to Jeremiah. He might need her in the middle of the night, and she was afraid she wouldn't hear him. "Scoot on now. Go to bed and rest. Doctor Tim will probably be back out here tomorrow, and I am sure he will check you over. Maybe you will be able to return home."

"Maybe so, but you got to promise me you'll find time to continue your life story with me. I have found it fascinating."

Chapter 10

Justice, a longtime friend of Rosie stopped by for a visit with Ollie. Bud Downey married Rosie and brought Justice and Rosie's two brothers with them to Limason. Justice and Ollie became friends immediately, even though Ollie wasn't sure about the rumors that Justice was a voodoo queen from Louisiana and could perform hocus pocus on people and turn them into frogs or whatever she felt.

Justice arrived after breakfast with three fried chickens and a bowl of chicken and dumpling. "Lordy, woman, what time did you get up this morning and start cooking?" Before Justice could answer, Ollie ushered her into the kitchen. "It's so good of you to think about us. How did you hear that I was taking care of Hope and Jeremiah?"

"Now Ollie, you know how gossip travels from town. Bud saw Will in the dry-goods store yesterday and he said that Jeremiah wasn't feeling well, and Hope had fallen out there in the road. I felt you had your hands full with Rae still out of town."

"I only started taking care of Jeremiah late yesterday, but I am very worried about him. He had a restless night and he's worn himself out coughing, so he's still sleeping this morning."

"How's Hope?" Justice asked.

"Good morning, Miss Justice. Believe it or not, I am feeling well. I know I am going to need your help. You helped me deliver my other two and now that I am having twins, I will want you beside me every minute."

"Doctor Tim might have something to say about me being in the way," Justice laughed.

"I am the one having the babies and I will tell him today that I will need you nearby." Hope walked slowly over to the kitchen counter and poured herself a cup of coffee. She sat closed to Justice and whispered, "I will want some of your special seeds to help with the pain, like before."

Justice smiled and gave Hope a nod. "I'll take care of you, for sure. Twins might not be an easy delivery."

Hope was slathering butter on two biscuits that Ollie had taken from the oven. She stopped and stared at Justice. "Should I be worried?"

Justice smiled and shook her head no. "Like I said, I will be near." She watched Hope fix her plate with the two big cathead biscuits. "Now, Miss Hope, I know the babies are making you hungrier than normal, but you don't want to gain too much weight."

"Oh poop. You're spoiling my breakfast." Hope said as she lowered the hot biscuit from her mouth.

"Maybe so, but I want you to be in good condition when those two babies are ready to come out and meet their mama and papa. You don't want Doctor Tim to have to cut more than necessary."

"I know your right. Starting at lunch today, I will watch how much I eat."

The two laughed together. Ollie looked in on Jeremiah and he was stirring around under the tent. "Lie still, sweet man, and I will call Hank to come and assist you."

Justice walked to the side door and waved at Hank as he carried hay to a few of the colts in the corral.

"Coming!" he yelled and hurried to the house.

***

Doctor Tim drove his carriage into the front yard and hopped down with his black bag. "Morning everyone," he said as he entered the front door.

Ollie offered him a cup of coffee but he declined. "I'll get some later, but I want to check on Jeremiah."

Hank had helped Jeremiah back to bed and it had taken all the old man's strength. Stepping back and allowing the doctor to listen to Jeremiah's heart and chest, Hank stood over by the door with Ollie.

Doctor Tim expression was grim. Ollie asked, "How is he this morning?"

"Ollie, let the doc . . . finish."

Jeremiah was nearly out of breath. Doctor Tim had hope that the steam tent had helped, but his dear friend was worse, not better. "Jeremiah, have you been coughing?"

He only shook his head as Doctor Tim looked at the worried face of Ollie.

"He coughed most of the night until he tuckered himself out. He wrestled with the covers and tried to sit up," Ollie said, as Doctor Tim listened to Jeremiah's back.

"Woman -- how do you know what---I did?"

"I knows because I slept right there in that bed next to you, like I plan to do until you're better." Ollie attempted to straighten his covers.

***

Justice was sitting at the kitchen table when she saw Claire, Jesse, and Rae's daughter, come to the door. "Morning, Miss Claire," Justice said.

"It's so good to see you, Justice. How are Bud and Rosie doing? I haven't seen them in a while."

"They're fine, but I have been expecting good news about you and that sweet man of yours."

"Oh, Justice, every month I am hoping for that same good news, but after nearly two years I feel like giving up. I want a child so bad, but I try not to show disappointment around Albert. He wants a baby, too."

Justice moved closer to Claire. "What would you say to a toddy that Ollie and I can make for you to drink? You can't say anything to anyone."

'Would it be dangerous?"

"Now Miss Claire, we would never give you anything that might harm you or a baby. Goodness, girl, if you can't trust us, then its best you not have it."

"No, I mean yes." She looked around the room, making sure no one overheard their conversation. "What will Ollie say about me drinking it?"

"Ollie loves you. She will help me. We gave it to another gal in the church, and it was no time till she had a baby on the way."

"Let's talk about something else. Ollie and I will speak about it later. She is working hard to get Jeremiah well. He's in a bad way."

"Oh, I didn't know he was here. I came out to see Ollie, Hope, and the kids since Mama and Papa are still gone. I think they will be home in a day or two."

***

Doctor Tim entered the kitchen to get a cup of coffee with Ollie on his heels. "Willa, Jeremiah is asking for you. Go see want he wants." Ollie watched the child race out of the kitchen, and then she focused on Doctor Tim.

"What else can we do, Doctor Tim? He's not any better since he has been under the steam tent."

"You're right, He's not better. In fact, he's much worse. His heart is so weak. I don't know what to do for him." Doctor Tim wiped his hand down his face. "I'll send Hank to go for John, Katie, Tater and Missy. I wish Jesse and Rae were here."

"Tim, my boy, are you telling me that you're afraid my dear friend is going to die? There nothing more you can do for him? Please, please make him better."

"Ollie, I'm not God, but I think we all need to pray to Him for help."

***

A few minutes later Jeremiah whispered something to Willa and when she smiled, he knew she would take care of business for him. In less than five minutes, the child was back and handed Jeremiah a sheet of paper and a pencil which he quickly slid under his covers.

"Olli . . .e, come here!" Jeremiah called with a struggling voice.

"I'm here, my love. I'm here."

"Ollie, come nearer." He was out of breath. "I have always wanted to ask—you something important and now, since it not too late . . ." He slowly slid a white piece of paper on his chest. He turned it over. It read *Marry me.* "I want you to be my woman . . . forever." Looking at his Ollie, he couldn't help smiling. She was sweet and pretty with her white short curls. She brought such happiness to him and everyone on the ranch. Ollie had taught him to laugh and deep down his heart smiled every time he sat and drank his morning coffee with her. Right now, his deepest regret was that he was going to have to leave her. He knew that she would be well taken care of, but he was the one who wanted to be

54

here with her forever.

"Oh, Jeremiah, don't be silly. We don't have to marry. Besides, I feel like we have been married for years." She took the sweet note out of his hands and pressed it to her chest. "You're going to get better, and then we'll talk about a real marriage and a honeymoon. I just ain't going to allow you to leave me-- all alone."

"You won't---never be alone. Family loves you too much. Please say you'll marry me....now. Send someone after the preacher."

"I'm here, Jeremiah," the preacher said from across the room. "I came to see you." He walked over to the bedside and took his friend's hand and squeezed it firmly. "I will be more than happy to perform a beautiful wedding ceremony for you."

"I am going to sleep now. You—Woman, put on your— prettiest dress," Jeremiah whispered to Ollie. He closed his eyes while tears streamed down Ollie's black cheeks.

"Please, Jeremiah, I must hold you in my arms, I have to once more. His face was only inches from hers. She gazed down into his face that had become so familiar over time.

The preacher turned to everyone in the room and motioned with his hands for all to exit and give the couple privacy.

"Kiss me, sweet woman," Jeremiah said so softly for her ears only to hear.

She brought her lips down over his. This may be one of their final kisses and she wanted to remember it the rest of her days. There were no shyness between either of them. They wanted to hold each other until the end of time, but Jeremiah struggled not to cough. He patted Ollie on the back, and after his coughing spell motioned for her to go and get dressed.

"Make me a happy man. I will be here waiting for my bride." He closed his eyes and rested as she hurried out of the room.

"Girls, Justice, help me. I can't let Jeremiah die. Justice, please make a special toddy that will help him." Ollie sat down in her rocker and placed her face in her hands and cried.

"Ollie, I would do anything to help your man, but I have no medicine that will make his heart stronger. Doctor Tim says that he is weak, and his lungs are filled with mucus and fluid." She walked over to the rocker and patted her friend on the shoulder. "Come on now. Marry this wonderful man that you have shared many mornings with over the years. Let's make you a beautiful bride." Justice took her arm and pulled her out of the rocker and pushed her toward her room.

***

Claire cried as Hope opened her arms and raced to Will who had been outside taking care of the animals. "Oh, Will, I can't believe that our Jeremiah might die soon."

Willa and Jay rushed to Will. Both were openly crying. "Papa, help Jeremiah get better," Willa said as Jay wiped tears from his eyes.

Will scooped up both of his children and looked at his sad wife. "I know, sweetheart, Hank told me, but you have to think of yourself and our babies," Will said with a large lump in his throat. "Please settle down and rest."

"Tomorrow, I'll rest, but Ollie needs me, Katie, and Claire to help her get dressed for the wedding. Jeremiah wants to marry Miss Ollie. Hurry and get cleaned up and please watch Willa and Jay. The wedding will be soon."

In less than thirty minutes, Ollie came walking into the living room wearing a soft, white blouse with a lace collar and light blue skirt. Her white, nappy curls, without the bandana that she always wore, were lovely. Her Rosie lips and beautiful white teeth were an added touch that made her glow.

The Black minister stood over Jeremiah's bed reading several Bible verses. He had his eyes closed and prayed the Lord's Prayer while Hank, John, Will, and Doctor Tim said it along with him.

Jeremiah held out his hand and Doctor Tim took it. "Where's my bride? Is she ready to be my woman?' Jeremiah coughed blood on his hanky. "Doc, everything I have and own, I want her--- to have it. See to it."

With a throat filled with silent tears, Doctor Tim whispered, "I will."

***

The minister gathered everyone together around Jeremiah's sickbed. Justice, Claire, and Willa hugged each other while Ollie entered the bedroom and walked slowly to Jeremiah's side. Jay covered his face in his papa's knees when the bride kneeled down beside her groom and took his hand in hers.

"Dearly family and friends, we are here to join Jeremiah and

Ollie in holy matrimony but before I do, I would like to say a few words.

God is Love. Whoever lives in love lives in God and God in them. Love is patient, love is kind. The Bible shares that love is more than a feeling. In Romans, the Bible says to be devoted to one another in love. When one fails, the other helps the other up.

"Love is completely humble and gentle. Jesus said, my command is this, "Love each other as I have loved you." Sighing, the preacher glanced around at the teary faces of many friends. "I know of no greater love than between my dear friend and Ollie. Even in their friendship, they were devoted to each other. It gives me the greatest pleasure to marry this couple.

He turned to the sick man. "Jeremiah, do you take Ollie to be your wife?"

"I do."

"Ollie, do you take Jeremiah to be your husband?"

"I do."

"God bless this loving union between Jeremiah and Ollie. I now pronounce you husband and wife. You may kiss each other."

Ollie leaned over and kissed Jeremiah on his sweet lips. Everyone in the room clapped and wiped tears.

Will motioned for everyone to leave the sweet married couple alone. Ollie continued to kneel beside Jeremiah, and she whispered to him for the first time in her life, "I love you."

"I know. You have—always—loved me, and me you. God has been good to us—your friendship has been my-- whole life. Sharing coffee-- every morning with you, talking over our plans for the day, and fussing about silly things." He began coughing and choking. After a few minutes or so, he continued, "You, Ollie have been my world since the first time I met you. ---I'm sorry I waited so long to ask you to be my wife." Squeezing her hand, he closed his eyes and his soul faded out of his tired old body into the heavenly world.

"No! Not yet, please, Jeremiah, not yet. Please hold on," Ollie cried.

***

Doctor Tim rushed into the bedroom and kneeled down beside his old friend. Taking the stethoscope from his neck, he placed it on Jeremiah's chest and listened. Silence, no heartbeat. He laid his head down over Jeremiah's chest and wept like a child. Something he had not done in many years.

Feeling the bed shift, Tim glazed into Jess's red –rimmed eyes. Jess had told him that Claire had rushed up the hillside to his house and told him to come, that Jeremiah was in a bad way, and there was going to be a wedding. He'd told her, "Go back, and I will bring Mary Beth. We're coming."

"Tim, isn't there anything you can do?" Jess asked, not realizing that his wonderful childhood friend had already passed.

"It's too late, son. He's gone."

"No, oh no. God—bless-- my old warrior," Jess mumbled through tears as he held Jeremiah's hand.

Mary Beth, Claire, and Willa held each other and cried. Will held Hope and Jay as all three shed tears. Everyone loved the wonderful old man who had come into their lives over twenty-five years ago.

Tim thought back about his friend's life. Jeremiah had been a friend and protector of Rae's aunt, Katie Brown, after her husband died. They learned that Herman Summers, Rae's stepfather, had kidnapped her in hopes of forcing her to marry him. When the men came into the ranch house to capture Rae, they were forced to take Ollie with them. Katie and Jeremiah came from Peamont, Texas to help find the girls. After the girls were rescued, Katie fell in love with John Johnson, Jesse's foreman and they married. Jeremiah stayed and helped the new couple open a successful flower farm. John and Katie had one child, Missy, who married Tater, Rosie Downey's brother. What a legacy this Black man's life had been to all of them.

***

The next day, Jesse and Rae arrived home on the afternoon train from Dallas. They had been gone for three weeks on their twenty-fifth wedding anniversary trip. After they'd married, they never had the time to go on a real honeymoon. Jesse had promised Rae that when the time was right, he would take her anywhere she wanted to go. Rae always wanted to travel to the beautiful state of California, so they visited the West Coast for weeks.

As Jesse waited on their luggage, the train master offered his condolences to Jesse in the death of his friend, Jeremiah. "We plan to be at his funeral tomorrow."

58

Jesse stood frozen and stared at the busy man. "What did you say about Jeremiah?"

"Don't tell me you didn't know? I'm sorry to have broken the bad news," he said as he told the young assistant to hurry. "Go to the livery and get Mr. Maxwell's horse and carriage."

Jesse sat down on a barrel on the train depot. Rae walked over and asked him what was wrong. "You're as white as a sheet."

Jesse pulled Rae into his arms as he laid his head on her chest and she ran her hands up and down his back, silent until he was ready to tell her.

Chapter 11

Today had to be next to the worst day in Ollie's life. The worse day was nearly sixty something years ago when she lost her baby boy to typhoid fever. Now today, Jeremiah, the love of her life, was being laid to rest.

As Ollie strolled slowly down the aisle to the front of her church, she wasn't surprised to see all the benches packed with Black and White friends. Many of the men stood against the walls, and children sat on the floor in front. Jeremiah was a friend to the whole community. He had a heart of gold when it came to someone in need. At Christmas, he helped build toys for all the little boys and donated money to purchase turkeys and hams for many families. He made sure that the church ladies were making dolls, doll clothes, cradles and special dresses for the little girls.

If a farmer needed help with planting or harvesting their crop, if he couldn't do the job, he hired extra help for that farm. He always saw that the widows in his church area were taken care of. Jeremiah always placed money in the church offering to make sure no one for miles around went hungry, but he never boasted about his good deeds. Everything he did, he did because God spoke to his heart, and it was never spoken of to anyone.

But today, the people spoke of all his good deeds. Their presences proved that even though Jeremiah never bragged about what he did for others, each person on the receiving end of his charity knew where it came from.

As the minister spoke of Jeremiah and how he was received into heaven already, he asked if anyone would like to say a few words.

Surprisingly, Willa raised her hand. Will pulled her hand down. She turned to her papa and said, "But Papa, I have to tell everyone about my friend. Please," she begged.

The minister walked to the edge of the platform and motioned to Will to allow the child to come up front. Will said to be sweet and stood Willa on her feet. She took small steps up on the platform and looked out over the large congregation.

"Jeremiah was my only Black friend. My -- storyteller has left me and my brother, but he will *always live* in my heart. Miss Ollie told me that, didn't you Miss Ollie?" Willa pointed at Ollie as she wiped tears from her face. She shook her head. "He kissed my booboos," holding out her arm to show a bandage. "He even stole cookies out of Miss Ollie's kitchen for me and hid me from Papa and Mama when they were mad at me. I am going to be in big trouble without Jeremiah. I already miss him."

Many people wiped tears while they watched the beautiful little six-year-old hurry off the platform and rush into her papa's arms. Will lifted her up and they took their seat. Will whispered in her ear, "Good job, and I love you."

The minister, walking back to the center of the platform, cleared his throat, and wiped his eyes with a large white hanky. He asked if anyone else wished to speak. People murmured and looked around.

Jesse slowly stood and walked to the front. He shook the minister's hand and turned to face the congregation.

"Jeremiah, *what can't a person say about the short, stumpy, old man?*" Several people laughed. "Jeremiah was more than a friend to many of us. He was family. No family could have a better companion, a better friend. He came into our lives over twenty-five years ago, and in no time, he made a place in our hearts.

"At our breakfast table, there's an empty chair, where he shared coffee with Miss Ollie every morning." He cleared his throat and smiled over at Ollie. "There wasn't anything he wouldn't do to help us. Miss Ollie fussed at him many times, for working so hard for others. He was a brave little man, too. Hank and Jeremiah helped my son find two of the worst men in the country, who had harmed a lady, and they saved my son's life. Both of these old men are mighty Warriors." Jesse coughed and looked down for a few seconds. "Jeremiah died a warrior with a soft heart for everyone in need. As my precious granddaughter just said, Jeremiah is going to be missed by everyone who knew him.

There is an empty chair at our table, but he will live forever in our hearts.

"As I look out over this room filled with men, women, and children, I am not surprised at your presence, and Jeremiah would be very pleased. To help celebrate Jeremiah's memories, my men have been up all night smoking a large side of beef. After this service, everyone is invited to come to my ranch and enjoy a large spread of food. I hope all of you will come."

***

A few days later, Ollie and Will walked out to the small family cemetery to place fresh wildflowers on Jeremiah's grave. "I know he would be surprised to know that you buried him in the family graveyard," Ollie said with a little chuckle in her voice.

"Why would he?" When Ollie didn't answer, Will said, "Jeremiah was family. When the good Lord calls you home, you will be laid to rest right beside him. You would like that, wouldn't you?"

"Sure would, but what do you think others will feel about us Blacks lying in this pretty cemetery next to your grandfather, Papa and Mama?"

Will had bent down to place the lovely flowers on Jeremiah's grave. "Ollie, I'm surprised at you. You should know that we Maxwell's don't see a person's skin color. We look at their souls."

***

Doctor Tim had ordered Hope to walk a bit every day, but not on the sandy road that ran from her house to her folks' place. She fretted most days until Will would take her to see Rae. With a full-time housekeeper, she had very little to do. It was too hot to cook big meals, so most of the time they ate at Jesse's and Rae's table. Hope enjoyed helping Ollie and Rae cook and listen to the gossip that the men carried from town.

Hope thoughts went to Miss Ollie. No one said anything to Miss Ollie about the passing of Jeremiah. Everyone tried to go on with their normal routine, but the old man was surely missed. Aunt Katie and John worked hard on their flower farm. With the late spring and early summer, this was the busiest time for them. Missy was busy taking care of her young son. They depended on Tater for help with the packing and selling to the customers who wanted a wagon bed full of flowers. John had said that business was good, but not having Jeremiah's help, they were going to have to hire another man to help them.

After John and Katie had left for their flower farm, Hope sat at the kitchen table with Willa, who, like most little girls, wanted to sit at her mama's feet and listen to all the gossip. Many times, Rae and Hope had to spell words so the little nosy girl wouldn't know who or what they were talking about. But Willa was a smart child, so she probably knew everything.

***

After supper, Jesse asked Will to ride out with him to the pasture and get a head count of the new calves that had been dropped. Jesse wanted to take the cattle by train to Fort Worth and sell. He wanted to brand the young calves and round them up into several large pens in the pastures. All this needed to be done in the next few weeks. And Jesse wanted to have this chore completed before it was Hope's time.

"Well, Jesse, do you think we need to hire a few good men to help? John is so busy at his place and Bud has been harvesting many of the farmers' corn crops. Without Jeremiah, we will need help with the branding for sure."

"Tomorrow, we will go into town and post a sign to hire some men. The sooner we get started, the sooner we will return from Fort Worth with full pockets," Jesse said.

***

The men saddled up and rode out to the big pastures while the ladies helped Ollie clean the kitchen.

"We have enough baked apples for lunch tomorrow," Ollie said."Come on over here, Ollie, and continue with your story. Will and Papa Jesse will be gone for several hours." As Hope guided Ollie to her favorite rocking chair, she told Rae, "Miss Ollie has been telling me about her childhood, about when she first came to work for the boy's grandfather, then later worked for their parents, Jake and Missy."

"Really? I have heard a little about Ollie's life, but not about Jesse's folks," Rae said. "Ollie, come on over and sit down and take a load off your feet." She placed a foot stool in front of Ollie's rocker.

***

Ollie sat down and sighed loudly. "Lordy, it always feels so good to sit." She smiled at the girls. "Let's see, I remember where I left off. Missy, the boy's mama, was very weak. Once in a while she would ask to go to town and church, but she only wanted Jesse to help her. I stayed home from church to take care of Will because Missy wouldn't allow him to leave the farm. She was afraid he would catch something."

"How old were you then, Ollie?" Rae asked.

"Oh, I guess I was thirty-five or so. Will was small." She looked to the ceiling trying to remember. "Jake continued to work on the house. The men he hired had already built two other bedrooms onto the back and installed two water closets. The house didn't look like the old soddy- house any longer. Jake was ready to rebuild the kitchen, but Missy had a hissy fit. She didn't want strange men in the house, and she had no place to go to get out of their way."

Jake did most of the repair work himself and he did a good job. Missy wasn't happy with anything that he did to improve the room. One day she moved her things into the big bedroom in the back of the house and locked the door every night. Poor Jake. He was still a young man and needed his wife, but he stopped trying to tell her goodnight and he tucked the boys into bed himself. I cooked the food that she wanted, but she only nibbled at it. After a while I noticed how frail she was getting. I told Jake that she could hardly walk to the water closet, so he asked the doctor to come out and check her over. The news was bad. She had consumption, and her pulse and heart were weak. He told Jake that her days were numbered. The doctor tried to talk with her about how to get better, but she just turned her head toward the wall, refusing to listen.

The doctor gave me instructions to help make her better, but she only screamed for him to get out of her house. She yelled, *'That man's so dumb he couldn't pour piss out of a boot!'*

Well, Lordy, I didn't know what to do. I had never heard Missy use any kind of foul language or say anything unkind about another person. Mr. Jake apologized over and over to the doctor, but he swore he wouldn't be back if she felt that way about him.

"Our poor Missy died the following Sunday evening. I believe she knew she was dying because she had me comb her hair and put on her nicest gown and robe. She told me to leave her alone. Later, thinking she might be asleep, I went to check on her. I used my key and opened her door. Her pretty hair was spread across the pillow as she lay as sweet as an angel with the quilt pulled up to her chest. When I walked over to her bed, I could tell she was too still. I placed my hand on her forehead, and she was already cold. In her right hand was a bloody handkerchief.

Mr. Jake was devastated. He blamed himself for her death. He said she was too weak to have another child, but gracious, after four years, she had time to get her strength back. The doctor said he had told her that he was sure she had tuberculosis, but she only laughed. He said that she threatened to spread ugly rumors about him if he told Jake that stupid diagnosis. The doctor also told her that she needed to move to Arizona or New Mexico where the air was drier. It made the doctor sad that Missy didn't trust him and wouldn't listen. Believe it or not, I felt sorry for that doctor. Missy was a terrible patient."

Ollie continued to rock. "Lord, the following days were so sad. Jake didn't know what to do with himself. The boys and I went about every day, kind of like we had been doing before Missy died. She never played with Will, but she showered Jesse with attention. Of course, he was older, and I would find him crying on his bed or out in the barn. Jesse took her death really hard. Time always helps us to accept death, but that doesn't mean you still don't miss that person.

"Jake filled his days remodeling the inside of the house. He hired two men, one of them was Hank, and they helped him and Jesse knock out walls and rebuild the kitchen, pantry, and dining room. He always wanted a large stone wall with a fireplace, so he spent many hours polishing and smoothing the stones and you can still see how nice the wall looks today. After the kitchen was completed, Mr. Maxwell asked Hank if he would like a job on the ranch, and Hank has been here ever since."

"Mr. Maxwell would shower, dress in nice clean clothes and ride into town on Saturday night. Sometimes Hank would go with him, but they never spoke of any single women that either one of them might have spent time with. At church, Mr. Maxwell sat with the boys and wouldn't speak to any of the ladies. He was a recluse. All he cared about was his cattle ranch. A few years later, he bought a few thoroughbred horses for Jesse. The boy always loved horses, so his papa bought some so he could learn to work with them. As the years went by, Jesse grew into a fine young man who worked beside his papa every day. Hank was the overseer of the fields. He worked beside three young Mexicans boys who came every day and went home in the evening."

"What did Will do every day?" Hope asked, wondering about her husband as a young boy.

"Oh, he went to school. He wanted to quit and become a ranch hand, but Jake wouldn't hear of it. That was a big fight for sure, but Jake won that battle." Ollie wiped her mouth and sighed big.

One day, Mr. Maxwell went riding by himself to check on a few new calves. Around suppertime, he had not returned. Jesse was worried about him. and he asked Hank to go with him to look for his papa. A few miles from the ranch, they found him lying in a ravine. His neck was broken. A small calf lay on its side, tangled in some briars.

If I recall, Jesse was twenty and Will was about twelve. Lordy that Will thought he was grown, and he and Jesse had many loud arguments. I thought they might kill each other, but Hank always came in between them.

"You know, Miss Ollie, I have been married to Jesse for twenty-five years, and I have learned so much about his childhood today. I have asked him over the years about his mama, but he only says that she was pretty and sweet. Nothing else. I did ask how long he had been on the ranch and his answer was forever." She laughed.

"I think Will was about sixteen when we came to the ranch. I remember he was very nice to me," Hope said.

"Listen, I believe the boys have returned. Golly, I have been running off at the mouth for too long. I bet they would like to have something sweet to eat. Come on Rae, dish up some cobbler and fresh coffee." Ollie pushed herself up from the rocker and waddled into the kitchen.

Chapter 12

Claire pulled her carriage up to the picket fence at her parent's ranch. Rae saw her daughter drive up and she rushed onto the walkway to give her a big hug. "Oh, Claire, I have missed you so much. I brought you a little something from California."

"I missed you and papa, too. Don't ever leave for weeks again," Claire said, smiling. "I felt lost knowing that you were gone. Yes, I know I could have driven out to see Hope and Ollie, but this place isn't the same without you here."

"This place is different every morning without Jeremiah sitting at our kitchen table sharing coffee and fussing with Ollie. We try not to mention him because it makes her so sad."

"Oh, I have a large package for her. Mr. Zackery stopped me as I was coming out of the post office and asked if I was coming out to the ranch soon. I told him I was on my way this morning and he asked me to give this to her."

She reached down into her big bag and pulled out the package. "I have no idea what this could be but let's go in and give it to her." Claire placed her arm through her mama's arm, and they walked into the house.

"Good morning, Miss Ollie," Claire called.

"Oh my, young'un, it's so good to see you. I didn't get to visit with you last time you were here."

"Mr. Zackery, the lawyer, asked me to give this to you. I have no idea what's in this big package. Come and sit down at the table and open it."

Ollie took the package and read her name written across the front. She smiled and tore open the top and pulled out two pieces of white paper. "She squinted her eyes and moved the paper away from her and then brought it back to her."

"Would you like for me to read it to you, Ollie?" Rae asked.

"That would be nice. These old eyes ain't what they used to be."

Rae looked at the top of the first page and said, "Ollie, this is Jeremiah's Will. Goodness, it is dated five years ago and then amended in June, 1894 to change last names of some of the beneficiaries." She glanced at Ollie and Claire.

"Go on and read it. See what that old goat was thinking."

"It is his handwriting and signed by a lawyer, John W. Wilson. Oh, I remember him. Jesse and I had him transfer land to Will and later to Jess. A nice man,"

"Go on Mama. Read what Jeremiah wrote," Claire said, watching as Ollie wrung her hands.

"He writes, 'to whom this may concern, I leave twenty thousand dollars, in the First National Bank of Limason, to my beloved friend, Ollie Pritchet. *Twenty thousand dollars!* Oh, mine, he says he has more." Rae was flustered. "At present I have thirty-five thousand dollars."

"My goodness! Where did Jeremiah get that kind of money? I knew he never seemed to have money problems but he never spoke about being rich. And you said this was written five years ago?" Ollie fanned herself with a hankie.

"Yes, that is what written across the top. Let me continue. 'I leave each of the following people two thousand dollars: Jesse Maxwell, Will Maxwell, Jess Maxwell, Hope Maxwell, and Claire Maxwell. I leave five thousand dollars to my dear friend, Hank. At the time of my death, I should have more money, if God's willing, and that money should be divided between any grandchildren that may have come from Will, Jess, Claire and Missy for their education. I have jewelry in a bank deposit box kept at the bank. My wishes are for Jesse to do whatever he wants to do with the pieces.

'I leave my share of the Flower Farm to John and Katie Johnson. The flower farm's property is cleared of any debt. I paid it off several years ago. Money paid monthly by John and Katie, to the bank has been placed into a saving account for them. The saving account is in their name, John and Katie Johnson.

I leave my five acres connected to the Downey's farm to Tater and Missy Downey with my wish that they build a house and live on the property.

In Peamont, Texas, I leave my fifty acres, to be sold and money used to help repair my church and build a schoolhouse and hire a teacher for the Black community. Deed is in bank's deposit box. On this date, January 25, 1890, I bequeath the above and request that Jesse Maxwell see that my wishes are fulfilled.

One finally word: I love Ollie Pritchet and all the Maxwell family. I love Katie Johnson like my very own daughter.

Jeremiah

***

"Mercy Ollie, where do you think Jeremiah got all that money and the money to buy all that property?"

"Well, I wouldn't know for sure. He has been here for over twenty-five years, and I never really saw him spend a lot of money. He worked for Katie's first husband for years, and he had a successful business. Once, he said something about being in partnership with Katie's husband, but I didn't question him. For years, he was paid a small wage to work for Jesse and also helped with the flower farm. Shoot, he talked about investing his money, but I didn't know what that meant."

"Well, it doesn't matter where he got it; he had it and now he is leaving it to all of us." Claire was thrilled. "*Two thousand dollars* is like a dream come true. Albert is going to be so pleased, because he watches every dime we spend. Even though we have a beautiful house his parents built for us, we don't make big salaries. Now we will have a nest egg."

"Ollie, what will you do with twenty thousand dollars?" Rae asked, grinning.

"First thing I want to do is give some to Sadie, an old lady in my church. She's crippled and takes in washing from some of the field hands on several farms. I would like to make her life easier."

"I'm not surprised," Rae laughed softly. "I know you will do great things with your gift from Jeremiah. You will make him proud," Rae said, as she went into the kitchen to look at the roast in the oven.

"Just wait until the others come in to lunch. They'll be surprised. Hank is going to be thrilled for sure. Oh my," Claire commented. "I wonder how much money Hank has saved over the years."

"Oh, honey," Rae said, "Hank has never made that much money working here on our ranch. I know he doesn't have a lot of expenses, but who knows what he does or who he helps. He's a good-hearted man, just like Jeremiah was."

"Now, you two listen to me. I don't care that the family knows about the money Jeremiah has left all of us, but we must keep this quiet. Don't let the children know or anyone outside of the family. All my friends already think I'm a rich, old woman," Ollie said, smiling.

"Mama, I am not staying for lunch. I want to get home and share the wonderful news with Albert. He is going to be sad, happy and surprised all at the same time. He thought the world of Jeremiah, just like we all did."

"Clair, child, I will walk you to the porch. There's something I want you to do." Ollie and Claire walked outside, and Ollie looked over her shoulder to make sure Rae didn't hear what she had to tell Claire. "I want you to stop by Bud and Rosie's place. Justice and I talked. She has made you two toddies to drink. Now, don't question her about what's in them. Just do like she tells you, and we feel it will help you to conceive soon."

"The drink isn't dangerous, is it? I did ask Justice and she said it wasn't."

"Child, would we ever do anything to harm a hair on your head. Justice knows what she's doing. You can't speak of this to anyone, now, you hear?"

"I trust you." Claire turned to walk to the barn to get her horse and carriage. "I sure hope these toddies work. I want a baby so bad."

Ollie blew her a kiss and watched Hank hitch her horse to her small, black carriage.

Chapter 13

Claire rushed into her house and placed both of the toddies in the ice box in their big pantry. She made a few ham sandwiches, deviled eggs and placed bread and butter pickles on a plate for Albert's lunch. She hurriedly scribbled him a note saying that she had a few errands to run and she wouldn't be home to eat with him. "You will find your lunch in the icebox. Love Claire."

***

Albert had been busy all morning at the bank, but he was starving. "I'm going to lunch now," he told the bank manager. "Be back soon."

Once he arrived home, he found Claire's note. He was disappointed that she wasn't home. Since it was summertime, he enjoyed sharing lunch with her. He went into the pantry, opened the small icebox and pulled out a covered plate with his lunch. He noticed two tall glasses of something chocolate so he grabbed one of them and took a big drink. *Man, this chocolate has a kick to it, but it's really good.*

After eating his lunch and drinking the toddy, he thought about the other tall glass in the icebox. He decided that Claire wouldn't care if he drank some of hers. She barely eats and drank enough to keep a bird alive. So he indulged some of hers.

Once back at work, he was feeling good and little frisky. Light on his feet, he found himself whistling. The bank manager and teller kept looking at him, probably wondering what had put him in such a good mood.

Miss Liverpool came into the bank, requesting to talk about a loan for her dress shop. She was led to Albert's office, and he offered her a chair. She was a pretty, petite lady and Albert suddenly felt himself becoming very uncomfortable from his waist down. He pulled his chair closer into his desk and gave himself a shake. "Now Miss Liverpool, how may I assist you this fine afternoon?"

Once their business was finalized, Albert was in a strange predicament. When he stood, he placed her file in front of his private parts and walked her to the door. Something was terribly wrong, so he announced to the bank teller that he needed to rush home. "I'm not feeling well."

The bank teller stood at the window and watched Albert run down the street toward his house. "What happened to Albert?" the bank manager asked.

"Something peculiar. Not really sure, but it came on him after Miss Liverpool entered the bank." The men watched Albert until he was out of sight.

***

Albert rushed into his house and raced up the staircase to the master bedroom. He went into the water closet and examined himself. He couldn't find anything wrong, except he was in a scary, crazy-like mood. He placed his face into his palms and started bawling. He couldn't remember when he cried last. Leaning down he placed his elbows on his knees and ran his fingers through his hair pulling it out from his ears. Beads of sweat popped out on his forehead. A strange sensation flowed over him, and his mood changed.

Albert moved slowly out of the water closet, took off his glasses and removed his suit coat. Suddenly, he wanted to take off all his clothes. He removed his vest, shirt, belt, and pants. He pulled off his white union undershirt and looking in the mirror, then flexed his muscles. He felt a little on the wild side. Reaching for his undershirt, he tied its long sleeves around his neck like a cape. He leapt on the bed with only the cape, short union underpants and long wool socks. Feeling like the king of the jungle, he jumped up and down on the mattress like a little kid.

***

Claire opened the door and walked into the kitchen. She saw that Albert had been home and placed his dish and a tall glass by the dry sink. Oh no, she thought. Albert drank one of her toddies! She went to the icebox and sure enough, one of the toddies were gone and the other only had only a few sips left in it.

Hearing a loud noise coming from above, she hurried to the entrance hall and called up the staircase. "Albert, are you home?"

The bedroom door flew open and Albert slide across the floor at the top of the stairs. He was undressed, almost, but the lower part of his body was at full attention. Surprised was the only word that came to her mind.

"Albert, sweetheart, did you drink my chocolate toddy?"

"Yes, my Fair Lady!" he answered her with a gallant bow. "It was delicious. You must get some more." He practically danced down the long staircase and grabbed her around the waist. "Come, we must go to my hideaway and make mad passionate love." Before she knew what had happened, he grabbed her into his arms and raced back up the stairs, stumbling several times, but they reached the top and lay on the floor.

"Where are your glasses?" she asked.

"I don't need them to see you my fair lady." He stood and pulled her into their bedroom. He started to unbutton her shirtwaist, but his fingers were numb, so he tore open the blouse and buttons flew across the room.

"Slow down, Albert. Talk to me." Claire removed her skirt and the torn blouse when he pulled her toward him. She had never known Albert to act so impulsive.

Slowly, Albert backed into the foot of the bed and sat down. He held his face in his hands and began to cry again. "I don't know what's wrong with me. One minute I am a mighty warrior, and the next, I'm crying like—a stupid baby. Help me Claire, help me."

Claire stood in front of Albert as he wrapped his strong arms around her waist. She held his face into her body. "Oh, Albert, I'm sure it's the drink you had for lunch. Surely, it will wear off soon."

Albert pushed her away, suddenly becoming a wild man. He wore a silly grin and wide eyes, then picked her up and tossed her on the bed. Straddling her, he ripped off the rest of her clothes and became a roaring, raging bull.

Claire didn't know whether to be afraid or laugh. Everything was happening so fast.

He entered her unprepared body and collapsed on top of her. "Aww, that was wonderful."

"Albert? When he didn't answer, she said his name again. She said, over and over. He lay as still as death.

Claire tried to awaken her adorable husband, but when she couldn't, she became very afraid. She slid off the bed, grabbed her long, satin robe and rushed downstairs. Flinging the door open, she practically flew off the porch and leaped through the hedges that divided Doctor Tim and Hannah's home from theirs. Just as she started to bang on the door, Doctor Tim drove his carriage into his circular drive.

"Oh, Doctor Tim, please come. It's Albert. He's in our bed and I think he's dead!" She cried.

They hurried into Claire's house and stopped. There on the foyer floor, Albert laid spread-eagle on the floor with a grin on his face.

"I though you said he was in your bed?"

"He was when I left. I guess he wasn't dead after all."

Doctor Tim felted all over Albert's body for any broken bones. Albert reached for Doctor Tim and attempted to pull him down on top of him. "Come on baby, let's do it again."

Doctor Tim leaned down and smelled Albert's breathe. "What in the world did he drink?" he looked at Claire for an answer.

When she stood and looked away, Doctor Tim stood up, too. "Claire, what did Albert drink? It was mighty potent for sure."

Claire refused to answer. She was too embarrassed to tell the truth.

"I can't help this young husband of yours unless you tell me. You know I will not speak about this to anyone."

"Ollie and Justice made me a couple of toddies to drink to help me conceive. They were only trying to help *me*. . Albert wasn't supposed to drink it or even know about them."

"How did Albert come to drink them?"

"I brought them home this morning and placed them in our icebox to get cold. I was to drink one after lunch and then sip on the other before I went to bed tonight. Albert came home for lunch and I guess he thought I had made them for us."

Doctor Tim looked down at Albert, all cuddled into a ball on the hard floor. "Go get a pillow and blanket to cover him. Do you have any of the drink left?"

"Yes, it's in the kitchen by the dry sink. He drank most of both of them. He said they were delicious."

As Claire covered her wild man, Doctor Tim pulled out a hair in the chocolate drink. "I think this is a hair of some kind. This toddy is loaded with whiskey, too." Doctor Tim laughed. "Justice will not tell me what's in the toddies, so it's no use in my asking. Albert will not die, but his private parts will take a while to get back to normal. He doesn't need to go out in public until tomorrow, so let's get him back to bed.'

"It will be easier to carry him into the spare room down here. I will stay with him to make sure the King of the Jungle remains home." Claire laughed.

Chapter 14

After a long hot day, Jesse told Jess and Will to bring their wives to supper. "John, Katie, Tater and Missy are coming over, Bud took a note into town to Albert, Claire, Tim and Hannah to be here, too." Jesse turned to walk to the house, he called to Hank. "Hank, get cleaned up and don't be late. This dinner is important."

"It's only a Tuesday night. Is there something special going on that we need to know about?" Jess asked.

"There is something very special that all of you need to hear, but Ollie and I want you all to hear it at the same time. The girls are making a big stew--nothing fancy, but plenty of it."

"Should we bring something?" Will asked.

"No, it's too late to ask the ladies to prepare anything. Just come." Jesse strolled toward the house while Jess and Will walked up the lane to their homes.

Hank went into the barn to take a quick bath and change clothes. He pondered what this special news was all about, but knowing Jesse, he wouldn't spit a word out until it was time.

Hours later, Jesse held open the front door. "Come on in and let's eat. I'm starved." He pulled out chairs for Ollie and Rae, while Will helped Willa and Jay take their place at the table. Katie hugged Hope, Claire and Mary Beth before she sat down next to Willa. John motioned for Missy to sit down while Tater had to whisper a joke to Jess and Albert. "If you men are ready to stop clowning around, I'll ask the blessing."

After Supper was over and the ladies had pitched in and cleaned off the table, washed and dried the dishes, the men brought in chairs from the dining room so everyone could sit down in the large living room.

"Ollie wanted me to invite you all here this evening to hear the reading of Jeremiah's Will." A hush went across the room. "Jeremiah was a very generous man, we all know that. I want you to know that Ollie and I had no idea how wealthy Jeremiah was. He wrote his will over five years ago, and last year he amended it to change some of the last names, but I can tell he put a lot of thought into what he left each of you." Jesse looked around the round at his family and read, "To whom this may concern, I leave twenty thousand dollars, in the First National Bank of Limason, to my love, Ollie".

No one said a word. Jesse hesitated before continuing.

"I leave each of the following people two thousand dollars: Jesse Maxwell, Will Maxwell, Jess Maxwell, Hope Maxwell and Claire Maxwell." He stopped and peered around the room. No one said anything or moved. "I leave five thousand dollars to my dear friend, Hank."

Hank leaped from his chair and yelled, "Holy . . . ! He can't do that. He didn't have that kind of money, and besides, what in the world am I going to do with it?"

"Hank, Jeremiah had plenty of money, and you were his best friend. Now, calm down and sit. Let me continue, please."

"At the time of my death, I should have accumulated more money, God's willing, and that money should be divided between any grandchildren that may have come from Will, Jess, Missy or Claire for their education or plans that their parents agree upon.

"I checked at the bank, and Jeremiah has over eighteen thousand dollars and that money will be divided among the four: Will, Jess, Claire, and Missy."

I leave my share of the Flower Farm to John and Katie Johnson. The flower farm's property is cleared of any debt. I paid it off several years ago."

Katie busted out in tears. "Oh my, what a thoughtful old man. I loved him so much."

Jesse continued, "Money paid monthly by John and Katie, to the bank has been placed into a saving account for them. The saving account is in their name, John and Katie Johnson.

"My Lord, Katie, we've been making payments on our property for years. There will be a might large sum in the bank for us," John stated.

"Well, whatever the amount of money is in the account, it is yours. This is what he wanted." Jesse looked around the room and all the ladies were crying silent tears.

"I leave my five acres connected to the Downey's farm to Tater and Missy Downey with my wish that they build a house and live on the property."

"Oh my, Tater, you hear that. Now we can build our own home."

'In Peamont, Texas, I leave my fifty acres, to be sold and money used to help repair my church and build a schoolhouse and hire a teacher for the Black community. I am asking Will to oversee the construction of these building.'

"On this date, January 25, 1890, I bequeath the above and request that Jesse Maxwell see that my wishes are fulfilled. In the margin of this will is where he signed to have it amended to show the changes of last names."

One finally word: I love Ollie Pritchet and all the Maxwell family. I love Katie Johnson like my very own daughter and Missy like my granddaughter.

"I pray that you all will be pleased with what I left each of you.
Jeremiah

Everyone sat in stone silence. Even Willa and Jay didn't move a muscle. Finally, Ollie said, "I think we should pray. Everyone bowed their heads and Ollie spoke softly,

"Lord, we want to thank you for our beloved friend. Our hearts are broken because he's not with us in person, but his spirit shall live forever in our hearts. We are all thankful that he remembered us and has helped these young people with their future dreams. Bless us all tonight that we will use his gifts wisely and in his love. Amen"

"Thank you, Ollie. I do have something important to say. Please don't talk about Jeremiah's will to anybody. The community doesn't need to know what he left any of us, especially Ollie. All her Black friends already thinks she's rich. When I sell his property in Peamont and hand over the money to Will to oversee the repairs to their church and the construction of the school, then, it will be just fine for them to know that Jeremiah remembered them." Jesse looked at all the children and they gave a nod.

Everyone gathered back in the dining room for peach cobbler

and coffee. Hank was still sitting in the living room all alone. Will walks over to him and asked what was on his mind.

"On my mine, are you kidding? I ain't never had more than a hundred dollars saved up at one time in my life. Now, I have five thousand dollars. What in the world was that old fool thinking to leave me such a windfall?"

"He was thinking that his old friend didn't need to worry about his future. If and when you want to stop working and just sit around on the porch with Ollie, you can." Will smiled and looked at Hank.

"I guess, but Will, I never knew Jeremiah had so much money. We never discussed money or even the future. I just figured we would sit on the front porch and tell lies till one of us just up and died."

Doctor Tim walked over and pulled up a chair next to Will and Hank. "I want to tell you both something. I am sure that Jeremiah had been ill for a long time. His lungs were too weak, and his heart was giving out on him. If we think about it, we know that he didn't take long rides out in the pastures and carried buckets of water out to the cattle. He had started slowly down, thinking that no one would notice. I had told him a while back to slow down, but I had no idea he was as sick as he was."

"Doctor Tim," Katie stood next to his straight chair. "I was going through Jeremiah's clothes last night and I found his pocket watch. He had this piece the very first time I met him. I would like for you to have it." She held the old gold pocket watch out for him.

Doctor Tim looked down at the shiny gold pocket watch with a long gold chain. "I remember Jeremiah wearing it every time he was in his Sunday dress. "I would be honored to have it, but Ollie might like to keep it?" He peered up at Katie.

"Ollie and I both want you to have it."

Tim took the watch and held it tightly in his large hand. "I will always cherish this gift. Thank you." He took the watch and hooked the chain in his vest pocket. "I will have it on me from now on." He stood and walked over to Hannah. "We had better get on home. Duty calls early in the morning," Tim said as he took Hannah's hand.

Chapter 15

Jesse was in the corral, preparing to take his herd of cattle to the train depot. They had to be herded in the cattle cars and taken to Fort Worth to sell.

Will came riding up on his big bay, prepared to leave. "Jesse, I'm praying that this will be a quick trip. If something happens with the sale of the cattle, I will have to catch the train and come home. Doctor Tim says that Hope won't be delivering the twins for at least six weeks. He promises to keep a close eye on her every couple of days. But you never know."

"You can return home whenever you need to, or if you had rather stay home, John and Jess will understand. I can hire a couple of men in town to go."

Will held up a palm. "No, I want to go and I'm sure Hope would be disappointed if I stayed. She says I am driving her crazy."

Jesse laughed. "Rae said that she is going to tell Hope and the kids to come and stay here with them. We have plenty of room, and I will feel better if she stays down here with the Rae and Ollie."

"I told her to plan on staying here, but she can be so stubborn. I was sure that Rae might insist, so that makes me feel better. Hope really wants to be here too."

Jesse slapped the rear of one of the cows. "All right, let's get these cattle moving toward town. The sooner we leave the sooner we will return.

"Where Jess this morning?" Will asked as he looked up the hill toward Jess's ranch house.

"He's in the house talking to Rae about Mary Beth. She is planning to go back to nursing school. Jess is trying to be happy about it, but he's not ready to accept the idea of living alone for the next year or two. I think he wants Rae to tell him to come and live here with us while she's away."

"Here he comes. When will she been moving back up north?"

"Not really sure, but it will be soon. Let's not ask about it. He will tell us what he wants us to know." Jesse turned his horse around and saw Rae and Ollie standing on the porch blowing kisses, giving them a sendoff.

***

Once Hope saw Will off for a couple of weeks, she gave her housekeeper instructions before she left to be with Rae and Ollie for the day. She would get Hank to come to her house later and get their carpetbags. She had planned to stay with Rae and Ollie while Will was gone on the cattle drive, but he had made her mad earlier, so she didn't tell him. Let him worry about her while he was gone.

The morning was beautiful and Hope watched Jay and Willa race to Ollie, jumping and skipping all the way. Ollie had a cup of coffee waiting for Hope on the porch. The kids had gone into the kitchen to get something sweet from Rae.

***

"Willa," Rae asked, "Why do you keep scratching your head? Come over here and let me look at your scalp."

Rae moved Willa's hair all around and lifted the hair off her shoulders and glanced at her hairline. "How long have you been scratching?"

"I don't know. Just started, I think."

Rae took Willa outside on the porch where the light was better. She looked deeper into the child's hair.

"Hope, I 'm afraid that this little bugger has head lice. We are gonna have to do something to get rid of them now."

"No," Hope screamed. "Let me look!" Hope struggles to get out of the rocker as tears formed in her eyes.

"Oh, mama, don't cry. My head ain't hurting."

"Ollie, you gotta help. What do we do to get rid of them? I don't want to have to cut her beautiful curls. No, I will not do that."

"Give me a minute to think. I do remember having those critters in my head when I was about ten. Lordy, I had them bad. I had been playing with some of the field-hand children. When I kept scratching, the old cook grabbed one of my pigtails and looked at my hair. At that time, I had bushy hair so on of the housemaids plaited my hair in about six long pigtails. The old cook took me to the bath house and used a pair of scissors and cut off all my pigtails.

Then she pour kerosene all over my head and rubbed it in. She rubbed it on my scalp and on my neck until my skin felt raw. Then she placed a big white towel over my head and made me sit with it on my head for about forever. Finally, she rinsed my hair over and over until it was shiny. She then took the scissors and cut my hair as short as she could to make it even. My short hair curled ,and I have worn it like this all my life. Except, as I got older, I covered it with a bandana."

"But Ollie, I am not cutting her hair. We can do the same treatment but no cutting. What do you think, Rae?"

"Let's try it for sure. We better do Jay's hair too."

"No! I don't want that stuff on my hair. I'm not itching."

Rae stood over Jay and parted his soft brown hair and looked at his neckline. "He's right. He doesn't have them."

"Let me go see Hank this morning and get him to pour some kerosene in a jar. I will go get some old towels to wrap her hair when we placed the oil on her head. We won't cut her hair, Hope. So, just sit back down and let me take care of Willa."

After Hank retrieved the kerosene, Rae took Willa to the back porch and worked the oil into her hair. After wrapping her hair with towels, Rae brought out a plate of donuts and a cup of milk for the child to enjoy while waiting for the treatment to work.

***

"Hank, I need you to drive me to Hope's house so I can tell Mary Lou that she needs to scrub Willa's bedroom. Her tick and mattress will need to be burned."

Hank helped Ollie from the carriage, and she entered the house. Where was the young housekeeper? As she stood in the foyer, she heard sounds like a rutting hog. Something wild was surely in Willa's room. She eased the door wide open and was surprised to find Hope's young housekeeper all wrapped in a young man's arms, lying on top of Willa's bed.

"What's going on here?" Ollie yelled as she stood in the doorway. The couple was so involved in their lovemaking that they didn't hear Ollie come in. The young girl, Mary Lou, pushed her young lover off of her and grabbed a light blanket and covered her naked body. The boy landed on the floor, snatching his discarded pants.

"Answer me now. What do you think you're doing? Don't start lying to me either. I'm so mad I'm fixin' to lose my religion!"

"Well, uh, I was making up the missy's bed when he came to see me." She pointed at her young lover. "He started helping me with the covers and suddenly a, uh, *big, wicked snake* appeared, and the next thing just happened. We had to try to make it go away. We landed on the bed, and that's the God awful truth, ain't it Willie?"

The young boy shook his head up and down, like a bobble head. Ollie glared at the two who was shaking like a dog pooping watermelon seeds.

"Get your clothes back on your skinny behind and you, boy, had better get that wicked snake back in your pants and get your rag tail out of this house." Ollie walked further into the Willa's room and both of the young'un jumped into action. As Mary Lou dressed, Willie gave her a wide space and raced out on the porch.

Ollie joined her, hands posted on hips. "Gal, don't ever come back to this house again."

"But Miss Ollie, what am I gonna tell my folks? I need this job."

"Chase after that young buck with the wicked snake and ask him," she said. Ollie walked out of the house and told Hank that she needed him to help her carry all the bed linens in Willa's room to Rae's. "We need to roll up her bed tick and mattress and burn them."

The front door slammed, and Mary Lou jumped off the tall porch and raced through the woods toward safety.

"What in the world has gone on here?" Hank asked. "Why isn't that gal helping you?"

"Didn't you see that boy?" Ollie asked.

"Yep, he was running like something scary was after him."

"Well, let's let just say if you're gonna dance, you gotta pay the fiddler. Well, those two just did a jig and had to pay up," Ollie said as she went back into the house.

Chapter 16

Doctor Tim put his stethoscope back in his medical bag. "Hope, I must say you sure have two strong heartbeats. I'm very pleased that you're doing well, and the babies are too. Now don't get frisky and attempt to do any heavy housework or stay on your feet too long each day. Good meals, strolling around on level ground and resting every day are your orders to follow. I will be back out in a day or two,"

After a light lunch with Rae, Hank and the children, Ollie followed Doctor Tim out on the porch. "I just wanted to ask if you have seen Claire lately. Since she lives next door, I was wondering if you have seen her or Albert. She hasn't been out in a few days, and I was kinda worried about her."

"As a matter of fact, I did have to run over to their home a couple of days ago. I have been meaning to talk to you and your friend, Justice." He glanced over Ollie's shoulder and then pulled her off the porch to get away from the open door. "Claire told me about the *toddies'* you and your witch doctor, hoodoo friend made for her. Unfortunately, Albert came home for lunch and drank nearly all of them."

"Heaven help him," Ollie whispered. "He's all right?"

"He is now. But Ollie, look at me. You and your friend have got to stop practicing . . . *hocus pocus* on people."

"Do you mind telling me how the toddy made him feel?"

"Feel! He was a raving bull one minute, king of the jungle next, and then babbling like a babe. Claire didn't know what to do with him. I put him to bed and told her not to let him out of the house for a day.

"Oh, my goodness," Ollie shook her head side to side. "We were only trying to help Claire. She wants a child so bad."

"I know, but you have to let nature work miracles. No more toddies, please." Doctor Tim walked to his carriage and waved as he left for town.

***

After two days of travel on the train, Jesse left Will, John and Jess with the cattle and went to make arrangements for the corrals to place the herd. It wasn't long a tall, lanky older man with a long-handle mustache came back to the cattle cars and started giving Jesse's hired men orders. A long ramp was placed at the first cattle car and the beef came charging off the train. Will, Jess, and several of the young men Jesse had hired, began driving the herd alongside the tracks to the stockyard. It seemed to take forever for all the cattle to unload.

Jess sat in his saddle staring out into space. He was daydreaming with his eyes wide open about his lovely wife. Will called to him to be careful and watch some of the older cows, but Jess seemed to be in another world. His Mary Beth was his world, and she would be leaving him as soon as he got back to Limason.

Will rode his big bay beside Jess to get his attention. "Hey lover boy, get your mind back on the job before someone gets hurt. These cows can get out of control pretty fast with all that crowd of city folks gathering around."

"Sure, I'm sorry. Just thinking about home."

"I understand, but let's get these cows into their assigned corrals," Will yelled to him.

Will did understand how Jess felt being away from home. He couldn't stop thinking about Hope. He needed to be at her side every day, especially since she was going to have twins. Lordy, that woman could make him so mad so fast, but he loved her more than life. He had loved that little gal since she was three years old, and he was only fifteen. She was the prettiest little girl he had ever seen and today, she was beautiful. The older and more mature she was, the prettier she become. Please Lord, let this be a quick, successful trip so they could get home soon, he prayed silently.

As evening came, the herd was all settled in their corral pens and the men were hungry and exhausted. After checking into the finest hotel that Fort Worth had and having a nice hot tub bath, the men felt human again after removing tons of dirt and grit off their bodies.

86

Will, John and Jess went into the hotel restaurant and ordered the biggest steak the placed served. Jesse came in and ordered the same. "Well, fellows, we can catch the train home tomorrow. I settled with a buyer and got top dollar for our beef. It seems up north, there's a shortage of high-quality meat."

A big-belly waiter carried a platter of steaks and boiled potatoes to the table. Jesse came in and ordered the same.

The four men stretched out their long legs and patted their stomachs. "Well, boys, I'm going over to the telegraph office and send a note to the girls that we'll be home in two or three days the most. I don't know about you two, but I'm taking this old body off to bed. See you at breakfast, and then I'm going to check out the shops."

As Jess, John and Will started back upstairs, Jess said that he was going to go into the saloon and have a night cap before retiring.

"Since when did you start indulging into hard liquid?" Will asked. John was surprised at Jess's statement, too.

"Just one drink might help me relax and not think about Mary Beth. One drink won't kill me," Jess said, trying not to get angry with Will.

Will gave Jess a salute as he waltzed around a saloon gal who was giving him the once-over. He tipped his hat and smiled as he hurried up the staircase behind John.

***

Jess walked into the saloon and strolled over to the chrome bar. He asked for a whiskey and looked around the room. A crowd of men were gathered in a circle and tossing cards into a hat and each man was given a card with the same number on it.

"What's going on?" Jess asked as men continued to toss cards and pay a dollar for the numbered cards.

"A man can toss a card into the hat and later, a number will be drawn from another hat. He will win all the money if he has the correct number card. Easy and fun. The pot can get up to a thousand dollars. You should toss a few cards into the hat."

"When will the man draw the number to see who the winner will be?"

"He going to draw in about ten minutes. You best hurry if you want a chance!" The men were excited, drinking and laughing.

Jess reached deep into his pockets and gave the man who was making change a ten-dollar bill. He received twenty cards, two each identical, and he immediately toss ten cards. He received many different number cards. He placed the other ten in his vest pocket and walked over to the bar and asked for another drink. It wasn't long before a man announced that he was going to pull out a number.

The men gathered around the hat with the number cards in it. One of the saloon gals counted the hat full of dollars. The winning pot had eight hundred and fifty-three dollars in it. The old man pulled out a card. He held up the card and yelled, "Queen of diamonds!"

Many men cussed and tossed their cards on the floor and lumbered to the bar. Jess flipped through his ten cards and laughed out loud. "Hey, I have the Queen!'

A man ran over to him and looked at his number card. "Well, congratulations, young man. You're the winner. Come over here and collect your winnings."

Jess wished Will or Jesse were down here with him. He took the money and felt too keyed up to go to bed. He tucked the money into his wallet and placed it in his vest pocket while several men gathered around him. They patted him on the back, so Jess told the bartender to set up drinks for these men. After feeling a little light-head, he said good night and walked up the staircase to his room. Boy, the guys are going to be surprised with his wild story about winning the money.

During the night, a man opened Jess's door and entered. Jess always a light sleeper, he sat up in the bed. "Who are you? What do you want?" he said, rubbing his eyes to clear them. The few drinks had made his head fuzzy.

The sound of gunfire, then a bullet hit Jess in the shoulder, knocking him off the bed. It was hard to see in the dark, but Jess saw the shadow of a man pick up his vest and empty its pockets.

"Hey, you have no—"

Just then the intruder rushed over to the door and made sure it was locked before he climbed out the front window onto the balcony.

***

Will, John and Jesse heard the gunfire and immediately rushed into the hallway. Since Jess didn't come out of his room, Will knocked on his door and jiggled the doorknob. When there was no answer, he kicked in the door, slamming it against the wall.

The light from the hall showed Jess lying on the floor with blood covering his chest, arm, and neck. "Get a doctor!" Will yelled to the men as he lifted Jess like a baby onto the bed.

John turned up the lantern, while Jesse immediately checked Jess for breathing. "He's alive. He took the bullet in his shoulder, thank the good Lord."

Somebody had summoned the sheriff and he arrived the same time the doctor did. "Move back and let me look at this young man," the doctor ordered.

Jesse and Will stood at Jess's bedside and watched the doctor closely.

"It's not too bad. Believe me, I've seen worse. He's going to be fine, but I have to move him over to my infirmary. Are you his kin?"

"Yes. He's my son. This is my brother," Jesse answered.

"Here comes someone with my stretcher. You two help place him on it and carry it behind me. I need to extract that bullet as fast as I can."

"Does anyone have any idea what took place here?" The sheriff looked around at the people gathered in the hall.

One of the men said the wounded man had been in the saloon, then said that he had a lot of money on him when he left a couple hours ago." He was the winner of the big pot of money. Nearly one thousand dollars. I saw him put it in his vest pocket."

The sheriff looked around the room and saw Jess's vest lying on the floor. "Is this the one he was wearing?"

"Yep, that's it," the man answered. He added that he shared a drink with Jess after he had won the money.

The sheriff checked the vest pocket, and it was empty. "I guess this is a case of burglary and armed robbery. He must have awakened the young man and then shot him. Must have climbed out this window," he said as he looked down over Front Street.

Once Jess was in the small operating room, Will told Jesse that Jess had gone into the saloon for a night-cap. I was surprised, but he said he needed a drink to help him sleep. He can't keep his mind off Mary Beth. My guess is he got into a betting game and won."

"From what that man said, it would seem so. I never knew Jess to be a gambler. Guess we live and learn about people when you go off with them," John said.

"I bet he won't be able to travel tomorrow. Do you think I could leave you two here and catch the train home? Like Jess, I'm worried about Hope."

"Maybe I can buy one of those sleeping compartments for Jess to use while traveling home. Doctor Tim will make sure he's fine once we arrive there."

"Sounds like a good plan. I really didn't want to leave you and John here." Will hung his head down and wiped the sleep out of his eyes. Man, he had just gotten to sleep when he heard the gunfire in the next room.

The next morning, Jesse carried a sleeping Jess onto the train. After a few hours of traveling, Jess started to wake up.

"Lie still, son," Jesse said.

"Hi, Pa. How long have I been asleep?"

"Ever since you got shot last night, and a long time today. The doctor doped you up pretty good after he took the bullet out of your shoulder."

"The medicine must be wearing off because my shoulder hurts like the dickens."

"You can have some more medicine after you have eaten a bit of food and taken care of your personal needs. I can help you to the water closet, and I will have John or Will bring you something from the dining car."

Once Jess had taken care of his personal needs, and washed his face and hands, John brought him a ham and cheese sandwich with a bowl of hot chicken soup. After he finished with his simple fare, he eyed his father and the two others. "I need some medicine. The pain was almost unbearable.

As Will prepared him a large spoon of sleeping medicine, Jesse asked him if he could remember anything about the man who shot him.

"I heard someone come into my room. The light from the hallway let me know it was a stranger. I asked him who he was and what he wanted. He laughed and then shot me as I was getting up. The darkness made a shadow of the man's face, but he wore a messy top hat. You know, one that gentlemen wear with an evening suit. His jacket had a high collar. That's all I remember."

"Do you think you would recognize the man if you saw him?"

"No, I don't think so, because it was dark. But, Pa, not many men wear top hats these days in Texas." He opened his mouth and Will spooned the medicine into his mouth. It wasn't long before Jess began to relax.

***

Will and John went into the dining car to get something to eat before returning to their seats. They had to pass through the car where men smoked, read newspapers and played cards. One of the men laughed and raised a high bet causing Will to notice him. He stopped in his tracks causing John to run into him.

"Hey, give me a warning next time you plan on stopping. I nearly busted my tooth on the back of your head."

Will made no comment while wiping the back of his head and continued to walk out of the moving car. "Did you see the man with the top hat?"

"No, I only saw the back of your head when you stopped walking."

"A man wearing a top hat and a high-collar coat was playing cards, and he was betting big. I would wager that's the man who robbed and shot Jess."

"Let's get our food and act natural as we come back through this car. I want to tell Jesse before we make a move."

***

"Jesse, let step out on the back of the car. The air is nice and fresh."

"All right, fellows, what's going on? I know you both are as tired as I am and ready to settle in for the night." Jesse smiled at a few passengers as they walked past.

"While we were walking through the car where the men smoke and play cards, I noticed a man wearing a dirty top hat and a high collar coat just like Jess described. And, the man was betting big. I think he may be the man who shot Jess and robbed him."

"Sounds like it, for sure. Let's go and I'll sit in on the card game and try to get the fool to talk. Men who have a large amount of money like to brag. John, if you don't mind, stay in the sleeping compartment with Jess. There's room to lie down if you want to.

Will and I may be more than a minute or two."

Before Jesse left the sleeping car, he strapped on his gun and hostler.

"Why are you wearing your gun?" Will asked, his eyebrows furrowing.

"I just might need it, and I want to be ready to arrest that fool."

Jesse and Will opened the door and entered the smoky car. Several men were sitting at the card table playing five card stud. The man wearing the top hat had a pile of greenbacks in front of him. "Can anyone sit in this game?" Jesse asked.

"Come on and sit down." The big guy said as he moved his cigar around in his nasty mouth. "I need some fresh blood. I've about drained these fellows of all their money."

"Here, have my seat," a tall, young man stood and walked out of the car.

"See, what I mean?" The big mouth laughed and waved for Jesse to take it.

Will walked over and sat down on a comfortable couch next to a window, but close enough to keep his eye and ears on the game. He picked up a day-old newspaper and flipped it open while watching Jesse take a seat at the table.

"Your friend don't want to play? Got plenty of room."

"No, he's not one for gambling," Jesse said, laughing a little. He reached into his vest pocket and pulled out a hundred dollars and place it in front of him. Will noticed the other men eyeing Jesse as the man dealt a hand for each player. The guy with the top hat won easily and laughed big. "You might need more money soon, if my luck continues."

"Your luck looks pretty good; that's for sure," Jesse said.

"He had a lot of money to start with," the player on the right of Jesse said.

"Really? Where did you get all your money to play with?" Jesse asked as he looked at his second hand of cards. "Did you sell cattle at the stockyard today?"

"No, man. I ain't working that hard to earn money, when there are easier ways of getting it." The man turned up a shot of whiskey and swallowed it down with one big gulp. He reached for his bottle and poured himself another one, then held it up at Jesse and asked if he wanted a drink.

Jesse ignored the man and kept his eyes on his cards. The man murmured, "suit yourself" and downed another one, then poured himself another before setting the bottle back on the table.

"What brought you fellows to Fort Worth if you aren't in the cattle business?" Jesse asked.

"I'm in the lumber business," one of the men answered and another said he was just passing through from up North.

"What kind of easy business are you in that lets you make all your money?" Jesse eyed the man with the top hat.

"You sure are a nosy fellow, if you ask me. What's your business here in Fort Worth?"

"Oh, I bought nearly six-hundred cattle into the stockyard and sold them to a northerner. I got a good price for them too."

"So, you're carrying a bundle home." The man grinned.

"Yep, you can say that, but I'm going to take a little more with these four aces." Jess spread his cards out in front of him. The big guy's face turned a brilliant hue of crimson.

The men tossed their cards on the table and stood. "That busted me, so I'm turning in for the night." The stumpy little man lifted his britches up and tipped his hat at the men as he left the car.

***

The longer the top hat guy sat, the madder he seemed to get. "There's no way you could have drawn four aces." He glared at Jesse with hatred in his eyes. "You cheated, and you're not going to get away with it." The man shoved the table toward Jesse as he reached for his gun.

Jesse was ready and had drawn his colt 45. He pointed at the man's heart before he knew what had happened. "I didn't cheat, but I know for sure you're the one who shot and robbed my son last night. You're going to jail, Mister," Jesse said, as Will grabbed the man's gun.

Jesse grabbed the man and jerked his jacket lapel back. Reaching deep into his pockets, he pulled out Jess's flat wallet with several hundred dollars still in it. "Looks like you've had a spending spree, my friend. My son had over eight hundred dollars when you robbed him."

"No, he didn't have . . . ," Suddenly, even in a drunken state, he knew he had said too much.

"That's all right. You already gave yourself away, but my son recognized you before you crawled out his window. You'd better be glad you didn't kill my boy."

"There's no way. He was unconscious!"

'Sorry, my friend, he was able to describe you before he passed out."

"What are you going do with me?" He asked while holding his hands in the air.

"My brother is going to get the conductor. He will have a place we can lock you up until we arrive in Limason. The sheriff can take care of you once we arrive there."

Much later, Jesse and Will returned to Jess's sleeping compartment and found John asleep at the foot of Jess's bed. The men smiled and returned to the passenger car and stretched out on some empty bench seats and slept.

Chapter 17

"Mary Beth, you can wait one more day until the men get home. Jess will be so disappointed to find you gone. He going want to tell you goodbye for sure. Please change your mind."

"No, Mama, it will be better this way. Jess doesn't really want me to go to nursing school. Well, that's not true. He doesn't care that I become an educated nurse, he's just selfish. Jess doesn't want to be left alone for a year." Mary Beth's eyes filled with tears.

"Your papa is gonna be sad too. He wants the best for you, but you did choose to marry Jess when he wanted to get you into another school. Now, you're running off without a word to both men that loves you."

"Are you going to the train depot with me or not? The train will be here in less than thirty minutes. I need to go now if I am going to purchase my ticket and catch it."

Hannah placed a shawl around her shoulders and picked up a small traveling bag, held the door open, and watched her daughter walk onto the boardwalk. In less than a half hour, Hannah stood at the train platform waving goodbye to her spoiled daughter."

After the train pulled out of Limason, Hannah asked the station master what time the train would arrive from Fort Worth. "It will be here close to four p.m., Mrs. O'Riley."

Thanking the old man, Hannah walked back to the doctor's office where she had a few patients waiting. Doctor Tim was in the kitchen having a cup of coffee."

"Hi Sweetheart. I wondered where you got off to. The patients said you would be right back. Where's Mary Beth?"

"Mary Beth is on the train heading to Ohio to attend nursing school. She wasn't supposed to leave for two weeks, but she received a note from the school, telling her she could start classes if she arrived the day after tomorrow. She was eager to go. I tried to make her stay and talk to Jess before she left, but she said this was the best way, since he didn't really want her to go."

"But, Hannah, he seemed to be all right with her attending school last week."

"Mary Beth said that he didn't want her to go, but he agreed to it. I know Jess wanted to make her happy, but they haven't been married long."

"He's not going to be happy to find her gone when he returns from Fort Worth.

"I told her that, but she didn't seem to care." Hannah said, lying her face on her sweet husband's chest.

***

The train whistle blew over and over. "Wonder why the engineer is blowing that whistle," Jesse said as he leaned out the window.

"Maybe something is on the track, "Will said, as he got up and nearly fell forward as the train pulled to a stop in Limason.

As the porter rushed through the passenger cars, Jesse stood in front of him to stop him. "What's happening that the whistle is blowing enough to wake the dead all the way to the next town?"

"Why, your son is on the train. He's safe and sound, and the townspeople are here to welcome him home." The porter stepped around Jesse and rushed off to the front of the train.

"Come on, fellows. Let's go make sure Jess is dressed properly and help him off the train. Lord have mercy on my hide. I didn't telegraph Rae and tell her that Jess had been shot. When she finds out, she is going to lay into me for sure."

"What about Mary Beth? She'll be upset too." John gave a small chuckle and walked into Jess's sleeping compartment.

Once the train had settled at the train's platform, people were standing nearby, sitting on their horsebacks, or keeping their seats in their carriage. Doctor Tim and Hannah were pushing their way through the crowd, waiting for the men to get off the train with Jess.

"There they are!" Hannah's said rushing through the crowd. "Jesse, over here," she shouted.

***

As the men maneuvered through the well-wishers, Doctor Tim stopped a young boy and gave him a dollar. "Run to the livery and tell Sam to have my big carriage brought here as quickly as he can."

When he saw Jesse, Tim patted him on the back. "Welcome home. We understand that Jess got hurt," he said, as he approached Jess. "How are you feeling son?"

"I hurt like the . . . devil, but other than that I'm fine." His head craned around Hannah and Doctor Tim. "Where's Mary Beth? Looking around Hannah and Doctor Tim, he asked where Mary Beth was.

"Look, here's my carriage. There's enough room for all of us to ride in. I will take you boys to the livery where you can retrieve your horses."

"Great, Tim, I appreciate you coming to meet us. Jess really didn't need to ride a horse yet." Jesse said, "Stop, Tm, I need to tell the sheriff something."

After Jesse explained about the man who shot Jess and how he admitted his guilt, he told the sheriff that the man was being held prisoner on the train. I will come back to town tomorrow and give you a full report, but I need to take my boy home."

"I'll take charge of the prisoner from here. We might have to take him back to Fort Worth, but we'll know all about that later."

"Mrs. Hannah, where is Mary Beth? Is she still angry with me?" Jess asked.

"No, I am sure she's not mad at her charming husband. You just sit back and relax and when we get you to bed, Doctor Tim and I will tell you what she's doing?"

"I don't know if I like the sound of that." Jess laid his head back against the leather upholstery and closed his eyes. He soon fell asleep, and when Tim hit a bump, his eyes flew open, and he cried out for Mary Beth. Everyone looked at him. "I guess I was dreaming out loud. The medicine I've been taking helps with the pain, but I've been having crazy dreams," Jess said.

After arriving home, Jesse was correct about Rae being upset that he didn't telegraph her about her baby being shot. She would have been better prepared for his arrival home. Rae instructed Hope to begin cooking all of his favorite foods for supper.

Ollie and Rae took full charge of Jess while Doctor Tim

examined him. No prince would have been treated more royally. Once Tim announced that Jess was going to recovery, the ladies settled down.

Rae moved Hope into Jess's old bedroom so he would be closer to the front room. "That's fine with me, Rae. Now that Will's home, I will be staying at home with him and the kids. I'm so much better."

"You are better, but no housekeeping, heavy lifting, ironing, or anything that will cause you to get overtired. Will, if she doesn't obey my orders, she may have to come back and stay here so Ollie can watch her."

"I'm not a child, Doctor Tim. I know when I'm tired," Hope pouted.

***

Will took Hope into his arms, standing behind her. He leaned down and whispered, "I'm glad you want to come home with me tonight. I've missed my little woman."

Hope whirled around and pulled him into the kitchen pantry. She giggled all the way. Will kicked the door closed. He pulled Hope into his arms and kissed her like there was no tomorrow.

She moved as close to him as her big belly would allow and whispered, "I missed you something awful. I'm sorry I was ugly to you when you left. I didn't mean to be," her eyes lowered.

"It's all right, sweet girl. I didn't want to leave, and when Jess got shot, I was afraid we were going to have to stay. Actually, I told Jesse I needed to leave and come home. He was nice about it and said that John would be with him. Luckily, the doctor said Jess could travel in a sleeping car." He nibbled on her ear and placed kisses all along her neck to her collarbone.

"You're sexier than socks on a rooster, my dear husband."

"Gracious woman!" Will tossed back his head and laughed. "I can tell you been hanging around Ollie too long."

***

Later that evening, Doctor Tim and Hannah shut Jess's bedroom room for some privacy. Both took chairs and pulled them beside his bed. "After you left to go to Fort Worth, Mary Beth received a letter from the nursing school. It stated that she could begin classes in a couple days, instead of having to wait for the fall session. She was excited, but sad too." Hannah said.

98

"Mary Beth wanted to go early and so she could complete the year sooner. She didn't have time to wait for you to return and talk it over with you," Doctor Tim said.

"So, she discussed it with you?"

"No, I wasn't here, but she talked to Hannah." He looked at his wife.

"Jess, I pleaded with her to wait for your return, but you know how headstrong she can be. She became angry with me and said that you really didn't want her to attend the school."

"That's not true. But I did want her to wait. We haven't been married that long, and the house is not even decorated the way she wanted it to be. Having a nursing certificate is all she had on her mind." He stared at the ceiling while Doctor Tim and Hannah looked at each other. "As I lay in the bunkbed on the train, all I could think about was Mary Beth being at the train station, waiting for my return. We had so many plans for the future. Now, she's gone with no explanation, no goodbye. All I have is a cold, empty house to return to."

"Jess, we're sorry that she left without saying goodbye, but when you're able to travel, you can go on the train to see her. I know she will be thrilled to see you."

"Yes, maybe I'll do that as soon as I am up and around." He turned his face to the wall.

"I knew his feelings were going to be hurt, and now with his injury, it makes matters worst that she's not here to care for him," Hannah said, once they'd left the room.

"This is all part of growing up, sweetheart. He's a man now, and he has settled things with our daughter. We can't do it for them." Doctor Tim pulled Hannah into his arms and said, "Let's go home. I'll be back tomorrow."

Chapter 18

Ollie was in the kitchen cleaning a bushel basket of fresh strawberries that Katie and Missy had dropped off after they had made a trip into town. Rae had gone down in the cellar and selected the jars that needed to be brought up.

Rae hurried up the ladder and headed out to the barn. "Will and Hank, I need the jars in the cellar brought up to the back porch where I can wash them to use for canning the strawberries. If you fellows do this job fast, Ollie will make a couple of pies for lunch."

The two men did what she asked. They filled two tubs with water and placed the jars in them to soak.

"Will, how is Hope this morning?" Rae questioned as she watched him.

"She's frustrated because she has to hire another housekeeper. I am going to take the wagon and bring her down here. Hope wants to talk to Ollie about some young gal she knows who could use the job.

***

"Will watched a wagon pull into the yard. He called Rae over to the door. "Do you know these two ladies?" Rae wiped her hands on a dishcloth and shook her head no. Will walked out on the front porch and watched a woman rein in the two big mules.

"Invite them down off their wagon. I have some lemonade if you don't mind chopping some ice and bring it up from the cellar."

"Hello ladies," Will said, noticing one of the ladies was a young girl about fourteen or fifteen, and the other was a much older woman.

"Hello, young man. Are you the owner of this fine ranch?"

"Well, I am part owner. Why don't you two come and sit a spell? The lady of the house will bring you a glass of lemonade while Hank waters your mules." Will offered the older woman a hand while Hank walked the mules over to the corral.

Will left the ladies as he hurried into the cellar and chopped a bucket of ice and carried it into the kitchen. Rae poured glasses of lemonade and carried them out to the front porch. "Hello, my name is Rae Maxwell. Please enjoy a glass of cold refreshment."

"Well, this is mighty fine. My grand-daughter and I haven't been treated so well in a long time. Most folks won't even allow us to stop at their places."

"I had no idea our neighbors were so unfriendly." Rae said, glancing at Will. "Will, go to your house and get Hope. I know she is ready to come. She can help Ollie and me." Turning back to their visitors, she asked, "What can we do for you?"

"Well, to tell you the truth, we're down on our luck. We are both in good health and need work. My granddaughter is sixteen, and I'm close to sixty, but I'm strong as a horse, a good cook, and housekeeper. I've trained my granddaughter well. She can cook, clean, and loves gardening. She is educated too."

"Granny, you make me sound like you're selling a horse."

Rae smothered a laugh at the young girl's remark. "What is your name and where are you from?"

My name is Mrs. Mildred Miller. My granddaughter's name is Lucy. We left our home in Tyler, Texas, because rustlers came and killed my man and stole all of our cattle. The sheriff never found the ones responsible. After a while, I couldn't keep up the place. I had no money to pay wages so I sold the house and we've being traveling in this here wagon ever since. We.ve bout spent all of our funds, so we are in need of work."

"Here comes my sister, her two kids and her husband, Will, whom you met earlier. I don't guess you have any references?"

"What's that?" Mrs. Miller responded, peering at the approaching wagon.

"People you have worked for before might have written a letter saying what a good worker you have been," Rae tried to explain.

"Well, I ain't ever worked for nobody, but myself and husband."

Will helped his family to the ground and drove the wagon to the barn. "Hope, this is Mrs. Mildred Miller and her granddaughter Lucy. They are looking for work."

"Praise the Lord. I need help, now. I can't believe in just a few days how messy things have become at the house. By the time the kids and me make their beds, I'm exhausted."

"Just a minute," Rae said. "Ollie, can you come out here please?" Rae trusted Ollie's opinion about people. She was a good judge of character.

"Lord have mercy, I didn't know we had company. Howdy, I'm called Ollie."

"Mrs. Miller and Lucy, Ollie has been on this ranch many years. She raised our husbands, mine and Hope's. Ollie knows everyone for miles around." Rae turned to Ollie. "Ollie, Mrs. Miller and Lucy are looking for housework."

"Now, Ollie, I know you had someone in mind to work for me, but I would like for this young lady to have a chance," Hope said, then turned to Lucy. "How would you like to work for me? I have two children, and I am going to have twins in several weeks. As you might guess, I need help with the house and later with the babies. Do you think you could help me? We can tried it for a couple of weeks, and if we don't get along, we can go our separate ways.

Lucy's hands framed her face. "Oh, my, I love babies and kids. I never had brothers and sisters but plenty of other kin. I helped Aunt Marie with her children, didn't I, Granny?"

"Rae, didn't Missy say that she need help with her baby boy and the house while she helps Katie with the Flower Farm?"

"Yes, she was talking about getting some help this morning."

"Why don't I ask Hank to ride over and invite Katie and Missy to come back here for a few minutes to meet Mrs. Miller?"

"Lucy, I would love to have you live-in with us, and I know Missy has room for your grandmother. You two can't live in that wagon." Hope took Lucy's hand, noticing how clean it was even thought she had been driving those mules.

***

Ollie went back to the kitchen and prepared three strawberries pies to go in the oven while she stirred a large pot of chicken and dumpling for lunch. She rolled out several dozen buttered biscuits, covered them with two dishtowels, and set them on back of the stove. She had left-over ham from breakfast, so she prepared more slices to go with the biscuits. Who knew how many she would be serving for lunch.

***

After Katie and Missy met with Mrs. Mildred Miller, the ladies were excited. Missy assured her that she had a nice room for her to live-in, and they would discuss her hours after she settled into the routine. On the way home, Missy expressed to her mama that she was sure Jeremiah would be happy to know that she was using some of his money to make their lives better and someone else's too.

After lunch Will helped Lucy retrieve her personal items out of the covered wagon. Lucy was thrilled with Hope's lovely home and the idea that they would allow her to use the small carriage to go and visit with her grandmother. Will assured her that she would be their housekeeper, not their slave. She would be treated well and given a fair wage.

***

Hank drove Mrs. Miller's covered wagon to John's and Katie's Flower Farm while Missy and Katie followed behind. Missy showed Mrs. Miller all around and helped her settle in.

Tater was thrilled to meet the older lady and introduced their young son to her. Mrs. Miller immediately picked up the toddler and gave him a squeeze which he seemed to like.

John told Mrs. Miller that he would park her covered wagon in his old barn where he had buckets, wheelbarrows, bags of dried manure and other needed items for the farm. It would be out of the weather, and in the future, he would make repairs, if she decided to sell it.

Mrs. Miller walked with Hank out of the barn and thanked him for all of his help.

"You're more than welcome, Mrs. Miller," he said tipping his hat.

"Please call me Milly," she said with a shy grin. "I hope we will be good friends."

John had witnessed the exchange and slapped Hank on the back. "Come on *good friend,* let's get back to work."

"You ain't nothing but a smart ass," Hank murmured as he leaped onto the horse like a man half his age.

Chapter 19

"Oh, what a morning. This rocker feels so good with my big fat ankles propped up," Hope declared. "It sure feels good to know that I have help. The kids love Lucy already. She helped them clean their room, washed a load of clothes, ironed a batch of clothes, and made lunch. Now she's on the porch watching them play while she's knitting a shawl for her granny. I am thrilled we hired her."

"I hope you let her know that she doesn't have to cook the supper meal. If she wants, she can help Rae and me, but she doesn't have to. It's good that she keeps your home nice and clean and helps with the kids," Ollie said.

"How is Jess this morning?" Hope asked Rae, while shifting to get comfortable in the rocker.

"Jess's doing well," Rae commented. "He had breakfast at the table and walked to the barn earlier. Now he resting. Doctor Tim said that he had lost a lot of blood, and that is why he's still weak."

Hope glanced at Ollie. "Now, come and sit with me. You have to tell me more stories about living with Will's papa before he passed away."

"Let me get a fresh of coffee. Rae, you want 'a sit a spell?'"

"I can't right now. I'm riding into town with Hank to buy a few supplies. Also, I want to stop and visit with Claire. Maybe we can have lunch with Albert today."

Settling into her rocker, Ollie took up her crotchet and hummed for a second. "Let see, one day I was hoeing in the garden. It was a lovely day, not too hot, when two Black boys rode up on a big, flappy-eared mule. Will was playing at the edge of the garden, while Jesse was at the edge of the corral washing down one of his horses. "I stopped my hoeing and asked them fellows what they wanted.

'We came for a young woman called Ollie. Miss Runner needs for her to come to Waverly Plantation.'

'Why? What's going on there that I'm needed? I ain't been back there since I left there nearly a dozen years ago." The boys just sat staring at me."

"Runner says for us to make you come. She needs you bad."

"Well, boys, I can't just up and leave. My boss man ain't home now. Besides, you two ain't gonna make me do nothing.' I pointed my hoe at the boy that was talking. 'I'll ask my boss man if I can come, and if he agrees, then I will hitch up a wagon and come as soon as I can. Now, you'd best climb down off that mule and go sit under those trees. I know you have had a long ride and have to be hungry. I'll bring you out something to drink and eat, that's if you sit and behave yourselves.' As I turned to go inside, Jesse was standing behind me with a double barrel shotgun pointed at the two young boys.

'Ain't no need for that, Jesse? You can stand here and watch them, but don't dare point that thing at them again. You probably done scared them senseless' I said, chuckling. "I know he scared the bejesus out me.' I asked him where he got that gun.

'Pa keeps it loaded in the barn all the time. It's hidden so Will can't mess with it, but Pa has taken me to the woods several times and taught me how to use this gun and his rifle.' I was happy that Jesse knew how to shoot, but I wish I had known. I did tell Mr. Maxwell when he got home."

"Did you go to Waverly and find out what the lady called Runner needed with you?" Hope asked.

"Yes, I asked Mr. Maxwell if I could have time off and drive to Waverly. He said I could, but Jesse had to go with me. He would take care of Will. Mr. Maxwell didn't want me driving all alone that far from the farm. He told me that I needed to take some supplies to the folks that lived on the plantation. He helped me pack some sugar, flour, canned fruit, medicine, a basket of apples and picked corn.

I made a big basket of sandwiches, water, and fruit for us to eat on the trip, while Mr. Maxwell tucked several old bed linens that he had stored away in the back of the wagon. He called Jesse into the house, and he came out with a rifle slung over his shoulder, carrying several boxes of ammunition. He looked like a grown man instead of a thirteen-year-old.

'Pa said that I might need to hunt some meat while we are at the plantation,' Jesse said as he placed the gun under the bench. Assuring Mr. Maxwell that we would be returning in a few days, he waved goodbye. We followed the two young boys back to Waverly. I had no idea what was so important that I was needed after so many years, but I was kinda glad to return to the old plantation and see the old place and some of the people."

Ollie looked at Hope and asked, "How are you feeling? Are your ready for a snack? I've been running off at the mouth for quite a spell. I can get up from here and fix you something to eat."

"I am a little hungry, but Justice said I had better watch how much weigh I put on. So, I'm fine for now. I want to know why Runner needed for you to come to her. Please go on with the story." Hope leaned back and stared out the window at her children.

"Well, we stopped and ate the food that I had prepared for our trip. Lordy, those two boys were looking in my basket for more to eat. My food had been a treat to them. It was dark after we arrived at the plantation, but lights shone in the big house. The boys helped me down and led Jesse to the nice, big barn to park our wagon and unhitched our two horses.

Two ladies stood in the doorway of the house and stepped aside and let me enter. I didn't remember them but they knew me. 'I came to see Runner. Where is she?'

'Upstairs. The room at the top. Go on up. She's waiting on you.'

"Of course, Runner would have the Master's bedroom," Ollie said, chuckling. "I pushed opened the door and nearly fainted from the heat in the room. Two old cronies stood near the bed, and one of them was covering Runner with quilts.

'Runner, I'm here. What's wrong and why is this room hotter than hades?'

'We are removing the bad spirits out of her body. Who are you?' One old black woman said as she frowned at me.

'That's Ollie! She has come to help me deliver my baby. You—', Runner pointed at the woman and screamed, 'get out of this room and don't come back.' She fell back on the bed while

106

reaching her hand out for Ollie. 'Oh, Ollie, help me. I prayed, that you would come and care for me. Please don't let my baby die,' she pleaded.

'First thing we got to do is open some of those windows and get this heat out of this room' I started removing quilts off Runner's body. As I tossed the cover on the floor, I looked up and saw Jesse standing in the doorway of the bedroom. I called to him and asked him to help me open the windows.

The other woman in the room asked me what she could do. She said that she didn't like what that mid-wife was doing to Runner, but she was scared of her. I told her to bring some cool water for Runner to drink and several pans of hot water because we needed to bath her and put on a fresh gown. Then I told Jesse to go downstairs and get the boys to help him carry the food supplies to the kitchen.

'Oh Ollie, you brought food?' Runner tried to sit up.

'Yes, a few supplies I thought that your cooks could use.'

'We ain't got any cooks, not like it was when you and I were little.'

"I told her that I would take care of that kitchen once I took care of her. After I bathed her from top to bottom, she was still very warm. She told me that she felt sick ,and her head really hurt. I started looking in her hair and around her neck. There it was, the reason she was sick. Runner had tick fever. I got the other woman to help me, and we began picking ticks off her neck, back, under her arms and off her scalp. I had to use a hot stick to make some of the creatures turn loose. We were careful not to burn Runner, but those nasty critters can really sink into your skin. They will suck the blood out of a body, and you can see them easy because the swell up. We must have picked two dozen off her body. It wasn't long before Runner's fever had went away, and her head stopped hurting."

'Where in the world did she get so many ticks on her body?" Hope asked.

"Well, I understood that she and some of the other ladies had picked black berries. Any time you're in the woods or in tall grass, they will get on you. After checking over her body, I had to examine her to see how far along she was before giving birth. She was several hours away, so I went down in the kitchen and fixed some of Justice's special tea. It helps to relieve some of the pain."

Jesse had placed the supplies on the kitchen counter. One old woman sat in the corner and was shucking the fresh corn. She had placed a big pot of water on the stove to boil. 'Where are all the others?' I asked the woman.

"Oh, they'll show up when I get something fixed to eat. Well, no one will eat the food that I brought if they can't get their lazy behinds in here and help. I'll make sure of that,' Ollie said making the old woman laugh.

"I found an apron and pulled out the lard, sugar and flour. There was a little milk in the cellar. When I came up from down there, I went to the back porch and called Jesse. "Get some men to help you milk those few cows we saw when we passed the barn. I need milk if I am going to cook. Tell those men that if their women folks want to eat, they'd better come to the house and talk with me. I ain't feeding no freeloaders.'

"It wasn't long before about a dozen women came into the kitchen. 'Go wash your face, arms and hands and put on a clean apron or kitchen towel. We got some cooking to do to feed this bunch of folks. Some of you start peeling some of those apples for apple pies. Others can start making pie crust.'

"Jesse came to the kitchen and called to me to come outside. Well, I was surprised. The boys that had come to get us at the ranch stood holding up four dead rabbits. 'My goodness, Jesse. Where did those come from?'

'I showed these boys how to build a snare. We went to the end of the corn fields and set a few and it wasn't long before we caught these babies. We are going in the barn and dress them out. Do you want to cook them for dinner tonight?'

"I sure do. Cut them into small pieces because I will make a nice soup, a hearty stew, and put some in the dumplings. Thank you, boys, for all of your help. Oh, Jesse, if you catch more, skin them out and placed them down in the cold cellar.'

The dumplings were cooked, the biscuits were ready to go in the oven, and many pies were baked when the lady that was sitting with Runner called downstairs to me. I left the cooking to a few responsible ladies and hurried up to her, and sure enough, Runner was about to deliver her babe.

I had only helped bring one baby into the world, but God

helped me all the way. I had to cut her some, and I nearly fainted, but it wasn't long before a bald, black head made an appearance, and after a big push, the head and shoulders were out of the small body. 'One more big push, Runner, and we'll have a beautiful baby in my hands.'

Sure enough, in just one minute, I was handing over the baby to my helper, and I continued to work on Runner. The after birth nearly put me on my knees, but I had to finish the job. Runner lay crying as she looked her baby over. The woman took the baby and washed the little one and wrapped him in a small baby blanket.

That was the hardest thing I had ever done. I took Runner's hand and she said, 'I knew you would come and bring my babe in the world. Thank you, dearest friend,' and fell into an exhausted sleep.

"I sat down in a chair and cried my heart out. 'Why is you bawling? 'my helper asked.

'I ain't never done that alone before, and I felt the Lord sitting on my shoulders. I have never been so blessed.'

"Oh Ollie, I can't imagine how you must have felt. I was terrified when I was going to have Jay, and there were plenty of experienced people with me. I doubt I could help anybody have a baby," Hope said.

Ollie wiped tears from her eyes. She remembered that night very well. "Lordy, child, I am so thankful I never had to deliver another baby."

"Go on Miss Ollie. Tell me more." Hope said.

"The next day, Jesse let another boy ride one of our horses, and they went hunting. After a few hours, they rode into the barn with a big eight-point deer strapped to the back of Jesse's horse's rump. They pulled the deer up to the barn's loft and dressed it out. Then they chopped the deer meat into small pieces and wrapped it in cheese cloth and carried it to the cellar.

After I made sure Runner was going to be cared for, I gave her instructions how to dry up her milk when her baby started getting teething. The lady that helped me listened and said she understood what do to. I trusted this friend of Runner's to care for her because it was time for Jesse and me to return home. I missed little Will so much, and I was sure Mr. Maxwell was expecting us home.

Jesse had worked hard to help my people on the plantation. I was so proud of my young ward. He came with me a boy and was going home a man."

"Oh, Ollie, that had to be a trip. One you still remember. I can see Jesse doing all those things, even as a young boy."

Chapter 20

On the way into town, Rae asked Hank to stop at John's and Katie's flower farm. She wanted to check on Mildred Miller and see if she was working out with Missy and her baby, Johnny.

Hank pulled the two-horse team over to the corral. Rae leaped down with Hank's help and knocked on Missy's front door.

"Hello, Rae, please come in. You know you don't ever have to knock"

"I know, but Jesse and I were young once," Rae laughed. "I wanted to stop and check with you and Mrs. Miller to see how you are getting along."

"Oh, she is wonderful, and I am so glad that we were able to hire her to work. She is outside, walking Johnny around in the barn. Mrs. Miller says that babies need fresh air every day, and while it is still pretty, she enjoys taking him outside."

"Yes, the fresh air will help with his naps too. I remember Miss Ollie had me go outside with my two babies."

"She's a wonderful cook too. Tater is so happy that she is cooking our supper meal each night. I will try to learn from her, so my cooking will be better, but for now, I am too tried to stand over her and learn. I do help with the cleanup, but she's a neat cook. Lordy, I mess up every pan in the kitchen when I cook."

"I'd better be on my way. Do you need anything from town? We can always drop it back by."

"Thanks, but no. John and Katie went shopping a few days ago, and we're fine for now. Please come back when you can stay longer. Oh, how is Hope?"

"She's just fine and she is thrilled with Lucy. Hope has all of Miss Ollie's attention now. Miss Ollie is telling her about Jesse, Will and her own childhood. This morning, I left Will sitting in a rocker listening to some of her wild tales. Of course, Will was prodding her to tell stories about Jesse."

"Oh, I wish I had the time to sit and listen. I do love talking with Miss Ollie, myself." Missy waved goodbye to Rae.

As Rae was approaching the wagon, she saw Mrs. Miller holding little Johnny close to Hank. "Isn't he the cutest little fellow you ever did see?" Rae thought for a second that the woman was practically cooing to Hank.

"Are you ready, Ms. Rae? I already watered the horses. Nice seeing you again, Mrs. Miller."

"Milly, remember? Goodbye. Come back, you hear?"

After traveling away from the Flower Farm, Rae laughed.

"What's so funny?" Hank asked without even glancing at her.

"Mrs. Miller, oh, I mean, *Milly*. She's not very subtle, is she?"

"Oh, please, not you, too. John hasn't stop ragging me about her all week."

"Please drive me to Claire's home, and I will walk up town to the shops. You go and do whatever men do, and I will meet you at the café around twelve o'clock and you can have lunch with Claire, Albert and me. How's that sound?"

"Good, see you later." He stopped in front of Claire's lovely home.

"Oh, Mama, it's so good to see you. Hello, Hank. Are you leaving so soon?"

"I'll see you at lunch. You girls be good," he called over his shoulder as he drove toward the livery.

"Come inside, and let's have some tea and coffeecake that I made. It is so good. I got the recipe from one of my parents last fall, and I make it all the time."

"Is Albert at work?"

"Yes, I have so much to tell you, so I'm glad we have some time together."

After the tea was served and the coffeecake cut, Claire couldn't contain her excitement any longer. "Mama, I believe I'm with child. I know it will seem like it's too soon to tell, but I know my body. For two years, I have wanted a baby and every time it is close to my monthly, I can tell I am not, but this time it is different."

"How far long do you feel that you are? Sweetheart, please

don't get your hopes up so soon and be disappointed again."

"Mama, I have to tell you a secret. You have to promise, cross your heart and hope to die, not to tell anyone."

"Now, Claire, I'm not one of your childhood friends that are sworn to secrecy."

"No, it's more important than that." Rae's eyes were as big as saucers. "All right, I swear. Now tell me, please. I am getting scared."

"You don't have to be scared. I was scared enough for all of us when it was happening, and Doctor Tim didn't know what to make of it."

"Tim already knows you might be with child?"

"No, nobody knows, but me, and my body."

"Start from the beginning of your secret, please." Rae took a deep breath and sat back and listened to the wild episode that took place after Claire took the two chocolate toddies home that Justice had given her to drink to help her conceive.

"So, Claire, you never drank any of the special drink that Justice prepared?"

"No, Mama, Albert drank one and part of another. Man, he was feeling on top of the world, to say the least. He couldn't keep his hands off me. He was like the *king of the jungle* and well . . . you don't need to hear any more of his actions. Afterward, I thought he was dead, so I ran over to Doctor Tim's as he was driving up to his house. He ran over here, and Albert was lying in the foyer, spread eagle, that's what Doctor Tim said. We carried him into our guest room, and I slept with him, and he woke up several times and we, well . . . anyway, Mama, because of that night I know that my body is different. I should know in about four days. I am like clockwork when it comes to my monthly curse."

"Claire, your secret is about the toddies. Only you and Doctor Tim know that Albert drank them instead of you?"

"Well, Doctor Tim did tell me that he told Miss Ollie. She asked him if he had seen me or Albert. She was worried about me because she had told me to go by Justice and get the toddies. He told her that she and Justice had better not do anything like that again. But Mama, I'm glad they did. Albert was a *stud*! Oh, I'm sorry. I didn't mean to be vulgar."

"It's all right, honey. What a story. I'm sorry you have sworn me to secrecy because your pa would have loved hearing this, but a promise is a promise, and I will not breathe a word. I will pray that your hopes and dream for a child will come true in about four or five days. I want a grandbaby from you very much. Let's pray God will make this happen."

"I'm starving so let's eat our coffeecake and go shopping. I will be ready for a big lunch," Claire said as she took a bite of her cake.

Rae laughed. "I do believe you are eating for two already."

***

"Will, if you are going to sit around in the house today, you're going to help wash the lunch dishes," Hope said.

"I'm sorry, I cannot do that this time. I am heading over to Bud's house to pick up Boo. I promised Jay that I would take him and Boo to the river and catch a few catfish. Maybe we will have enough for a fish fry tomorrow."

"Is Jesse going with you?" Miss Ollie asked.

"No, he says that catfishing is too much work. John is working today on his flower farm, Hank is in town with Rae, and Jess is doing something up at his house. He still slinking around, so we are letting him be. Jesse don't want to leave you girls alone. He'll be in the tool room making some repairs and wiping down some of the leather items.

"Hey Miss Ollie" Will said as he started to leave. "I remember a good story to tell Hope about Jesse. Do you remember when Jesse was about sixteen? A saloon gal followed him home one afternoon?" Will laughed real loud and exited the house.

"I sure do. Boy Jesse was madder than an old hornet at me for several days, but he soon got over it.

"What happen Ollie, tell me!" Hope sat up in the rocker and smiled.

"Now, Sweetheart, let me finish these dishes. Willa, you come dry, and I'll put this roast in the oven to cook for supper. Sometimes, this here meat can be as tough as shoe leather if cooked too fast." Once the roast was in the oven, Ollie and Willa washed a dozen large, sweet potatoes, greased them down and placed them on the bottom rack in the oven to cook slowly. Supper was well on its way.

"Come on Willa, you might want to hear this tale. It's kinda funny and then it ain't." Willa grabbed a pillow and a small blanket and tossed it on the floor next to her mama's rocker. Ollie grabbed a glass of tea and sat down in her favorite rocker and smiled at the girls.

"Well, Jesse had gone into town to get some supplies. His pa, Jake, had let him go several times before and I didn't think anything about him being in town all alone. Shoot fire, we pretty near knew everyone in town for miles around.

Later that afternoon, after Jesse had returned home, I was raking around the front door when this carriage pulled to a stop. The young gal driving was a pretty little thing, but the closer she got, I could see her face was made-up like a clown. She wasn't dressed like a nice young lady either. She had on a red silk, low-cut, off the shoulders garment with a large gold ruffle surrounding the edge. Her bosom was pinched so tight, her puppies were protruding almost over the edge. When she stood, showing her tiny eighteen-inch waistline and her long black stockings, she looked just like what she was—a doxy from one of the saloons. She stood in the carriage, holding the reins, and asked if this was Jesse Maxwell's ranch.

"I said it was and wanted to know what she wanted with Jesse. She quickly told me to keep a civil tongue in my head and just go and tell him that he had a visitor." I looked her up and down and said, 'Child, you ain't dressed for visiting. You shore don't wanna be wearing that dress when Jesus comes back. You'd best just get on back from wherever you came.'

Well, goodness, you ain't never heard such nasty talk coming out a young woman's mouth. From the back of the house, Jesse came running and raced over to the gal's carriage. He didn't even notice me standing behind the fence. Before he knew it, he said, 'My goodness Susie, you look prettier than a store-bought doll. Here let me help you down.' He took her hand as to lift her to the ground.

'Stop,' I said. 'That little gal ain't staying. Beauty is skin deep, but ugly is to the bone, and that little hussy is about as ugly as they come. She is not getting down from that carriage.'

"Jesse, are you going to let your servant speak to me like that? I came all this way from town to see you, and I have only been insulted by that fat, Black woman.' Susie pouted her freshly painted red lips in my direction.

'Now, Susie, you can't talk that way to Miss Ollie. She doesn't mean you no harm. Maybe, it will be better for you to leave now, and I'll visit with you in town."

Before Jesse or the gal knew it, I grabbed the horse whip from her carriage and slapped it across Jesse's rump. He howled like a dog in heat. I told that young gal if she wanted some of the same just climb down off that carriage. She was not welcome, and Jesse wouldn't be visiting with her in town. I pointed to the gate. 'So, get your sassy behind and that carriage off our ranch.'

Well, Jesse didn't know what to do, but after that little hussy left, he was furious with me. But, he didn't voice his opinion of what I had done."

"My goodness, Miss Ollie. I bet Jesse was mad at you," Hope said.

"Mad isn't the word. He had a welt across his rump for a week, and his pa told him that he would have many more if he ever heard of him hanging out at a saloon. He took Jesse into the barn and told him about saloon gals and what kind of diseases he could get if he slept around with any of them. I believe that opened his eyes because he never met with that gal or any others that I knew about."

"Miss Ollie, what happened to her puppies?" Willa asked.

Hope burst out laughing. "Oh, honey, Miss Ollie was just using the word puppies to describe the girl's teats."

"That's silly. Why didn't she just say that her teats were about to fall out of her dress. I've heard that before."

"You have? Who have you heard say something like that?" Hope asked.

"Mama, I'm six years old. I have ears, and I hear everything." Willa lay her head down on her pillow and closed her eyes, obviously pretending to fall asleep.

Chapter 21

Jess walked around in his home fretting. He was so angry with himself and Mary Beth. He couldn't understand why she didn't wait a few days to tell him goodbye. They really had not settled their differences about her going back to school.

Oh, he wanted her to be happy, but he had hoped to talk her into returning to another school much closer, or at least wait until they had decorated their new home with the furniture and drapes she wanted.

His shoulder and arm was on the mend, and he could do almost everything but chop wood and get on his horse without assistance. But for now, he couldn't pull his share of weight working on the ranch. Jess was lonely, sad, and mostly mad. He had to do something.

Jess grabbed his hat, walked down to his Pa's barn, and asked John if he would saddle him a horse. He wanted to go into town. Maybe he would send Mary Beth a telegram after Miss Hannah gave him her address.

John helped Jess climb on his horse, and he rode straight for Limason. By the time he rode the ten miles, his shoulder was throbbing, but he didn't dare complain. As he walked toward Doctor Tim's office, he passed the saloon. He looked over the bat-winged doors and decided to go in for a beer. It had been months and months since he had a nice cold beer, and it was hot as hades, and it would taste mighty fine.

He strolled into the dim lit room and cradled up to the bar. "I'll have a cold beer," he said.

"Not so sure how cold it will be, young man, but here you go." He passed a tall glass of golden-orange beer with three inches of white foam on the top.

Jess took a big mouth full and nearly spit the warm drink across the room. Quickly he closed his mouth and swallowed big. It was the foulest taste he had in his mouth in a long time.

He tossed a nickel on the bar, turned, and walked back out the way he came. How in the world men drank that awful stuff he had no idea. He would never be a drunk if that's what he had to drink.

Walking down the boardwalk, he tipped his hat to several young pretty ladies who were definitely giving him the eye. Jess smiled and kept strolling until he came to the doctor's office. He pushed on the door, but it was locked. He peeked in the glass window and saw all the lanterns off inside. It was then he first noticed the sign that read, "Be back in an hour. Gone home for lunch."

Jess stood on the boardwalk and wondered when the doctor and Hannah had left. He rocked on his heels and thought he would go into the dry-goods store. He wandered past the post office, meat market, and came upon the picture window of the dry-goods store. In the window display, a lovely shawl was draped over a black velvet stand. Mary Beth would look pretty wearing that, he thought.

He entered the store as another man was coming out, so the bell over the door didn't jingle. Jess stopped and looked at the shawl in the window as he heard women speaking. "Can you believe that girl? Running off to Ohio with another man, pretending she's going to nursing school? Why she and that young man have been friends for years, but she married that rich, handsome Maxwell boy. I had hoped over the years that he would have wanted to court Martha Ann, but oh well, it wasn't mean to be."

"Are you sure she wasn't going to nursing school, Beatrice? I heard in church she was accepted, and she only has one year to complete her schooling."

"Well, they looked pretty cozy to me when they got on the train together."

Jess had heard enough. "Excuse me, ladies," he said, as he walked over to the counter where Mrs. Goodyear was ringing up another customer.

The two ladies chatting must have realized that Jess had heard every word they had said. As fast as they could, they left the store without the items they had chosen.

Jess watched the two hens rush out the door. "Hello, Jess, what can I do for you this fine, hot day?" James Goodyear, the store owner asked him, while stacking jars on the shelf behind the counter. Mrs. Goodyear had returned to the storeroom.

"Give me several jars of those preserves and a dozen peppermint sticks. Can you wrap those jars in some paper? I'm going to take them to Mary Beth at her school." Jess realized that he had just made the decision to travel to Ohio to see his lovely wife. He missed her, and he needed to hold her in his arms.

"Sure thing. Anything else?"

"Yes, I want that pretty white shawl in your display window."

"That's an expensive piece made by Widow Martin. She will be proud to see Mary Beth wearing it," The storekeeper hurried around the counter and picked out the shawl carefully from the display window. He folded it and wrapped it in some soft white material. "I don't want any of that print on the paper to rub off on this pretty piece."

"I appreciate that. How much do I owe you?"

"Do you want this on your pa's account?"

"No, this is my personal bill. I have cash to cover it," Jess answered.

As Jess left the store, he noticed Doctor Tim and Hannah entering their office. He juggled his packages and hurried to their office door. Using the toe of his boot, he tapped on the closed door.

Hannah hurried and opened the door and was so pleased to see her son-in-law waiting to enter. "Hello, Jess, come in please. Tim?" Hannah yelled and Tim came into the waiting room.

"It's so good to see you out and about. Come into the kitchen and have a nice cup of coffee. Hannah and I just came back from lunch. Wish we had known you were in town. You could have eaten with us."

"I must have just missed you. I went to the dry good store and purchased a few items to take to Mary Beth. I am going to check the train schedule and go and visit with her. We need to be together and talk. I miss her so much, but I need for her to know that I want her to finish school and I will be here working the ranch with Pa and Will. You know they made me a partner."

"Yes, and you deserve it. Jesse and Will both are so proud of the man you have become. A good hard worker."

"I came by to tell you both that I will be traveling in a day or so to see Mary Beth. If you have something you want me to take her, I will. I do need her new address. I understand that she rented a room near the college so I can stay with her when I visit. Is that correct?"

"Yes, she did. She wanted you to feel comfortable when you visited with her. I'm so pleased that you are going to see her. She will be thrilled," Hannah said."

Jess stopped by the train station and purchased a ticket to Ohio for the next day's train. He was getting excited about his plans to see his sweet wife. Hurrying to the livery, he asked a young man if he would help him with his packages as he stepped on the platform that ladies used to get on their horses.

Once in his saddle, the young boy stuffed a few jars in his saddlebags and handed him the soft package which he carried. He flipped the young man a fifty-cent piece and rode toward home.

When he arrived home, he broke the news to the family that he was going on a trip to see Mary Beth tomorrow. He asked Rae if she would help him pack his clothes and asked Miss Ollie if she would pack the preserves that he bought. Will you send some of your pickles to her, too? She loves them." He turned to peer at both of them. "Can you girls think of anything else I should take Mary Beth? She left so fast, I know she didn't take anything but her clothes."

Rae stood in front of Jess and nodded. "Of course, we will help you pack Also, I will pack some clean bandages for your wound. You need to be careful what you pick up. That wound is not nearly well, and you can break open the stitches."

Jesse walked into the room. "I'll drive you to the train station tomorrow in the carriage. You can rent a carriage when you return home, so you can stay as long as you like. This could be a second honeymoon for you and Mary Beth. Of course, I know she will be attending classes some during the time you are there, but you can sightsee while she is busy."

***

Jess's train trip was very successful. He had purchased a ticket with a sleeping car, so he was fresh as a daisy when he arrived at the college. He rented a one-horse carriage to take him to the college and use while he was moving around the city.

It was close to eleven a.m. when he arrived at the address where Mary Beth's rented room was located. The curtains were closed, and the place looked deserted. He saw a man working on the roof of the next building, so he walked over and called to the man. "Sir, do you know the ladies that live in these rooms?"

"Yep, who wants to know?"

"My name is Jess Maxwell. I am Mary Beth Maxwell's husband."

The man climbed down and walked up close to Jess. "Her man, huh? You don't look like the man who is there most of the time."

"Really?" Jess said. "Do you know when she will be home?"

"In classes now, I guess. All these girls walk to the college every morning and return different times of the day. Ain't sure what time that Maxwell girl will be home."

"Are you their landlord?"

"Yep, I am." He said, moving the ladder over a few feet.

"Can you let me in Mary Beth's room? I have my luggage and a box of goodies for her."

"Nope, I sure can't do that. I ain't sure you're her man. You can sit on her porch if you like, but I ain't letting you in her room. I've got work to do. So I need to get busy," he said, as he walked away.

"Is there a place I can put my horse and carriage while I wait? It's too hot for this animal to just stand here on the street."

The man looked at the horse and motioned for Jess to follow him." I have a small barn behind these rooms. Just walk around the house and you'll see it. You can give him water, oats and hay for a dollar a day."

"That's a little steep, don't you think?"

"Take it or leave it, I don't care." The old man said as he climbed the ladder to the top of the roof. He began hammering wooden tiles.

Jess remembered how far away the closest livery was and decided it was a better deal. "I'll take your offer. Do you want me to pay in advance for a few days?"

"Not necessary. If you don't pay, I'll have you arrested. End of the deal."

After Jess settled the horse and carriage in the barn, he went back and sat in a rocker on Mary Beth's front porch.

Giggling came down the sidewalk near Mary Beth's room. Jess stopped rocking and sat still in the chair. He waited and listened. Finally, Mary Beth appeared with a young man wearing a white doctor's jacket. He was holding her arm and telling a story about operating on a man. Another girl held onto his other arm. "The old fellow woke up on the table," he said, laughing.

Suddenly, Mary Beth stopped in her tracks when she saw Jess sitting on her porch. "Jess! Oh my Jess." She rushed up the steps and into his arms.

"When did you arrive, Jess? Oh, I'm so happy to see you," Mary Beth rubbed her face against his chest.

"Who is your friend?" Jess asked, watching the young man shift from one foot to another one.

"Oh, I'm sorry. This is Randall Woods. He's a doctor at the college, and he has been helping us girls with some of the lab work. He was walking us home. Judy just lives a few doors down from here."

"Nice meeting you, Doctor. You don't mind excusing Mary Beth and me, do you? We haven't seen each other for a couple of weeks. Goodnight," Jess gently pushed Mary Beth into her doorway and watched the young doctor leave.

"Oh, Jess, I'm so happy to see you." Mary Beth said as she leaned into Jess's arms. "I'm sorry," she said, as she jumped back and ran her small hand over his wound. "I didn't mean to hurt you."

"You could never hurt me, sweetheart," Jess said as he accompanied her into her room. Jess glanced around at the double bed with a wedding ring quilt on top. He moved her over to the edge of the bed, and they sat side by side.

Out of nowhere, thunder pounded the little room. Lightning flashed in the front window, and Mary Beth slid closer to Jess until the thunder stopped.

Once the rumbles stopped, she smiled and walked over to the window and looked out over the flashing sky. "I love storms," she whispered.

As she stood gazing out, Jess walked behind her and pulled her against his chest. "Come, sweetheart, I have missed you so much. He drew her to the bed and began untying her long blond braid. They kissed with pent-up passion as they began to undress each other.

***

For several days, between rushing off to school and coming home to find her sweet husband waiting, Mary Beth was so happy. She saw Jess early in the morning and when she returned, they spent most of their time in her room. During that time, Jess promised to wait patiently at the ranch until she returned home for Thanksgiving.

He described to her some of his plans to build a greenhouse so she could have her own vegetable garden. Will had asked him to help build a boardwalk for Hope and the kids between their home to Jesse's and Rae's. The sandy road with gravel and rocks was too hard to walk upon from one house to the other. Staying busy would help the time fly by and keep his mind off missing her so much.

"Don't get too busy and not think about me," she cooed.

"That will never happen. I miss you already, just knowing that I am leaving in the morning." Jess smiled at his sweet wife and said, "I forgot about the box I brought from home. I sat it in the corner. Hope you like what I brought."

Mary Beth practically squealed, "Oh, I love surprises."

Jess sat the big box on her dining room table and watched as she pulled out the preserves and candy. She reached for the white cloth.

. "Oh, my, how lovely." She held it out in front of her and quickly wrapped it across her shoulders. "This is perfect! I love it," she said as she rushed over to a plain mirror on the wall. "Thank you so much for thinking of me. I shall wear this every time I get dressed in my regular clothes."

Jess watched her waltz around the room with her new shawl as she placed the preserves and pickles on her kitchen shelf. "Mary Beth, I want to ask you something. This Randall fellow, how often do you spend time with him?"

"Oh, Jess, don't tell me that you're jealous?"

"Maybe, I am. You're my beautiful bride, and I don't like thinking that some other man is hanging around you daily."

"Please, it's not like that at all. He's very smart, and he already taken this lab class. So he's been helping Judy and me, that's all. He kind of likes Judy, and I am pleased that he does. They make a good pair together."

"If you say so. I can't help but be a little jealous. I miss you so much."

Chapter 22

Jess eased off the train and looked down the street. First thing he saw was Bud Downey and younger brother-in law, Boo, hanging a banner across the street. It was advertising the Fourth of July celebration that would be held at Jesse's and Rae's ranch. He had forgotten that the 4th would be in a few days. There was always a lot of work to be done when his family hosted the big celebration. They invited the whole territory.

He picked up his carpetbag and stood at the bottom of the ladder that Bud had climbed to hook his end of the banner to the hotel balcony. "Hello, Boo. Man, you must have grown a foot since I saw you last. How's everybody doing at your place?"

"Fine, Mr. Jess. We're getting ready for the big party at your folks' place. It is always so much fun."

Bud scooted down the tall ladder and shook Jess's hand. "Good to see you, boy. So pleased to hear that you were doing well enough to travel to see your pretty little wife. How's she doing up there all alone?"

"Just fine. Mary Beth is really too busy to be lonely. She has a lot of classes and studies all the time."

"She going to make a fine nurse," Bud said.

"Are you two heading home now or do you have more business in town? I thought maybe I could catch a ride to my place, but if not, I can rent a carriage."

"No problem. Let me toss this ladder in the wagon and we'll be off."

"I sure appreciate the ride. This way I won't have to return the horse and carriage tomorrow."

On the ten-mile ride home, Jess asked about Rosie and their little girls. Gracie was nearly three and Patty was almost two.

Rosie and Justice had their hands full with the two small children while Boo ran wild with Will's son, Jay.

"Everyone is excited about planning the big celebration. Rosie is determined to win the pie-baking contest, and Justice is sure her strawberry preserves will win a blue ribbon. "

"But, Jess, you and I both know if Ollie enters those contests, she'll win hands down." Bud smiled at Boo.

"Your ladies have learned from the best, so they might just beat Ollie this year. Besides, Ollie has been busy taking care of Hope and me. She hasn't even mentioned the celebration," Jess said.

Bud asked Jess if he wanted him to drive to his house or stop at his folks' place.

"I'll get out here, in front of Pa's house. They are going to want me to start staying with them while Mary Beth is away," he commented. "I have a big, lonely place without her." Jess slid down off the wagon, took his carpetbag from Boo and waved good-bye to them. "Thanks again."

Jay and Willa came flying out of the house and hugged Jess around the legs. "Here, give me your bag. I can tote it for you," Jay said.

John, Hank and Jesse, came from the corral and barn and greeted Jess. "Good to have you back, son," Jesse said.

"I bet you made your sweet wife one happy gal," Hank said, chuckling.

"Yep, she was very surprised, but pleased. We had a nice time together."

"I was prepared to take your rented horse and carriage back to town for you, but I see you didn't need to get one," John said.

"Bud and Boo were in town hanging a banner across the street, advertising the big 4th we are having here."

"Oh good," Jesse said. "We tacked up a few signs at the post office, bakery, and dry-goods-store, but that banner is the best. No one can miss it."

"There's my baby boy," Ollie said, as she stepped slowly off the porch with Rae directly behind her. Whenever Ollie walked outside, Rae was always near. At eighty, Ollie wasn't always sure-footed, as Hank always said.

"Come inside and let's eat. I have your room already for you to move in. We want you to move down here with us while your bride is away at school."

"Thanks, Miss Ollie." Jess turned to his mama. "I was hoping you wanted me to stay here. I'm so lonesome without Mary Beth."

Rae tucked her arm around Jess's waist and walked with him into the house. Hank took Ollie's elbow and helped her onto the porch.

"I sure hope Jess brought me and Willa something. This bag sure is heavy," Jay said struggling with the load.

John laughed as he lifted Willa in his arms and carried a handle of the carpetbag.

***

Will stopped Bud and Boo on the road leading to the Downey farm and spoke with them for a few minutes. He learned from Bud that Jess was home. "Come over tomorrow, and we will start digging two pits to smoke and cook the beef for the party."

"Sure thing. I might bring the girls over to visit with your family while we work."

"Rae and Hope will love seeing Rosie and her babies. It's been too long with Jesse and Rae having been gone nearly three weeks on their trip to California."

***

Activity abounded around the ranch, which made Ollie's heart glad. The men had dug the deep pit and placed the oak wood in the bottom to start smoldering. John brought the butcher from his meat store to cut up and prepare the beef to go on the big spit to turn over and over to roast the young cows.

Many of the young boys from surrounding ranches and farms brought their horses into the corral for the cattle roping, bronco riding, and barrel races. They teased each other and placed small wagers as to who would win.

Jess stood on the sideline and watched and listened. This would be his first year not to participate in any of the games. Rae had asked him to be a judge in the pie tasting contest and he didn't waste any time in refusing that job. There was no way he was going to have the women mad at him for not choosing their pie.

Hank had several young men helping set up tables and chairs under the shade trees and a big tent for the smaller children to play under with a two-foot-high fence surrounding it. They would hire some teenagers to help watch and play with the little ones while their mothers enjoyed the barbeque.

Justice rode over with Rosie and the children to visit with Rae and Hope. Will had made Hope lie down on the sofa while Rosie helped Rae peel dozens of eggs. Boiled eggs were always a favorite on the table. Ollie had already prepared eight strawberry pies and placed them down in the cool cellar. Many of the neighbors would bring all types of potatoes salad, steaming buttered corn, baked lima beans, and cakes of cornbread. Pies and cakes of all kind would be on the dessert table. There would be enough food to feed an army.

Ollie pulled Justice aside to talk in private about Claire and the two toddies that she had made. Claire was coming today, and Rae said that she had a big surprise. Ollie was whispering to Justice about Albert drinking the toddies when suddenly everything went black. Someone was pulling a prank on her and she said, "Stop clowning around, its' too blasted hot to have this thing on my head." She tried to push it off when she felt a blow to the side of her head, and the next thing she knew, she was on the damp, stone floor.

Justice said something in French and down she tumbled on top of Ollie. Suddenly an old, rugged voice said, "Come on, let's get them to the horses. We got my woman. You carry that one."

The Indians. Two of them. Both women tried to fight, but seemed to only hit each other until the men separated them. The two old men placed Ollie across the front of a saddle with the saddle horn in her belly. The other man sat Justice up in front of him and the men rode away from the ranch at full speed.

***

Willa always tagged after Ollie, and it was a good thing she was following after her today. She saw Ollie lying across an Indian's horse. She was trying to scream but her words were muffled under the cover on her head. Justice was waving her small arms and attempting to remove the pillowcase off her head, but the Indian kept slapping her hands.

"Mama, mama!" Willa raced into the house and ran to the sofa where Hope was almost asleep.

"Willa, be quiet. Can't you see your mama is sleeping and so are the babies?" Rae said.

"But, Rae, Indians got Ollie and Justice. Indians. Help! I saw them ride off with them."

"Oh, Willa, what an imagination you have, "Rosie said.

"Please Rae, come and help me tell Papa. Miss Ollie is gone with that old Indian who came here while you were gone. They were going to cut my pigtail, but mama wouldn't let them."

Hank walked in the door and picked Willa up. "Why are you crying, my little doll?"

"Oh, Hankie, Indians took Ollie, That old man who wanted her to be his wife. Remember? He took her from the spring house."

Rae frowned. "Hank, take her outside and go find Ollie and Justice. Show that child that they are all right, please, before she wakes Rosie's girls."

"Come with me, and let's go find the two old hens," Hank said, as he carried Willa to the spring house.

"See, they aren't here. Those Indians took them. They placed pillowcases over their heads and rode that way."

Hank sat Willa on the ground and looked down at all the fresh horse tracks surrounding the door of the spring house. Ollie's pretty white bandanna lay on the ground. Hank picked it up and said, "Come with me, child. We got to find Jesse."

***

After what seemed like hours, the old Indians stopped their animals and removed the pillowcase from Ollie's head. She stared wide-eyed at the front of a large brown and white deerskin teepee. A young Indian maiden came out and laughed.

"So that is what you went hunting for. A big fat woman and a scrawny one that couldn't carry a bucket of water." The young maiden scoffed. "I hope you don't think I am going to take care of these pigs."

The old Indian let Ollie slide to the ground. He jumped down and caught her before she landed on her backside.

Ollie rubbed her belly. She felt like she had been stabbed in the middle and she was going to make someone pay for treating her so rough. She peered at the old Indian man who stood toe to toe with her.

The other Indian removed Justice from his horse and stood her on the ground. With so many young and old Indians standing near as she straightened her dress and apron, she eased over to Ollie. She had heard Bud said not to show fear when someone was

129

mistreating you.

Ollie watched Justice bit on her trembling lip. "We'll be fine, Justice, These three Indians' *cornbread ain't done in the middle,* if you know what I mean. They came over to the ranch a few months ago. They wanted to buy me from Jess because they like my biscuits."

"For gosh sakes, see if you can make them some more, and let's get out of here. Surely, we will be missed by the others at the house soon."

"Not sure how long that will be, but I'm certain these men won't hurt us. That little gal might think she can scare us, but we'll take care of her. You have your bag of goodies in your apron, don't you?"

"I never leave home without it," Justice said, patting her apron pocket.

"Move," the older Indian said, waving his hand toward the teepee.

Ollie walked inside the brazing hot structure with Justice on her heels. He pointed at the fire and the spider skillet. "Cook," he said as he rubbed his stomach.

Ollie looked at his necklaces and beaded vest. She remembered it from the last time he stood at her kitchen table, sticking his fingers in her hot soup.

"Justice, this old fool wants me to cook biscuits like he ate at the ranch when they came to get some cattle. I fed them and Jess took them out to the pasture and gave them a dozen head of cattle. He offered to buy me. He said I could be his wife."

"He's the chief of all these other Indians? Just think, you could be his woman and be his queen," Justice laughed. "You would be a very important person, living out here."

"You're nuttier than a fruit cake, woman. Indians don't have Kings and Queens," Ollie said, as she kneeled down on the ground. "Lord, oh mighty. I ain't sure I will ever be able to get up. Tell that old Indian at the door that I need milk, if he wants me to make biscuits."

Justice walked to the door of the teepee and tapped the guard on the shoulder. He jumped and drew back his tomahawk as to hit her with it. "This old man is deaf. He nearly peed in his pants when I touched him." Justice giggled like a schoolgirl. Finally, she made the old man understand what she needed.

Later, after the three men ate their fill of hot biscuits and milk gravy, the older man eased up to Ollie. Picking at her while curls, he said, "You my woman now. I find man for her soon," he said as he nodded towards Justice.

"I'm sorry old man. I ain't gonna' marry you or any man. Now, that I have cooked for you, take us back to the ranch."

"No! You stay with me." He got real close to Ollie, ran his hands through her white curls as she flinched and attempted to move away. "I *like to sop* you up *with another biscuit.*"

"Shoot fire, you old fool," Ollie pushed him away and howled with laughter. "You're about as romantic as a cross-eyed mule."

The old man looked dumbfounded. "Two Teeth said that to his woman. It worked for him. His woman immediately cut her wrist, pulled him close and they bled together. She shares her blanket with him now."

Ollie scooted further away from the older man's hold on her. "Look here now. I don't care what the other Indian said or did to get his woman. Justice and I are going home." Ollie looked to Justice, and mouthed, *do something.*"

Justice looked around the room. Two old squaws were sitting on a blanket, making pine straw baskets. Slowly reaching down into her apron, Justice pulled out two firecrackers and tossed them into the fire. Loud explosions and crackling of the fire sent everyone running out of the teepee.

"Now, that's just a little magic that she can perform. The next one, she might hurt somebody." Ollie yelled to the chief.

The young Indian maiden rushed over to the teepee. "Many white men are coming with rifles. We must hide."

Many of the Indians began to move away from the door of the teepee. "No, don't go anywhere," Ollie yelled. "It's our men. They have come to take us home."

Hank was leading the small army of men from the ranch and those working the barbeque. Jesse leaped down and stood in front of Ollie and Justice. "Are you girls alright?"

"My woman." The older man stood as tall as he could in front of Ollie. "She can go," the old Indian said, pointing at Justice. "She's bad. White Curls, she stays."

"Listen old man, you can't have our women. No one is staying and if you want to live another minute, you best move away from them." Hank grabbed the old man making his necklaces and beads rattle.

"Now Hank, calm down. The girls aren't hurt."

"Hank's right, Jesse. This old man tried to get Jess to sell Ollie to him months ago. Jess told him no then, but it seems he didn't take Jess seriously," John said. "We gave them a dozen head of beef."

"I see," Jesse said turning from John. "Listen old man, this woman belongs to me. You cannot have her. If you touch her again, you'll be sorry."

The older chief walked to Ollie. "I never harm you," he looked at all the men. "Can I come to your ranch again and get more biscuits?"

Ollie smiled at the old creature and nodded yes. "Come anytime."

"Saddle up fellow, we've got a lot of work to do before tomorrow." Hank yelled as he placed Ollie and Justice in the carriage that a man drove behind them. Hank knew that Ollie wasn't able to ride a horse home.

Ollie sighed as she sat down in the carriage, rubbing her stomach and said to Justice, "That Hank is always thinking what's best for me since Jeremiah isn't here anymore."

Chapter 23

The fourth of July was nearly a perfect day. Hank couldn't be happier. The sky was a beautiful blue and the sun shined directly overhead. All the families in a twenty-mile radius were in attendance. Many of the men had stayed up during the night turning the spindle on the beef. The ladies of the community had brought hot dishes and desserts. Rae and Ollie had organized the time for most of the food to be placed on the tables to be served.

Hank headed to the corral. With the firing of a pistol, the young men lined up to ride the bunco horses. Loud laughter could be heard coming from the corral as the young men took turn tiring to stay on their horse for eight seconds. Bets of money were passed back and forth among the men.

The little boys were lined up for rope calving. They would wrestle it to the ground and tie its four legs together. The boy who did it the fastest would be the winner. Jay was beside his best friend, Boo, hoping that he would win the covet blue ribbon.

Hank's eyes lit on the picnic tables. The jars of preserves and best pie contest took place before dinner. Several ladies proudly wore their ribbons during the day. Katie was disappointed that her pear preserve recipe didn't win, but two judges told her that they were delicious.

Hank was over at the children's tent as Mrs. Miller passed Tater's and Missy's toddler, Johnny, to one of the teenagers.

Mrs. Miller latched onto Hank's arm and smiled sheepishly at him as they strolled over to the big tent where the food tables were set up. Hank tied to shake the older woman's hand loose without being rude, but to no avail. He helped her to a chair, but she pulled him down beside her. "Now, Hankie, let those young men do all the work today. You just sit here with me and visit. Tell can me all about yourself."

As fast as lightning, Hank leaped from the chair and told those sweet, pouty lips he had to go take care of some business. "This is practically my ranch and big celebration, and I have many things to take care of."

Making sure the older woman wasn't following him, he hurried into the house and found Rae. "You've got to help me. That woman will not leave me alone. She's worse than a clinging-- leech!"

Rae laughed and looked into Hank's red face. "Oh Hank, calm down. Mrs. Miller has got a crush on you. You should be happy that a pretty, older woman wants your attention."

"Just listen to you, Rae. That woman is after my money."

"How in the world would she know that you have 'money', as you put it?"

"People gossip and I believe old Mr. Taylor at the dry goods store probably told her."

"How would he know about your finances? Good gracious, aren't there any secrets in this town?" Rae said, shaking her head.

"No, I believe she wormed the info about my finances maybe from Missy. She did mention something about me being able to keep a woman in fine things. I believe she put that dress she's wearing on my bill, without my permission."

"Surely, she wouldn't have done that, would she?" Rae asked, giving Hank a puzzled glance.

***

Lucy was standing in the pantry and couldn't help but hear the conversation between Rae and Hank about her grandmother. She wasn't surprised at all that her sweet Granny would have done just that. She was sorry now that she had told her about everyone inheriting money from their friend who had died several months ago.

Hank was complaining again. "Rae, she is out there right now clucking all about how sure she is that I like her a lot. I might even want to get married. I can tell you now I ain't going anywhere near her again, much less marry that woman. You've got to put a stop to that woman, or I'm going to hurt her feelings!" Hank stormed out the side door and limped across the yard to the barn.

Lucy came out of the pantry and stood at the door with Rae,

watching the old man huff and puff as he rushed into the barn.

"Mrs. Maxwell, I'm the one that told Granny about Mr. Hank having money. Miss Hope told me all about your family inheriting money from a friend. She made me promise not to say anything, but Granny and I share everything. I am worried about her now. You see, my grandpa has returned. He wants Granny to go away with him. He's awful sorry about how he treated her in the past. They don't have much money, so I guess she thinks she can get some from Mr. Hank. I wouldn't be surprised if she might have stolen money from the flower farm."

"Oh no. Surely, she wouldn't have done that. Aunt Katie hasn't mentioned anything about money missing," Rae said, as she sat down in a kitchen chair.

"Grandpa told me that if they had a small nest egg, we could move on and settle somewhere. He ain't a lazy man, but he does like to drink, too much. I told Granny that I don't want to go away with them. I would like to stay here and maybe get a school teaching job. I am educated and I have worked as a teacher's helper before. But I don't want to leave Miss Hope, especially in her time of need."

"Oh, Lucy, you can stay with us as long as you like. In the near future, the school board might have to hire someone to help my daughter, Claire, with her students."

"That would be grand, but I have got to stop Granny from taking advantage of people," Lucy said. She might go to jail and grandpa would just leave her again for sure."

***

Hank was furious, and madder than an old setting hen. He would like to strangle that old woman for not setting the women straight. They didn't know what they were talking about. When the women mentioned there may be a wedding in the near future, Mrs. Miller didn't deny anything.

Gosh darn it, he had only spoken with that woman on two different occasions. He was sure she was up to something, and it did involve him. Just as he decided to go back outside to the corral and watch the calf roping event, a sweet voice came from the shady side of the doorway.

"Hank, dearest, I have something important to talk to you about. Will you stand still long enough to discuss a little business deal with me?" Mrs. Miller stood close enough to him that he smelled a sweet vanilla scent.

"What kind of trouble are you trying to stir up about me now?"

"Sweetheart, you are a dear man, and I am in need of some help. Wouldn't you like for me to disappear out of your life forever? With me gone, let's say, out of the picture, the community will stop gossiping about us."

"Gossip I might add, you started." Hank took a deep breath and gestured for her to speak her peace. "Get on with your plan. I just told Mrs. Rae that you were up to something, so whatever you have on your mind won't be a surprise to me. I wasn't born yesterday."

"I need to get away, or go away. You see, my husband has returned, and he wants me to go away with him. You know, start over."

"Your husband? We were told he was dead. You're supposed to be a widow woman on hard times."

"I am or was on hard times until Missy and Hope gave us a job. But, my husband isn't dead, He just up and left Lucy and me to fend for ourselves. I have used all of the money that I had hidden away from him."

"So, the old goat has returned, and you want to leave with him. What about Lucy? Is she going to leave Will and Hope, without any help, when she has her two babies?"

"No, Lucy wants to stay here, that is, if they will allow her, too."

"Let's get down to the facts, woman. What do you want from me?"

"I need a little nest egg to be able to leave with my man. He promises to get a job wherever we land. I can work too, but we need traveling expenses. You have money and if you really want me out of your life, you will help us . . . with expenses."

"How much will it take to send you and your dearly-departed husband out of my sight before I strangle you?"

"Two hundred dollars, will send us a far piece away, out of your sight."

"You ain't planning on traveling cheap," Hank said sarcastically.

"I could ask for more, but I am not attempting to rob you."

"Stand right here. I'll be back in a few minutes." Hank turned and rush into his bunk house room. He tossed back a board on the floor and reached down for the box where he stored all his important papers and extra money. He counted out the money she had requested and stood to find her standing in his doorway.

"Now, I see, I will have to invent another hiding place. I can't be having you return and rob me blind.' He handed the woman the money and quickly said, "After this shindig, I want you gone. While you are mingling with our guests, I would appreciate it if you said something about your husband returning. I don't want my friends thinking I have been playing tootsies with you while you're still married." Hank stared hard at the woman and dared her to refuse his request.

"Tonight, I'll tell Tater to get your covered wagon ready to move out. Your mules have been taken care of and he will hitch them up for you. I better not ever lay eyes on you again. If I do, I'll tell the sheriff that you and your *lover* robbed me. Got that?"

"Hank, I will always remember our special friendship," she said, as she walked out of the barn, holding her head up like she was royalty.

***

After dinner was served to all the guests, dancing was in full swing on the sturdy platform that Jesse, John and Hank had built twenty-five years ago for Jesse and Rae's wedding. Over the years, the men had kept the frame and flooring in good condition to be used over and over.

As the men played guitars, fiddles and mouthorgans, Hank saw Rae signaled John and Katie in to the house. She relayed the story that Hank had told her about Mrs. Miller leaving tonight with her husband, and she told them that Lucy was staying with Will and Hope.

Hank had ridden over to Tater's to help him with the woman's covered wagon and mules. He didn't tell Rae that he gave the old woman money to leave as he was embarrassed at being blackmailed.

He was thrilled he didn't have to worry about a woman trying to nab him. He was going to be very cautious as to how he spoke to the ladies in town from now on. It hadn't occurred to him that he had so much charm.

***

At lot of laughter was heard coming from outside. Everyone rushed over to the bedroom window and looked at the table where Mrs. Miller was sitting. "That must be her husband," Rae said. "You think we should invite them in the house?"

John and Katie looked at each other and Katie said, "No. She embarrassed Hank and I'll glad she is leaving."

***

Late into the night, as all the close neighbors had left for home and the ones that had traveled far were settled down in their covered wagons that formed a circle in the open pasture, Jesse and Rae had a long discussion. She told him about Mrs. Miller, her dead departed husband, who came back to life.

***

As Jesse and Rae prepared for bed, Rae remembered that Albert and Claire had not announced their big surprise. "Oh, Jesse, I've got to go see Claire," she said as she grabbed up her pretty, silk robe.

"Hold your horse's woman," Jesse said. "If it's what we think it is, it can wait until morning. They have already gone to bed, and you don't need to disturb them. It's a grand surprise and they're eager to tell us, but let them have one more night alone, together, sharing it only with themselves. It can wait." Jesse said as he held his lovely wife in his arms and nuzzled her neck, cheeks and eyes. He moved her to the bed and blew out the lantern.

Chapter 24

Late into the night, after the yearly barbeque was completely over, Will had bedded down Jay and Willa on the two sofas in the living room. He walked in Hope's bedroom and looked down at her. She laid perfectly still, except for her big belly moving up and down. She had the quilt pulled up under her arms with her long blond plait placed over her left breast. She was a beauty.

Will stood over her remembering how beautiful she was after giving birth to Jay and Willa. During the birthing, she would scream like a wild woman, but minutes afterwards, with Justice soothing her, she became calm and the prettiest little mama a baby could ever have. He did wonder what Justice said to her, but he didn't ask. After removing all his clothes, he slipped under the covers next to Hope. Her eyes slowly opened, and she gave her handsome husband a sweet smile. "How are you feeling tonight?" Will asked.

"Tired, and my back hurts a lot, but I am trying to lie still. That helps," she relied. "I guess I walked around in the yard too much and ate more than I should have."

Will moved closer and his mouth covered hers, urging her mouth to open a little further as he placed his lips over hers.

Hope's body appeared to come alive with desire and her breathing grew faster as did his.

Just then, a blood curling scream came from Hope's mouth as she twisted in the bed, "Pain, my Lord! A pain like no other shot up my back." She could hardly speak.

Will slid off the bed onto the hard floor, nearly breaking his knee cap. He grabbed his denims and pulled them on just as Rae busted through their bedroom door.

"Are you in labor, baby?" Rae said, not giving Will a glance.

"I must be or Will just stabbed me in the back with a knife," Hope said, hardly able to breathe. "I'm wet too. I' couldn't get up quick enough."

"I'll send one of the men after Doctor Tim," Will said, as he hopped around the room with one boot on.

"Get Justice. I want Justice here NOW!

***"

Screams from the house could be heard at the bunkhouse. Hank came flying through the back door with part of his nightshirt stuffed into his pants. "I'll go get Justice, if Jesse can get Doctor Tim," Hank said.

Ollie stood in the doorway of Hope's bedroom and said that she would get everything ready for the birthing.

With this being Hope's third child, Ollie had everything all ready from the previous birthing. A big oilcloth and many old sheets that could be thrown away, were placed beside her bed until they were sure she was in labor.

A couple hours later, Will stiffened at a whimper that escaped Hope as pain consumed and gripped her body.

"Push down Hope. That's it. You can scream if you want. I don't like you being so silent," Doctor Tim mumbled.

Screams did come, one after another, sending chills down Will's spine. *God, I wish it was me having these babies.*

Hope reached and grabbed Justice's small hand and squeezed it. A frown from pain crossed her face, but Justice continued to use soothing words to help calm the soon-to-be-new mother.

"Open your mouth, Miss Hope." Justice waited until Doctor Tim was busy with his instruments, before she pushed a few little pellets of medicine under her tongue. "Keep your mouth closed and allow the medicine to do its job." Justice whispered and placed the rest of the medicine back in her apron pocket.

For the longest time, Will paced while Hope twisted and turned on the bed, while Doctor Tim pleading with her to lie still. Eventually, Hope's smile replaced her painful expression, the writhing stopped, and she lay perfectly still. All the terrible pain had begun to fade, and she was able to relax.

Doctor Tim was surprised at Hope's sudden calm, but he was happy. "Okay, push now. One of the baby's crowning.

The head merged and, a scream did come, causing Will to sit

down in the chair beside the bed. He thought he might pass out, but swallowed hard and held onto his precious 'wife's hand.

In a matter of minutes, a beautiful, but bloody baby girl was out, and then with the next baby following so close, Dr. Tim had to quickly place the babe in Ollie's hands. In a flash, her little brother slipped out. Justice took the baby and wiped his mouth out as he announced his arrival with a hardy scream.

"Oh, Hope, we have one of each. Just what you wanted." Will wiped at his eyes that were full of tears.

"Of course, you always give me what I what.' She closed her eyes and fell into a deep sleep.

Doctor Tim immediately listened to Hope's heartbeat and smiled broadly. "She's just worn out. Sleep will be good for her while I clean her up. Ollie, you and Justice bathe and dress the wee ones while Hannah helps me with the afterbirth."

Will was ushered out of the bedroom. He walked into Hanks waiting arms. He placed his forehead on Hank's chest and mumbled, "I promise, this will be the last time I put Hope through that kind of pain."

"Congratulations my boy," Hank said with a chuckle. "A fine son and daughter. A little brother for Jay and baby sister for Willa. If you remember how spoiled Hope was, you can just figure those two in there are gonna be something else," He patted Will on the back.

"I was really scared this time, Hank. But you know when the pain is so bad, and you are sure she can't endure it much longer, Hope gets really calm. It's like a miracle."

Ollie and Justice carried the babies into the living room to allow the family to see them. Jess and Hank stood side by side to view the babies and beamed as proudly as if they were responsible for them being born. The ladies walked over to the children and pulled back the blankets and let them see the wrinkled red faces of their little sister and new brother. "Gosh, Miss Ollie, was I ever that little?" Jay asked.

Will took a chair and sat near a window. He saw that dawn was breaking. Everyone in the house had to be tired. He smiled to himself, so proud of his new babies. He felt like he could wrestle a bear despite how exhausted he was. He began to stand when his weight on his hurt knee nearly made him fall on his face. With all the excitement of the babies being born, he had forgotten that his kneecap felt like it was broken.

Rae peeked around the corner of the kitchen where she was putting on a pot of coffee. You got up too quickly, I see." She smiled at Will and told him to go lie down in the twin bed next to Hope's. "You need to sleep while she's resting. There's enough of us to take care of the children, big and small."

"If you are sure, I will, but I need to have Doctor Tim check my knee. I fell off the bed when Hope screamed from pain, and I think I may have cracked it. I want to thank him for everything, too."

"Tim and Hannah are going to rest at Jess's house this morning. Tim doesn't want to be too far away from Hope when she awakes. He wants to keep an eye on her and the babies."

"Is he afraid of something happening to her?" Will asked, suddenly nervous.

"No, Will," Doctor Tim answered from the doorway. "Hope has been through a hard birthing, so I want to be here to check her over before I travel the ten miles to town. Just being cautious."

"I appreciate everything. I know Hope trusts you with her life. We are all very fortunate to have you and Miss Hannah with us. Before you retire, could I get you to look at my kneecap? I fell on it and it hurts like the devil." Will said, as he attempted to stand.

"Come into the bedroom and let me examine it. Hannah, gather our things and wait for me in the kitchen with Rae," Doctor Tim said.

After a thorough examine, Doctor Tim determined Will's kneecap had a large crack across the top. "You're going to have to stay off it for a while. Maybe two weeks before it heals. That had to hurt when you did it."

"It did, but with Hope in so much pain, I didn't have time to do anything about it."

Once Will's leg was wrapped, Doctor Tim and Hannah walked out into the morning sunrise and went up the hill to the lovely house that they had built for Jess and Mary Beth's wedding present.

"Pa," Jay walked over to Will while he was enjoying a fresh cup of coffee.

"Hey buddy, why aren't you asleep? I know you must still be

tired."

"A little, but I have been thinking about something important." He looked at his pa and then turned his shoulders around to see if anyone else was listening. "Pa, can men have babies?"

"What?" Will asked, trying not to laugh because he could see how serious this question was to Jay. "No son, only mama's have the babies. When a Pa and Ma love each other, they make a baby, but the mama is the only one that can bring it into the world."

"So, I don't have to fret over having a baby and going through all that pain?"

"No, God didn't make a man's body to have a baby."

"Man, that's a load off my mind. I don't believe I would be strong like Mama. Her screaming really scared me. I sure hope our new babies will know what she's done for them to get here."

"Your mama is going to need a lot of help in the future with the new babies. I hope *you* will remember what she has been through, and you and Willa will help care for them. I am sorry you had to hear her. If we had known that she was going to go into labor, you and Willa would have been at Aunt Katie's."

"Pa, I'm sort of glad I was here. I hope mama won't ever have to go through that again. What do you think?"

"I love all my babies 'son, but I'm like you, I don't want this to ever happen again." Will reached for Jay and pulled him on his lap, careful not to harm his hurt knee. He pressed his small head into his chest and told him to go to sleep.

Chapter 25

Early the next morning, after a thorough examination from Dr. Tim and Hannah, Hope woke again to the sound of her two babies. She attempted to sit up and get a closer look at them. Rae held the boy child while Ollie cooed to the baby girl.

They were feeding the babies a sugar tit. Hope's milk had not come down yet, but the babies had to be fed. Justice had stayed all night and she was prepared small bottles of diluted cow's milk. Dr. Tim had told the ladies that Hope would not be able to breast feed both babies at one time. "Prepare small bottles to help her feed the babies," instructed Doctor Tim.

Justice carried in the small bottles and gave Ollie and Rae one each. Both held the nipples to the small pink lips and they both took to it just like they had hoped.

Hope sighed and watched Rae and Ollie give her twins their first real food. "You know, Will and I have talked about names for the babies. What do you think about Olivia Rae after you, Miss Ollie? Jesse told me that your real name is Olivia Pritchet." When Ollie sat speechless, Hope continued. "We thought to name our new son, Jeremiah Hank Maxwell and call him Jerry. What do you think about these names?

"Oh, Miss Hope, are you sure you want your baby girl named after me?"

"Yes, I can't think of a better role-model for my child to follow than you and my precious sister, Rae.

"Hank is going to be very proud, and Jeremiah would be honored. Jerry is a perfect name to call your new son. How does Will feel about not naming the boy after him?"

"He is the one that suggested both names. Willa is already named after him, so he wanted to have Jeremiah in our daily memories."

"You know, no one ever called me Olivia until the foremen at Waverly Plantation called me to come and get my Freedom Paper. My mama never called me anything, but Ollie."

Rae placed the baby on her shoulder and patted his back until he burped. Ollie did the same and everyone laughed. "We will have to feed them again in about three hours. Let's try to keep them on a schedule. I was told that babies should be on a routine. I think that's what I learned years ago," Rae said, as she changed the baby's wet nappy.

Ollie looked at Hope who was soundly sleeping. "Having these two babies sure has worn this child out. Let's go and let her sleep." She carried one baby while Rae carried the other into the warm living room. Both babies were sleeping when Willa and Jay came into the room.

Ollie carried one baby while Rae carried the other into the warm living room. Both babies were sleeping when Willa and Jay came into the room. "Just look and be very quiet. You can hold their little hands when they wake up for another bottle."

"How many bottles will they drink during the day?" Jay asked.

"Oh, I'm not sure, but enough to keep them full and sassy," Ollie replied.

"Miss Ollie, you are so funny. Is mama asleep again?" Willa asked.

"Yes, she is. She's plum tuckered out, but she is going to be just fine in a few days."

"What do you think of the name Olivia for your baby sister and Jeremiah Hank for the little fellow? We will call him Jerry," Rae asked both children.

"I like the names. Did Mama and Papa choose them?" Jay asked. He was quick to ask questions.

***

Early that morning, Rae looked up from the stove to see Albert come tiptoeing in the back door. He looked down at the two sleeping beautiful babies. "Look at these little miracles," he said smiling. "How is Hope doing?"

"She's fine, but Albert, how is Claire this morning. Were you comfortable sleeping at Jess's house last night?" Rae asked.

"Yes, we were, but it looks like we missed all the excitement. I know Claire would have wanted to be here to help Hope, but I'm sure you had plenty of help. Did Doctor Tim make it back here? I saw him and Miss Hannah leave as we were walking to Jess's place."

"Yes, he and Miss Hannah, Justice, Ollie, Will and me. Like you said, she had lots of help. Once she was in labor, the babies came pretty quickly." Rae walked over to Albert and whispered for his ears only. "I'm glad Claire wasn't here. All of Hope's screaming would have scared her, if you know what I mean."

"So, you know what our big announcement is going to be?" Albert asked, a disappointed look on his face.

"Mostly, but I am her mother. And I thrilled to my toes. But it is your announcement to make at breakfast. Everyone will be tickled for you," Rae said, as she flipped over the flapjacks she was preparing at Hank's request.

Claire entered the kitchen wearing a pretty new dress, her long hair pulled back behind her shoulders. Her cheeks were glowing pink as she stood at the end of the table. She smiled at her papa and the whole group. "Albert stood and walked to Claire's side. He placed his hand around her waist and said, "Claire has something to tell you all?"

Claire saw Miss Ollie and Justice standing in the doorway with their heads together, smiling. Ollie waved her hand at her to go ahead and make the announcement. Claire smiled at Albert and said, and looking at Albert said, "We are going to have a baby this spring."

A loud applause broke out among the family members. Jess was the first to jump up and kiss his sister on the cheek and shake Albert's hand. After receiving hugs and kisses from the rest of the family, Ollie and Justice placed platters of flapjacks in the center of the table.

Claire hurried to Rae, Ollie and Justice and hugged them, then whispered, "I can't thank you two enough. I didn't drink the toddies, but Albert did. Whatever was in them, gave him whatever I needed to conceive. Of course, he doesn't remember that night and that's just fine. Its' our secret, and of course, Doctor Tim's," giggled Claire.

Rae nodded, rolling her eyes.

***

"Oh, mama, with all our excitement I forget to tell you. The new schoolteacher will be arriving tomorrow in Limason. She wanted to get settled before school starts in a few weeks. The School Board Superintendent, Mr. Wallace, wants me to meet her at the train and take her to her lodging. Doctor Tim said the school board can still use his house for the schoolteacher." Claire heaved a sigh. But I can't meet her. Doctor Tim told me to stay with you for a week. He doesn't want me riding back and forth to town. He wants me to rest and don't do any unnecessary riding. Mr. Wallace will be out of town and Mrs. Ellis has been down due to her back. There just isn't another person that I can think of that could meet her."

"Oh my, I can't leave Hope. I know there are many others that can stay and help her, but I just can't. I would never forgive myself if anything happened while I was away." Hope bled a lot while giving birth and Doctor Tim insisted she stay bed ridden for at least two weeks. "Jesse is a board member, and he can meet the teacher and help her get settled."

***

Early the next morning, Jesse went into town and met the 10 a.m. train. A tall, russet haired young woman stood on the platform. She was dressed in a layered, two-piece brown suit with a high-top hat adorned with a brown and white feather on its side.

Jesse walked over and asked if she was Miss Maybelle Sooner. "Yes, I am," she answered, giving Jesse the once over. She was expecting an old man or woman to meet her, not a handsome cowboy.

"Miss Sooner, my name is Jesse Maxwell. I am a school board member, and I came to retrieve you from the train and take you to your house. My carriage is parked there, next to the platform. I will collect your carpetbags and trunk."

Smithy was standing near the platform steps, and he offered her his hand and helped her into Jesse's carriage. Jesse thanked Smithy and after settling the luggage into the carriage, he drove down Main Street and turned onto a short side street. "Here is your little house. It's small, but I'm sure it is comfortable. It even has a porch swing and a small back yard." Doctor Tim keeps the little house in good shape with a fresh coat of paint and new window shutters.

147

"My, it looks very cozy. Thank you for bringing me to it," she cooed, batting her eyes at Jesse.

The young lady looked more like a spinster, maybe thirty years old or older. She wasn't a beauty but attractive enough. Her brown hair was shiny, even though she had it covered with an awful hat. Her body was very slim, but she was taller than the average young girl. She didn't appear to be shy, in the least. Jesse carried her trunk and carpetbags into the living room. "Where do you want this heavy trunk?"

"Please place it at the foot of the bed. It is very heavy, but you're so strong." She followed him into the bedroom, and he could feel her eyes on his back.

"The schoolhouse is two streets over, the post office is down that way and there's a nice café where everyone takes a meal. It's close to the bank on Main Street." Jesse started to the front door.

"Oh, Mr. Maxwell, I was hoping that you would take me on a tour of the school. Please . . . I need to see my workplace before I can plan anything, and I don't want to see it by myself," she said, looking like Willa when she wanted her way.

"Let's go then. I really don't have all day, but I will escort you to the schoolhouse."

"I knew you wouldn't let me down," she said as she hurried onto the porch.

'Shall we walk so you can point out the different places I will need to know about?"

"Walking will be fine." Jesse said, although he had no time for this. He pointed out the post office, the dry goods store, the bank and café as they passed them heading to the freshly painted schoolhouse. After arriving at the school, Jesse hurried up the steps and unlocked the front door. "Before school begins, the superintendent will give you a key."

Walking into the foyer, Jesse pointed out a room where the children hung their coats and removed their muddy shoes. "This front room on the right is Claire's room---she's my daughter and teaches the younger children up to the fifth grade. I am guessing you will be teaching the older students up to the eighth grade."

"Yes, that is what I was told. Oh, this is a nice room for smaller children. I hope my room looks *better.*" The unpleasant comment didn't go unnoticed by Jesse.

"Well, this will be your classroom. It does have a potbelly stove that the older boys come earlier to get a fire started so the room is warm. Our winters are really cold, and most of the students walk to school. We keep a supply of chopped wood on the back porch."

Walking around the room, she ran a gloved hand over the surface of a desk, her nose turned up. "There aren't any bookshelves on the walls. I cannot manage without them. Do you know if the superintendent will build some for me?"

"I'm sure if you mention this to Mr. Wallace, he will help you get whatever you need."

"Well, while teaching in my last school, no one would help me with my classroom. I had to use all of my extra money to buy whatever I needed."

Jesse walked around the bare room except for desk and chairs. There was a large blackboard, erasers and white chalk. The windows didn't have curtains or window shades, which he thought would help the room look better.

"Mr. Maxwell, this room needs several things. I have many books that I like to display for my students. I really encourage my pupils to read. The better they can read, the better they can do many other projects and excel."

"Oh, I agree with you about reading. I am sure I can get many bookshelves built in a couple of weeks. What else do you need?"

"Oh, I am so pleased that you will build me some shelves. I know I can depend on you. May I make a list of other things I need?" She batted her eyes at him again.

Jesse was sure this young lady was probably a good teacher but he was certain she was after a man – and it wasn't going to be him. He would have to bring Rae to meet this woman soon.

"If you have seen everything, we had best go. I have things to do while I am here in town." He stood at the schoolhouse door and waited for her to exit. As they walked down the steps, she stopped. "Could you take me to the store so I can get some supplies for my small kitchen? My cupboards are empty, and I will need a few things to help get me settled."

"The dry good stores is not too far from here, so we can walk. I need to pick up a few things while we're there as well," Jesse blew out a breath. He wasn't in the mood to hang out with this new teacher all day.

With the hot August sun beating down on both of them, the new spinster teacher looped her arm in Jesse's and smiled broadly at him as they walked side by side down the boardwalk.

Before entering the store, Jesse could feel many eyes watching him walking arm and arm with a total stranger. Many wondered what he was doing out in public with this other woman and not with his beautiful, beloved wife.

As they entered the store, Jesse introduced the teacher to Mr. and Mrs. Goodyear, owners of the nicest store in Limason. "Mrs. Goodyear, our new teacher needs a few supplies for her house. Can you show her around?"

"Of course, Miss. We have almost everything a person needs. This section of the store is for Ladies and little girls and behind it is the men and boys' items. Our fresh produce and can goods are in the front of the store. Here is a basket that you can place your items in while you shop. If you need to place anything on an account, you can fill out a form with Mr. Goodyear. I let him take care of people who want to buy now and pay later." Smiling, she walked back behind the counter.

"Oh, thank you, Mrs. Goodyear. I'm sure Mr. Maxwell will take care of my items today." She began to choose coffee, eggs, a quarter of milk, fresh loaf of bread, and a few pieces of fresh fruit. She placed a small bag of sugar in the basket and sighed. She carried her basket to the front counter and push it in front of Jesse. "I told Mrs. Goodyear that you will take care of my things today." She looked at him almost daring him to refuse.

"Mr. Goodyear, total the teacher's items up with mine, today." Jesse had no idea what kind of game this woman was playing, but he was going to take her to her house as soon as they gather her supplies.

After placing their packages in the corner of the store, she turned to Jesse. "I'm starving. Didn't you say there was a nice café down the street? Let's go there for lunch. I haven't eaten since supper last night."

"It will have to be quick. I need to get home. When I agree to pick you up from the train this morning, I didn't know I would be gone from home all day."

"I am so sorry. You probably wish you had not helped me

today. I feel like such a burden," She removed a hanky and wiped at her eyes.

Jesse looked up into the beautiful sky. "Lord, help me," he prayed silently. "Now, Miss Sooner, that isn't true. I was happy to welcome you to Limason. The other members of the school board were too busy, so of course, I volunteered to pick you up. I'm sorry if I have given you the wrong impression."

"Oh good. So you will take me to lunch?" The teacher glowed from her victory with Jesse.

"Yes, I am hungry too, so let go. You can walk from your small house to this café if you don't want to cook for yourself. After we complete our lunch I will go to the livery and get my horse and carriage and go to the store and pick up our supplies."

As they entered the café, the owner, Wilber Brooks, met Jesse and the stranger. He looked behind the couple for Jesse' wife, Rae. He had never seen Jesse with another woman.

"Hi Wilber. I have a new customer for you. This is Miss Sooner, the new schoolteacher. She will be taking some of her meals here at your café. I know you will make her feel at home."

"Yes, please come and have a seat. This is my best table." He pulled out the chair for Miss Sooner and handed her a menu. Turning to Jesse, he asked, "How is your little wife doing? Please give her my regards this evening."

"I will. What is your special today? We're kinda in a hurry."

"Roast beef with mashed potatoes and delicious gravy. Everyone is telling me how good it is." He kissed his fingertips and waved his hand all around.

"We'll have two of those and I will have a cold beer and Miss Sooner will have some hot tea?" Jesse looked at the frown on the teacher's face.

"I'm sorry Mr. Maxwell. I can't eat . . . that food. I must have something like roasted chicken with green beans."

"Jesse looked at the woman and sighed. "Can you make chicken in a few minutes, Wilber?"

"I will hurry. Do you want to wait and eat with your lovely companion?"

"I guess, but bring my beer now." Jesse was irritated to the bones. Maybe a beer will help calm him, he thought.

Once the lunch was over Jesse walked her back to her small

house. He hurried to the livery and got his horse and carriage, then returned to the teacher's house with her groceries.

After Jesse carried her package into the house she cooed, "Oh Jesse, I needed to stop at the bank and take care of business."

"Sorry, Miss Sooner. I've run out of time today. You can walk to the bank." He climbed into his carriage then turned to the teacher who watched him from the porch. "Miss Sooner, my name is Mr. Maxwell to you until we get better acquainted." He tipped his black Stetson and drove away.

Jesse shook his head at the time he'd wasted with a woman that had bought the worst out of him. He thought of a special saying that Ollie used to say about people ,and it certainly fit her. He looked up and thought about her words when speaking about someone you didn't care about. *"You don't have to eat the whole egg to know it's rotten."*

Yep, that's it. That schoolteacher had better be good to her students or she will be gone on the first train out of town. He would have Claire keep a close eye on her once they returned to the classroom.

Chapter 26

Claire was sitting at the kitchen table helping Rae peel potatoes for supper. "You know mama, have you noticed that papa hasn't said hardly anything about the new teacher, Miss Sooner? Even when I asked him a few questions, he only gave me real short replies. Pa didn't tell me what she looked like even when I asked him to describe her. He only said she is tall and looks like a woman. He hurried away so I couldn't ask him to explain further."

"I have asked him several questions about her but he only shrugged and walked away. I wondered if there isn't something he is not telling us about her? You know Jesse isn't a gossip, but I am, and like you, I feel that their might be something he isn't telling us," Rae said, standing at the kitchen counter glancing over at Ollie. "What do you think Miss Ollie? Is Jesse not telling us something?"

"I don't know for sure, but years ago when Will was little, he didn't like his teacher."

Hope's voice came from the bedroom. "Ollie! Don't you dare tell something about Will being a little boy and you don't let me hear it. I can't get out of this blasted bed so you girls come in my room. I want to hear all about my husband's childhood."

"All right, honey child. You have to keep your voice down before you wake your babies. We just got them to sleep."

A few minutes later, the ladies walked into Hope's room and sat down surrounding her bed.

Ollie sat down, picked up her knitting, and sighed big. "This chair always feels so good. Now, let me start back a little. Mr. Jake was on the school board, and they had a meeting about whether to repair the old building or build a new schoolhouse. Of course, the teacher at the time was Miss Abigail Thomson, was at the meeting.

"Well, one day, Will got into trouble with the schoolteacher. Miss Abigale Thomson was glad because she got the opportunity to drop by our ranch and have a private word with Jake. He was already leery of her because she flirted with him at one of the other meetings. That's what he told me."

"What is the world could she have done to him with so many others around?" Claire asked.

"Now Miss Claire, let me tell my story. You can ask questions later." Ollie smiled at her and went on with the tale. "Miss Abigale sat across the table, never taking her eyes from his body. Once in a while, her soft cowhide shoe would brush over the top of his boot, making him shift in his chair. He told me he wanted to jump up and leave. Jake told Mr. Jordon, 'I have other business to take care while I am in town. Let's get on with this meeting, please.'

'Hold your taters, Jake." We need to agree whether we spend money to build another room on this old building or build a brand-new building with more rooms added."

'If you can't afford to add another room, how can you build a new, bigger building? Common sense gives you the answer.'

'So, what is your answer to the problem?' Mr. Jordon huffed.

"'Do we have money in the treasury to build a new building?" Jake questioned the treasurer.

'Not to my way of thinking. Lumber prices are up, and other building materials are expensive too.'

'My answer is to repair the old building and add another room with a nice, large porch across the back. In the fall and spring, the children can sit outside and enjoy fresh air while in class. That should provide some space for the children.' Jake suggested as he looked at the others in the room.

'Let take a vote on Jake's suggestion,' Mr. Jordon said. 'I like his idea, and I will bring my men to help with the repairs.' Mr. Jordon looked around the room at the committee. 'All in flavor of repairing the old building and adding a new room and back porch give me a show of hands.' He peered around. 'Looks like everyone agrees with repairing the old building," Mr. Jordon tapped his gavel on the tabletop and said, "This meeting is adjourned."

Well, it wasn't long after the school board meeting, Miss Thomson came driving her small carriage out to our ranch. Will saw her coming so he hurried to the barn and hid. I figured something must be up when Will rushed out the backdoor. I went to the door and invited her in and took her shawl. Then I sat her at the table and offered her tea and some cake. 'Please enjoy your refreshment while I go and get the boys.'

"I hurried to the barn and called Mr. Jake, who moaned when he saw the small black carriage. He knew who it belonged to. 'What does she want?'

'She didn't tell me, but Will saw her coming and ran and hid somewhere in here.'

Will, get your butt out here, NOW!"

'Oh, Pa, I didn't do anything to her. She's just scared of frogs.'

'So, you put a frog in her desk chair?'

'No sir. I put them in her lunch basket.'

"Them? How many?

'Only four, Pa. That's not many.'

'One is too many if you are afraid of frogs, son." He looked at Will and shook his head. 'Let go inside and get this meeting over with.'

'I need to wash my hands before I meet with her,' Will said.

'All right. Hurry on into the kitchen and meet your teacher.'

'Will rushed into the front bedroom water closet and walked slowly into the kitchen. He stood behind me, like I was going to protect him.'

Jake asked, 'Why are we honored with your visit?'

'I'm sorry to have to come out here carrying this sad message about the misbehavior of your son, Will. He knows why I am here, don't you, sweet boy?"

"Jake didn't like the way she spoke to Will. Calling him sweet, was unnecessary. It was sarcastic. 'Miss Thomson, you tell me what did Will do in class?'

'He didn't do it in class, he did it to me. Will nearly cause me to have a heart attack.' She placed a hanky to her mouth. 'He placed a dozen big frogs in my lunch basket. I spilled my lunch everywhere, and then those green creatures were all over the room.' She patted her eyes as if trying not to cry. 'The girls were screaming and climbing on the tables and desks. It was awful, but *your son,--*' 'he laughed and laughed.'

'Did you punish him for doing that?' Jake looked at Will and then back to the teacher.

'Yes, I made him sit in a corner the rest of the day without his lunch.'

'So, since you punished him, what are you wanting me to do?' Jake was so angry with her for making Will go without food. He may be old enough to do mischief, but he was still a very young child who needed to eat.

'I want you to punish him and make sure he doesn't do something like that again.'

'All right. He will not do that again. I give you my word.'

'Well, what kind of punishment are you going to give him?"

'Punishment? None, because you already punished him.'

Miss Thomson was shocked with Jake's answer. She wanted him to whip Will to make sure he would behave in her classroom. The teacher leaped out of her chair, placed her hanky in her pocket, and patted her hair. 'I must go, but may I use your water closet before I drive back to town.

Will, show Miss Thomson the water closet in the front bedroom'

Will raced into the bedroom, opened the water closet door, and hurried back into the kitchen. A few minutes later, screams like the house was on fire came from the bedroom. Jake rushed into the room and found Miss Thomson bouncing on her belly on the floor with her skirt nearly over her head, showing her lily-white butt with her white pantaloons trapped around her ankles. "Get it, get it . . . off me!' She was kicking her ankles and slapping the floor with her hands like she was swimming.

'What is it?' Jake asked. 'Hurry, Ollie," he called, while pulling Miss Thomson's skirt down over her bare skin. He was holding his laughter in, but he wanted to howl.

I raced over to her. 'What's on you, Miss? I don't see anything.' Suddenly Will dove on the floor and came up with a two foot long, garter snake.

'Will," Jake grabbed him by the arm and gave him a shake. He whispered, "I am going to do something to you this time. Get that snake out of here before she sees it.' Jake kept his voice even. 'Miss Thomson, Miss Ollie is going to help you get yourself together. There isn't anything in this room or on you.'

'Jake left the room and closed the door, then he found his young son on the porch and whispered, 'Will, why did you do that?" he pointed to the bedroom.

'Pa, she's mean. She's got mean eyes, too. She is mean to some of the poor kids. Miss Thomson makes fun of what they have for lunch, when she has a nice full basket of goodies. She'll share her lunch with Dottie, who doesn't need it. Dottie is the daughter of Mr. Jones, the undertaker. She embarrasses some of the kids who wear the same clothes all week, even though they're clean. She will hit some of the boys with a ruler if they mispronounce a word while reading. She hasn't hit me because I read very well, but I feel sorry for little Joey, who stutters. The boys and I have decided to make her leave.' He mumbled, 'Beat me if you want, but I have got to help get rid of her.'

"Will, why you didn't tell me about her sooner. You had to know that I would never approve of her mistreating the children."

'Miss Thomason stood in the living room while I placed her shawl over her shoulders. She carried her hat in her hands, and her clothes looked a little rumbled. The teacher straightened her backbone and walked onto the porch. 'I must return to town. I would appreciate it if you will control your son's actions while in my classroom.'

Jake walked with her to her carriage, untied the reins, and handed them to her. 'Good day, Miss Thomson. I'm sure I will see you very soon.'

'I would like that,' she tugged on her collar and gave him a sweet smile.

'I'm not sure you will,' he responded, as he watched her drive away.

"Sure enough. It was long before Mr. Jake called an emergency board meeting and told the members what Will had told him. He said that he had gone to some of the other children's home and questioned the children in front of their parents. No one knew that Miss Thomson had being mistreating the children. Many of the parents said that their children didn't like school, and some of them had always loved going, until Miss Thomson. Once the meeting was over, Miss Thomson was fired and one of the mother's stepped in and taught the children until another schoolteacher was hired.

"Man, Jake said that was one mad woman when she got on the stagecoach and left Limason," Ollie laughed. "When the new teacher came, the children were happy and so was Mr. Jake. He could attend the school board meeting in peace," Ollie said as she continued to rock and knit without missing a stitch.

"Mean eyes? I have heard of that in a horse, but never a person. I am going to start looking for mean eyes in people. Especially those that work around children," Claire said.

Chapter 27

For several days straight, Jesse worked in the barn building bookshelves for two of the classrooms for the school. He had to complete the task for the new schoolteacher, he decided to build shelves for Claire's room too. He was going to let the teachers paint the shelves themselves before school opened.

Jesse called out Will as he passed the barn door. "Hey Will, how about you and Jess giving me a hand with putting these bookshelves in this flatbed wagon. I am going to take them to the schoolhouse and nail them to the walls in the classrooms today. This is one project I want to finish now. The teachers can paint them whatever color they want after I get them on the wall."

"Sure thing," Will said, as he called Jess to come and help. "Do you want me to ride into town with you and help unload the shelves? Hope is doing so much better, and she has plenty of help feeding the babies during the day."

"Sure, I would love the company. Go and tell the girls where we're going and let's hit the road. Jess and John, along with Hank, can take care of things around here while we're gone."

After Jesse and Will had carried the heavy bookcases into the schoolhouse, they stood around in the room trying to decide which wall would be best to hold the bookshelves.

***

Miss Sooner entered the building and saw Mr. Maxwell standing alone in her classroom. He was so handsome that she could hardly keep a civil thought in her head.

"Hello, Jesse," Miss Sooner cooed.

Jesse whirled around as she approached his space. "I believe I told you my name is Mr. Maxwell." He removed his hat and laid it down on a student's desk.

She ignored his response and continued to move closer to him. "So, you were eager to build my bookcases. I knew you wanted to see me again, but I wasn't expecting them until after school began."

"My daughter Claire, who you haven't met, will be teaching in the next classroom and she mentioned that she would like to have a bookcase, too. So, I wanted to move the shelves into her class while she is preparing her room for fall classes."

"Oh, I'm disappointed. I thought you hurried just for me," she pouted, showing him her rosy lips. "Can I help you with the shelves? I am very handy when it comes to using a hammer." She moved as close as she could to Jesse and gazed into his eyes, almost purring like a new kitten.

"That won't be necessary." He took her arms and moved her away from him, when Will entered the classroom. He stopped suddenly and looked at the couple who appeared to be in each other arms.

"Am I interrupting anything?" Will asked, his face showed anger.

"No, you aren't interrupting anything. Miss Sooner was offering to help, but I was just moving her out of my way. Miss Sooner, this is my brother Will, and he is here to help me. Would you show us where you would like the bookcases?"

"It is nice to meet you, Mr. Maxwell. Thank you for coming to help your brother. It is so very nice of him to build these nice bookcases for me."

Jesse glanced at Will and shook his head. "Where do you want these?"

"What do you think about one set on this wall, next to the window? I can use the top shelf to place a potted plant or two to make the room look a little homey."

"Great. Will give me a hand, and let's move the shelves over here, and you can hammer the boards to the wall," Jesse said to Will.

Once the two set of shelves were nailed to the wall, Jesse hurried to Claire's classroom. "We will put Claire's bookshelves under her windows. I didn't build her set of shelves as tall as the others, since her students are smaller. This way they can get a book and replace it without Claire's assistance."

"Miss Sooner, you can go to the dry goods store and get whatever color paint you would like. Just have it placed on the school board's bill. If they have any questions about it, they can ask me later."

"Oh, Jesse, you have been so kind, and I really appreciate what you have done. Do you think I might need help with the painting? I have never done anything like this before."

"If you can't paint them yourself, wait until school starts and have one of the older boys stay after school and do the job for you. I am sure they would enjoy helping the new schoolteacher. Good day to you, Miss Sooner." Jesse practically leaped off the steps of the schoolhouse.

***

His brother jumped into the wagon. Will hurried after him, almost afraid that Jesse would drive off without him. He waited until Jesse was out on the open road before he brought up the subject about the new schoolteacher. "What was that back there all about, brother dear?"

"What do you mean?" Jesse asked.

"Come on, I wasn't born yesterday. That woman has the hots for you and we both know it."

"I know. That woman freaks me out. She knows I'm married, but she comes onto me like I'm single. From the very first time I met her at the train station, she has made improper advances toward me. She doesn't seem to care that I'm a married man. Walking down the street, she grabbed my arm, and I could tell people were watching. I don't know what Rae is going to think if she gets winds of that woman acting like we are a couple."

"I suggest you tell Rae how that girl acts when you are around. Nip it in the bud, as Miss Ollie would say."

"Your right. I will talk to her after supper tonight. I don't ever want to be alone with that man-eater."

Will tossed his head back and laughed. "Who would think a man your age would have a young gal chasing him?"

"Hey, I'm not dead, yet. What if she was after you?"

"Hope would kill us both. Me first, and then her," Will laughed.

"I'm sure Rae will understand that I haven't encouraged her attention."

When Jesse and Will drove into the barn to put away the wagon and two horses, John told them that Rae and Claire went to town. "You guys must have just missed them. Jess is in the house with Miss Ollie and Hope. The babies have been so good today."

"Why did they go to town when they knew I was going? I could have gotten any supplies that Rae needed."

"Rae said that she didn't know you were going until after you had left. Hope needed some special medicine, and Doctor Tim said he would be in his office today. Since Rae has been in the house for many days, she decided to ride with Claire home."

"I didn't realize it was time for Claire to go home. I thought she would stay for another few days." Jesse said. He gave Will a knowing glance, and Will read it loud and clear. Rae's trip could end very badly for him.

Jesse headed for the barn, then glanced over his shoulder at Will. "I'm going to saddle my horse and ride into town and ride back with Rae. She knows that I don't like her riding back and forth to town alone."

"Good idea, Jesse. I'll help Miss Ollie prepare supper. I'm getting to be a pretty good cook." Will said as he began whistling.

"Sure, you are, just like I'm a *Romeo*." Both brothers laughed.

***

Claire pulled to a stop in front of the dry goods store and helped her mother down.

"Now, Claire, love, you go right home and take a good afternoon rest. Let your hired boy take this horse and wagon to the livery. You don't try to handle it yourself."

"I will Mama. I have to admit this ride has worn me out. I bet you will find Hank at the café this time of day. He likes to play checkers with old man Johnson and drink coffee. If you can't find him, I am sure Albert will drive you home."

Rae watched her daughter drive away as she entered the store just as a tall stranger was coming out. He nodded and held the door for her to come in. As she was smiling at the man, she heard a woman's voice say, "You should have just seen the two of them. Grinning and holding onto to each other like two lovebirds." As the words flowed out of the woman's mouth, she looked into the face of Rae Maxwell.

"Hello, Eloise. Please don't stopped your story. It sounds so juicy. Who are you ladies talking about?"

Eloise looked at Maria Waltham, and Mrs. Goodyear for help. "I was just talking about your precious daughter and her husband, Albert. We were told that they are going to have a baby, and they are acting like a newly married couple. They're so happy." Eloise was so proud of herself for her fast thinking. There was no way she wanted Rae to know that her friends were gossiping about her handsome husband and the new schoolteacher.

"You are all so right. I just left Claire. She was housebound for a few days because Doctor Tim thought she needed to rest since she is only a few weeks into her pregnancy."

"I'd better run. I am already late fixing the dinner meal. Thanks for the fresh carrots, Mrs. Goodyear," Eloise called as she and the other ladies rushed out onto the boardwalk."

Rae and Mrs. Goodyear watched through the display window as the ladies huddled together whispering. "Mrs. Goodyear, I understand that some medicine was going to be dropped off here by the stage master. Did it come?"

"Yes, it's here. I am sure once Hope starts taking it, she will get stronger and hopefully back to her old self. Well, her young self," Mrs. Goodyear laughed.

"Thanks. She is already doing well since she had the babies. You will have to drive out and visit with us soon. The babies are beautiful and so healthy."

The bell on the store door jingled and an unfamiliar woman entered. Rae turned to smile at the lady and thought to herself that this must be the new teacher.

The woman flounced to the counter. "Mrs. Goodyear, sweet Jesse told me to come here and pick out paint to use on the bookshelves he made for me. They are so lovely, and he was so nice building them so quickly for me. I just asked him a few days ago and he hurried and built them. He came early this morning and put them on my wall for me."

"We have about six different colors of paint. Come with me into the storeroom and you can look them over and decide. Mrs. Maxwell, I will be right back to help you with anything else you might want." Mrs. Goodyear glanced at the woman and led her into the back of the store. After the schoolteacher selected a color, she hurried out of the store.

"I'm sorry, Rae. That's one silly woman, if you ask me. Can I get anything else for you?"

"So, that is the new teacher. I asked Jesse about her, but he had very little to say. I wondered why?"

"There isn't much to say, if you ask me and maybe he thought the same. I do know that Will came into town with Jesse. I am sure he was at the schoolhouse the whole time with them."

"Why did you feel you had to tell me that? I trust Jesse—I have never had a reason not to."

"I don't know why I said that, but that silly gal is already the talk of the town.

"And Jesse's name is linked to hers?"

"I didn't say that? Don't put words in my mouth. I have already said too much."

"No, you have just opened my eyes to several things. I must go and catch Hank before he goes home without me. Thanks for the medicine—and the other information." Rae left with a steam of anger building in her body.

***

Hank and Rae were looking at the afternoon sun going down when they both saw Jesse riding toward them. "Oh, good. I see you caught up with Hank. I didn't want you riding home by yourself. Hey Hank, how about riding my horse and let me drive my loving wife home."

"Fine with me. Maybe she'll talk to you. She hasn't said a word to me since we left town. Be careful, boy. A storm is brewing," Hank said in a whisper, as Jesse held the horse while Hank mounted it.

Jesse leaped in the carriage seat and took up the reins. Rae sat as still as a frightened mouse, not giving him a glance. "Did you get everything you went in town to get?" Jesse leaned over to give her a peck on the cheek. Rae moved over quickly, dodging his affection.

Jesse looked up into the lovely sky and sighed real big. He pulled the carriage over to the side of the dirt road and said, "What have you got stuck in your craw? Get it out. I am about sick of women and their silly notions."

"Don't you dare speak to me like I'm a common ranch hand! If you think my feathers are ruffled, there are better ways of

164

approaching me." Turning to face him, she pointed her finger and jabbed him in the chest. "You got that mister?"

"Got it," Jesse said, rubbing his chest. Her finger was sharp, and it hurt like the dickens. "I'm sorry, sweetheart. I apologize to the way I spoke to you." He picked up her left hand and pulled it to his lips. "Please tell me what's wrong."

"I can't believe you don't have any idea why you and the new schoolteacher are the talk of the town. I went into the dry goods store and the ladies were discussing the two of you like you're the new lovebirds of Limason. What am I to think?"

"You have to know that none of that garbage is true. I have not done anything with that man-eater."

"Man-eater? Why are you calling her that?"

"Ever since that day I met her at the train, she has been batting her big blue eyes at me. She latched onto my arm when I took her to lunch, and every one of those lady friends of yours were watching."

"So, you have spent a good bit of time with that woman? Why didn't you confess to me that you were showing her around town when all I asked of you was to meet her at the train?"

"Confess? Listen woman, I didn't and still don't have anything to confess. I am not guilty of doing anything wrong. Now you stick that in your bonnet and do whatever you want with it. I am sick of this conversation."

Rae moved as far away from Jesse as she could and looked at the rumps of their two horses. Jesse slapped the reins over the back of the horses, and they took to a trot as soon as they managed to get in the center of the road.

***

The minute Jesse stopped the carriage in front of the house, Rae jumped out and rushed into the house carrying the small package she picked up for Hope. She handed the medicine to Ollie and hurried into the master bedroom and clicked the door lock.

Jess, and Hope were both holding one of the babies while Jay and Willa were getting dress for bed. Everyone just looked at each other. Jesse came in the house and headed straight to his bedroom. He turned the doorknob, but it was locked. He laid his forehead on the big wooden door and sighed. "That's just fine," he muttered. Whipping around, he strode into the living room, and for the first time noticed Jess and Hope. Smiling sheepishly, he walked over to Hope and took Oliva's little hand in his and gave it a little shake. "She's beautiful, just like her mama," he said. Turning, he looked at Jerry whom Jess was rocking to sleep.

"This is such a good baby boy," Jess said to his pa. "Do you want to hold him?"

"Not tonight. I've got business to take care of in the bunkhouse. I'll spend time with both of them tomorrow. Goodnight," Jesse said and strode out.

Watching Jesse walk out the back door, they all looked to the bedroom down the hall. Rae didn't come out. The room was silent.

Chapter 28

Early the next morning, Bud Downey came riding up to the corral. "Good morning, Jesse. I came from town, and I picked up your mail when I got mine. Mr. Goodyear said that Rae had left the store without getting yours while she was there yesterday. Here it is." He reached back to his saddle bag and pulled out several catalogs and a few letters.

"Thanks Bud. You want to come inside and get something cool to drink before heading home?"

"No thanks, I'd best be on my way. . Rosie has her hands full with those little girls of ours. That little rascal Boo is not much help, and Justice is getting on in years. I try to take one of them riding every morning just to give Rosie some peace. Ya'll come see us soon," Bud waved bye and left.

Looking through the mail Jesse saw a couple of letters for Jess. "Hey Hank, tell Jess I have some mail for him and to come and get it."

In a flash, Jess practically raced out of the barn to the corral fence where his pa stood holding a stack of mail. "Here you go son."

"Thanks Pa. There are two letters from Mary Beth. I sure miss that gal of mine."

***

Jess rushed into the house and flopped the mail down on the dining room table and rushed out the front door and went to sit in the porch swing. He read the first letter from his wife in a minute and then re-read it again slowly. Mary Beth missed him very much. She hoped his arm and shoulder were well. But all he read was she missed him.

He thought about the argument that he witnessed between his

167

ma and pa last evening. This was a surprise, because they have always gotten along so well. He continued to read about Mary Beth's classes and test scores. She was proud of herself and wanted to share how well she was doing with him. Of course, he never thought she wouldn't be anything but the star of her class.

He read the next letter and he wasn't pleased. She wrote about that male teacher, and how she was studying with him each week. She claimed the lab class was really hard, and he was a big help to her and several of her classmates. At least, she wasn't studying alone with him, he hoped. Then she asked when he was going to come and see her again. She didn't have any idea if she would be able to come home in September. Hopefully, he could come and be with her for another week.

He dropped the letter down to his lap and sighed. He guessed he would make plans and go see her, but he didn't want to surprise her this time. He wanted to make sure she would have time to spend with him. First, he would talk to Jesse and see if he could do without him soon. Just knowing that his lovely wife missed him lifted his spirit.

"Good morning, Jess," his mama said as she walked out onto the porch with a cup of tea. "May I sit with you for a minute?"

"Of course. I was hoping to get to speak with you without the others around."

"Really? Anything important you want to talk about," she questioned.

"Mama, I'm not a child anymore and I know that you don't have to tell me, but what in the heck was that all about last night?" Rae didn't answer, but continued to look out into the yard. "You rushing in the house and locking pa out of the bedroom."

"Why did you think I locked Jesse out of our room?"

"Ma, please. Ollie and Hope were sitting with me in the front room when you came storming in and hurried to your room. The click of the lock was like a small bomb going off. Pa followed and found the door locked. He looked like he had been whipped, the way he was hanging his head."

"Jess, you and Mary Beth have had differences. Your Pa and I are just like everyone else. He kept something from me, and I didn't like it. That's all there is to it. I'm going to talk with him later. We both need to just calm down."

"So, it's just a spat and both of you are guilty?"

"Well, I don't think I would say that I am guilty of anything, but I am willing to listen to your pa's side."

"Mama, come on now. Pa is just as stubborn as you," Jess grinned at his mama.

"Maybe so, but like I said, I will believe anything he tells me about this argument."

"Uh oh, here he comes. I am going inside and tell Ollie what Mary Beth's letters said. "Good luck," he whispered.

***

Rae took her right foot and kicked the floor to push the swing. Jesse watched his son hurry into the house while glancing at his wife.

"Good morning . . . . Darling," Jesse said sweetly.

"Morning, husband," Rae replied.

"May I sit with you?"

Rae didn't answer. She slid over and patted the seat of the swing. Jesse heaved a sigh and flopped down beside her.

"We need to talk about yesterday and come to an understanding. I am not sleeping in that blasted bunkhouse again when I have a perfectly good bed."

"Good, I missed you." Rae smiled at her handsome husband who had dark stubbles on his face.

"Rae, I didn't encourage that schoolteacher one bit. After taking her trunk and carpet bags to the house that Doctor Tim set up for the teachers, she said she was hungry and wanted me to take her to the café that I had told her about. I didn't know how to refuse, so we had lunch. She said she needed some items from the dry goods store so I took her there and introduced her to Mrs. Goodyear. The teacher purchased so many things I had to go and get the horse and carriage and come back and pick her up. Afterwards, she wanted to go to the bank and that's when I put a stop to her hanging onto me. I told her she could walk to the bank."

"Didn't you take her to the schoolhouse?" Rae asked, thinking that would be what she should have wanted to see right away.

"Yep, I forgot to tell you that first. Miss Sooner looked around and found the classroom not up to her standards. She fingered the desks and turned her nose up at the windows. Then she said that she needed bookshelves for her many books. She wouldn't stop

169

talking about needing them, so I said I would make her some. I decided to make some for Claire's room, too, so I needed to go ahead and make them because in a few days Will, Jess and I will be busy with the new calves that will be arriving."

"How did the ladies get the idea that you two were so called 'lovebirds'?

"Oh, hell Rae. I don't know. Miss Sooner did latch on to my arm as we walked down the boardwalk. Nothing I did, could make her turn me loose. I did tell her not to call me Jesse. Firmly I said, my name is Mr. Maxwell to you, but once in the dry goods store, she did call me Jesse. I wanted to strangler her right there on the spot. Your friends were watching and listening. I drove her home and said goodbye."

"I believe you Jesse, and I didn't want to believe everything I overheard the ladies saying about you two. But my feelings were hurt that you wouldn't tell me anything about the teacher."

Jesse stopped the swing and turned to take Rae's hands. Do you forgive me? I promise I'll tell you everything about another woman if and when you ask me." Jesse looked her in the eyes. "I know we're going to have to watch that woman. She's a spinster and searching for a man. She's not bad looking and she is probably smart. Maybe you girls can play matchmaker and get her hitched so I don't have to deal with her."

"You are willing to do anything to make her leave you alone," Rae laughed. "Don't you worry about that man-eater any longer? I will let her know that you belong to me."

Jesse glanced around and pulled Rae into his arms. "Really, will you show me – later that I'm yours and yours only?"

"Come on in and let me feed you—for now." Rae laughed, as she pulled Jesse out of the swing, and walked hand and hand into the house.

Chapter 29

After setting the babies down, Willa and Jay went outside to play in the tree in the front yard. A scream came from outside. Hope walked as fast as her body would move to the porch. "Ollie, Lucy, hurry. Willa is crying."

Lucy rushed out the door first with Ollie on her heels. They both hurried down the few steps to the yard and saw Hank limping as fast as his old body would allow. He rushed to Willa, as Jay stood looking over his shoulder.

"Oh, Baby, Uncle Hankie is here. Where do you hurt?"

"My arm!" She sniffed, glancing up at Lucy and Ollie.

"It hurts real bad," she said as Hank looked at it

Hank scooped Willa up in his arms being careful with her right arm. John came out of the corral looking very serious. "Should I get the carriage ready to drive into town to Doctor's Tim office?"

"Oh, John, where's Will?" Hope yelled from the doorway and then hurried to reach her daughter.

"Here I am honey. Sorry I was in the spring house straining the milk when I heard one of the children scream. I will hold Willa in my arms while Hank drives us to see Doctor Tim."

"Oh, my baby," Hope said, as she wiped Willa's long hair out of her eyes. "You like Doctor Tim and Miss Hannah. They will take good care of you. I will be waiting for your return. Be brave baby. Your papa will be with you."

"I will be mama. It's not hurting too bad now." Willa said holding on to Will's neck with her good arm.

***

As they drove away, Will asked his sweet daughter. "Are you in much pain?"

"Yes sir, it hurts like the devil."

"You told your mama that it didn't hurt too much."

"I know but I've gotta just suck it up." She rested her head on Will's chest and tried not to cry."

Hank glanced back at Willa and shook his head. "That little gal's sure been around Ollie."

After Doctor Tim examined Willa's arm and declared it broken, he set it in a sling. The arm had already become swollen, so he said that after the swelling had gone down, he would put her small arm in a cast.

Willa had cried while Doctor Tim examined the arm. After Will held her in his arms, she finally fell into a deep sleep. As they drove into the yard at the ranch, everyone was waiting to hear about the precious child.

"She's going to be fine and will get a cast on her arm in a few days. Willa is tired, but Doctor Tim said she could have ice cream tonight. So, I have got to get the salt and ice ready. I know you girls have the recipe."

"Of course, we do," Ollie replied. "I'm going inside and make my baby some of her favorite cookies to go with the ice cream."

Will carried Willa into Hope's bedroom and laid her on the twin bed that he used while Hope was recuperating from the birth of her twins. He guessed he would sleep in the bunkhouse for a few days until Willa was better. Hope would want her near at night. Lord have mercy, he thought. He was already feeling like a monk that he had read about in a book. Of course, he knew he couldn't make love to Hope but he had just got use to nuzzling with her every night.

The twins were growing and getting so big. They would soon be a month old and Hope was getting around much better. Doctor Tim had released her from bedrest and said that she could cook and do light housekeeping but no heavy lifting or riding a horse or in a carriage for miles.

Lucy was a big help with the twins during the day, but she was sleeping at Will's home every night. She walked up and help the girls with the babies, cooking and watching after Willa and Jay. Claire had sent a message by John that the school superintendent wanted to interview Lucy for the teacher's helper job. So, it looked like she would soon be gone, and more responsibility would fall on his shoulders again.

Even though Claire wasn't teaching school this summer, Doctor Tim had forbidden her to ride the long ten miles one way to their house so she couldn't help with the babies. Fatherhood was very hard sometimes but he wouldn't change any part of his life.

As Will and Hank were sitting on the back porch taking turns churning the ice cream, Hope sat next to Willa and the twins as they all slept. "Miss Ollie, did you know that man at your church that died last week? Homer Jordon, I believe was his name. Isn't he the big man that helped with a roundup a few years back?"

"Yep, that was him. He was a friend of Jeremiah's. I didn't know until Sunday, after church services, that Jeremiah helped Homer's family out many times. He gave them food, one of my hams at Christmas, and many other things they needed. He gave them money to purchase toys for the children. Mrs. Jordon told me she didn't know how they would manage now that Jeremiah was gone, too. Nearly broke my heart, but I told her that many others would step in and help them. You know I didn't know that Homer was the father of eight children when his first wife died. I didn't know anything about how much help Jeremiah was giving them, either. One day Jeremiah, just out of the blue, said that Homer told him that he was a lucky man to have me as a close friend. He told him that he had tried to court me after his wife passed."

"You mean that man with eight children really wanted to court you?" Hope smiled real big and looked around at her sleeping children.

Ollie looked to the ceiling and said, "I guess I was about thirty years old when Homer asked if he could call on me."

"Did you meet him at church?" Hope begged Ollie to tell more.

"No, it wasn't at the meeting house. One day, I went with Mr. Jake and the boys to town. The boys and I went into the dry goods store, and I bumped into Mr. Jordon going into the store as he was coming out. Lordy, I looked up at the most handsome man I had ever seen, with big brown eyes and a head full of black hair. His brown skin shined. He was certainly a handsome man."

"What did you do?" Will asked, as he came into the room and sat down.

"I thought you were helping Hank with the ice cream," Ollie asked, as she watched Will sit on the floor in front of Hope.

"The cream is ready, so Hank carried it to the spring house to keep cold. Go on with your story," Will said. "I remember Mr. Jordon."

"Oh well, as we stood in the doorway, he said that he was sorry and helped me inside the store. The clerk said, "Hurry and close that door. Girl, are you hurt?" he asked as he went behind the counter.

"No, Sir, I'm fine."

"Well good. Get your butts out of the doorway so my white customers can get inside." He practically growled and demanded to know if I had a list.

"Before I could answer, the big guy grabbed the little clerk and lifted him off the floor and said, "Don't you dare speak to this lady like she ain't good enough to be in your store. I don't believe Mr. Maxwell would appreciate you speaking to his help that way."

"It's alright. Please turn him loose," I said, as I jerked his arm, but he wouldn't let the man go."

"Out of nowhere, Mr. Jake appeared and asked what was going on. Lord! I was happy to see Mr. Jake." The big black man turned the clerk loose and told Mr. Jake the little weasel was being rude to me and he knew that he wouldn't like it.

Mr. Jake asked the clerk why he was being ugly to me. His face was red, and he stepped very close to the counter. He told the clerk that we came in that store every week and spent a lot of mone,y and no one had every mistreated anyone in his family and he wasn't going to allow him to do it.

"The small clerk backed up against the shelves behind the counter and started making excuses. He said he didn't mean to sound unkind. He was sorry and he would be more careful in the future."

Jake asked him to fill my list and be quick about it. He turned to the big man and thanked him. He took the boys into the back of the store and let them wander around and shop while I visited with the stranger. In a short while, the man asked if he could visit with me at the farm. I told him to come and have Sunday dinner with me under the shade trees and he agreed. Well, the boys sang all the way home. "Ollie's got a beau, Ollie's gots a beau, until Mr. Jake put a stop to it.

Sunday arrived and Homer came riding a big black mule. He brought me a handful of wildflowers. Mr. Jake said that we could eat inside the house with him and the boys but I said no. "We'll eat outside under the trees." It was a nice lunch and we talked and talked. I got to know him but I felt that he wasn't telling me something. He came several more times, and we took long walks. I had to admit I was smitten with this handsome man. He was gentle and kind. Sometimes Will would tag alone on our walks and Homer didn't seem to mind."

"I remember Mr. Jordon coming and you let me run and play while he held your hand," Will said, at the memory. "I told Pa that I was scared that Mr. Jordon was going to take you way from us."

Ollie smiled at Will and continued with her tale. "I could tell he liked children. But he never said anything about having any of his own. He only talked about his farm. He told me he had a place with ten acres of planted beans and corn where he sold some of the corn and some ground up for feed.

One Sunday afternoon, as we sat under the shade trees, he placed his big arms around my waist and pulled me into his arms. I was nervous, but it was time for me to allow him a little affection. Just as he started to kiss me, I noticed someone watching us. I pushed him away and pointed at the bushes about twenty feet from us. Homer stormed over to the brush, and I could hear him shouting to two small boys. "But Pa, Jenny's sick. Her stomach hurts her something fierce," I heard one of the boys saying.

"I jumped up from the ground and rushed over. There under a big bush was two small kids that looked identical. "What's going on Homer? Who are these children? And I heard one of them say that someone was hurting."

"Miss Ollie, these are my boys. Luke and Lewis. I have to go home. They have come after me. My daughter Jenny is not well."

Two boys and one girl, I thought. "How many children do you have?" I finally asked as I looked down on the two little tykes, who looked like two scared rabbits."

"Eight, I have eight children. I was going to tell you—soon."

"Well, I would hope so!" I turned to walk to the house. "Go get your mule and I will get my bonnet. I will get Jesse to drive me in our carriage. The boys can ride with me."

"You're going to my house?" Homer asked, clearly not understanding my actions.

"Your daughter is not well. We need to take care of her."

"Homer had to take her in to see Doctor Tim. She had a belly ache, thank goodness. I stayed with the children while he was gone into town. I looked the place over and fed the children that just sat staring at me.

"So, what did you think? Didn't you like him enough to marry him with all those children?" Hope asked.

"Listen to me child," Ollie said. "I already had a wonderful life. A nice home, a family I never had, clothes, and money. I didn't need a man to make me happy. This man needed a woman that loved him like a coon dog loved hunting. With that many children of all ages, she would need to be a better person than me."

"Now, Miss Ollie, there's isn't another woman better than you. I know you were younger but you would have been a great mama to each of those children," Hope said.

"Earlier I told you that I knew he was keeping something from me. Well he was trying to keep his children a secret until he felt the time was right between us. He should have told me straight up that he had those babies, and he was looking for someone to help him care for them, but he didn't. I was already happy with my life. I could have never married him if he had asked. There was no way I was going to leave Mr. Jake and my two baby boys.

"I was there when Jesse and Will were born, and I had helped raise them. I wouldn't have been happy caring for his children if I had left Mr. Jake and his two sons. I wasn't their mama, but I was the only one they had. No, Mr. Jordon couldn't have made me any happier. He later married an older widow woman who is still taking care of his and her children. She is a strong woman, and they had a good marriage. They needed each other."

"Miss Ollie, I wasn't very old, but I overheard you telling Pa that you weren't going to see that Mr. Jordon anymore. You would be with him and his boys until he ran you off. I went to bed a very happy boy." Will smiled at the old woman who was the only mama he really remembered. He wore his heart on his sleeve when it came to Ollie.

****

Willa woke up and smiled at her mama and papa who sit in the room with her. "I'm hungry," she said as she reached her good arm up in the air for someone to help her sit up.

"That's a good sign you're doing better. Your papa and Uncle

Hank have made you a special treat and Miss Ollie has made your favorite cookies." Hope said as she watched Will pick his daughter up out of the bed. Will carried her to the living room. Hank brought the big container of homemade ice cream and set it on the dining room table.

Jay and Lucy went into the dining room and took a seat at the table, while waiting for Hope to finish helping Willa in the water closet. Rae and Ollie dipped everyone a generous bowl of ice cream and placed the cookies in the center of the table.

Willa's eyes widened when she entered the dining room. "Oh, my, what a treat. Doctor Tim said I could eat ice cream, but I thought I would have to wait until I was back in town. Thank you thank you. Maybe I should break another arm next week," Willa laughed, and her papa tickled her belly.

Chapter 30

Albert drove Claire very slowly to her folk's ranch. Claire wanted to be with Hope and check on Willa, her precious niece. It was so hard not to be able to travel back and forth to her parent's home whenever she wanted to. Albert was so sweet. He had padded the carriage seats with several quilts. When she directed him to give the horses their head, he informed her that he was carrying valuable cargo, and he didn't want to damage it by going too fast. Claire laughed and sat closer to her sweet husband.

***

The men kept their distance while watching them. The men knew who Albert was but they needed to make sure that Claire was his wife.

After Albert shared the evening meal with Claire's family, viewed the twins and spoke to Willa, he left Claire to visit with her folks for a couple of days. The family assured him that someone would carefully drive her home.

"I didn't think we would ever get here," Claire laughed and told her family how careful Albert was driving to the ranch. "I believe I could have walked faster." Claire held Willa and looked over her small white arm cast. Jay had already wrote his name on it. "Would you like to sign my cast, too, Aunt Claire? You have nice handwriting, not a scribble like my dumb brother."

"Willa . . . you know better. Just because your arm is hurt doesn't give you the right to speak ill about your brother," Hope scolded.

"I will be honored to sign your cast. Do you have a special pen to use?" Claire asked.

Willa raced into the dining room and got the black pen and handled it to her favorite aunt. Claire drew a small heart and signed her name with love.

Lucy came in the house with clean clothes for the children. "Hello Miss Claire. I am so excited about my new job. I hope that maybe in the future the school might need me to fill another position at the school, too."

"What other position would you be able to do? You don't have a teacher's certificate," Rae said.

"At the other school where I worked, they had a lady that was called a school bookkeeper. She wasn't like a bank bookkeeper, but she kept a roll of all the children, and the future school students, their parents, where the children lived and any important information about the child or their family."

"So, if the school board hired you to do this exact work, when would you have time to keep the children's record?"

The lady at my school was the first one at school each morning, and if needed, she stayed awhile afterwards. Once the records are in order, the main thing is to keep them up. She would enroll new students and assign them to their new teacher. This does take time, but it doesn't take the teacher away from her classroom."

"Yes, I can see the need for someone to do that. Let me think about it some more and I will speak with the superintendent. You would only need about five more hours a week."

"The exact hours would really help me live on my own. Being able to share the schoolteacher's house will be a great help. I just hope the teacher is nice and will not mind me living with her."

Jesse frown. "If that teacher gives you any sass about sharing that house, she can just move out. That house belongs to Doctor Tim, and he allows the teachers to live there. Just let me know."

"Now Jesse, I believe she can talk to me about anything concerning her job just like Claire does." Rae grinned as she looked at her husband.

***

After a few more days of visiting with her family, and Hope and her children, Claire knew that Lucy was ready to go and see the schoolhouse. As they traveled back to town, Claire was driving the carriage slow and careful. The girls giggled and talked about everything. Suddenly out of the shade trees beside the road, two men rode their horses in front of the carriage. One man rode up beside them while the other held the lead horse's harness to keep the team still.

"What do you men want? Claire demanded, feeling around in her pocket for her small gun. Her papa had always insisted that his girls carry a weapon with them at all times. *Darn, it's under the seat.*

"We need you to go to the bank with us. Your husband, Albert, I believe is his name, and the bank president are waiting for us to arrive."

"You're lying. My husband would never have anything to do with the likes of you two unless he didn't have a choice."

"Well, you're really smart, aren't you? You're right. They don't know we're coming, and they won't be happy to see us. Now, do you want me to drive that little carriage or are you going to do it?"

As he waited for Claire to make up her mind, he glanced at his companion, sitting still beside the team. Claire slapped the reins and the team of young, trained horses took off, like they were in a race.

"Grab those horses. Get after them," the kidnapper yelled.

"Hold tight, Lucy, and feel around under the seat for my gun!"

Lucy scooted down on the floor and searched for a gun. "I got it," she said.

"Quickly, hide it in your pocket. They've caught the lead horse and now we won't have a chance to get away again," she said out of breath

"They won't know that I have it," Lucy said. She sat back up on the carriage seat and straightened her dress and shawl.

"Well, well, well, little Miss. You think you were smart, but we have you now." The grizzled man stopped his horse and handed the reins over to his partner. "Tie him to the back of this carriage." He looked both ways down the road and then jerked Lucy into his arms and gave her over to his friend. "Hold this young'un while I drive this little wild cat. They will not have a chance to get away from us again."

As Claire and Lucy arrived into town, the big guy drove the carriage around in the alleyway behind the bank. He jumped down and reached for Claire. She shrunk away from him, but she needed to be careful getting down. She had to remember that she was with child, and she needed to be very careful with her movements. She allowed him to help her down.

The man stood her on the ground, grabbed her two hands and tied them behind her back. The other man stood behind Lucy and the big guy tied her hands, too. She moved her wrists just as he finished tying the rawhide over her hands. Good, they weren't tied too tight, so she could free herself when it was time.

"If either of you make a sound, I will shoot that Albert fellow first. Got it?"

Both Claire and Lucy nodded their heads as they focused on each other.

The grizzly bear used Claire as a shield while kicking in the back door of the bank. With his hat in his hand and a briefcase tucked under his arm, the president of the bank was walking out of his office. He was preparing to leave for the evening.

Albert rushed to the back of the bank but stopped. Claire standing stiffly in front of a stranger. Albert froze as he saw his wife's ash white face.

"Albert, give these men what they want. Please don't give them a reason to kill you." Claire tried to get closer to Albert, but the man jerked her back to stand in front of him.

"Now, ain't that smart advice to give the love of your life?" The stranger said, as he pointed his gun at Albert's boss. "You, fat-so, get over to that safe—now."

"You're too late. I have already closed the bank's safe, and no one can open it until seven in the morning. Once it's closed and set, it can't be opened without an alarm alerting the whole town. I have no control over it."

"Well, Mr. Bank President, you better get over there and do something to open it. If an alarm goes off, I will shoot you dead." He looked at the others as the bank President moved to stand in front of the large, black steel safe.

****

Hank was walking down the old, gray boardwalk toward the livery to get his wagon. He had driven it into town early this morning to have Jules to repair the back wheel. Jules had assured Hank that if he didn't finish with it, he would place another one on it to get him home.

As he limped toward the livery, he glanced toward the

alleyway beside the bank. Standing as still as the night, were Jesse's two new horses attached to Claire's small two-seater carriage. As he approached the team, he noticed that all the shades of the bank were pulled down. A shadow moved inside. A sick feeling came over him. Something just wasn't right.

Leaving the team standing in the alleyway, he limped as fast as he could to the sheriff's office. "Murphy, hurry and come with me. Something is wrong at the bank and I can see movement inside."

"It's about closing time," Murphy said, as he walked to the window and looked toward the bank.

"Albert said the president of the bank will not allow them to pull the shades down until a few minutes after six. All the brown shades are down and Claire's carriage with her team still attached, is in the alleyway. Now, grab your shotgun and let's go."

****

"Man, are you hard-of-hearing? I just told you that I can't open the safe. If I could, I would give you everything inside. But, you must know, there isn't a lot of money in it. I placed a big payroll on the four o'clock train this afternoon. There's only several hundred dollars on hand for us to work with for a couple of days."

"You're lying and if you don't start turning that dial, I am going to shoot your clerk, Albert."

Claire moved to Albert, but with both of their hands tied behind her, there was no way to embrace. She leaned in to him and joined her Rosie lips over his.

"Get away from him, woman," the man said. "You lovebirds make me sick."

"Hey boss, why don't you let me shoot his woman? I bet he will remember the combination," he laughed, looking at Albert with a proud sneer.

When the man turned to look at his crazy partner, Lucy slid her hands free, grabbed the man and, with her long fingernails clawed at his face. Blood was flowing down his forehead into his eyes.

"What the hell?" the man screamed and pushed Lucy back away from him. Albert had freed his hands. He pushed Claire down to the floor and lunged to the other man who stood confused, peering at his boss.

***

Without announcing their presence, Hank used his big cowboy

boot and smashed in the lock on the front door. Sheriff Murphy rushed inside and, witnessing the confusion, he shot his pistol in the air, making everyone in the room stand at attention.

"Don't move or prepare to die," the lawman yelled.

Albert picked up Claire and held her in his arms. "Are you all right? I thought I was going to die when I saw those men holding you and Lucy hostage."

With everyone watching the sheriff, the grizzly guy angrily grabbed at Lucy. When he jerked her into his chest, she pulled out Claire's gun and it fired. Hank bellowed, and fell to the floor, then grabbed his good leg. The big guy pointed his gun but Sheriff Murphy shot him and he fell forward.

The big guy's partner yelled, "Don't shoot! I ain't armed." He leaned up against the wall with his hands in the air.

Sheriff Murphy used his boot and pushed the man over lying on the floor. "He's dead." Using his pistol, he pointed to the door and the other man rushed out of the bank onto the boardwalk running into William, the Sheriff's deputy. Several men and women had gathered outside of the bank's door.

"Take this man to jail for me, William. I've got a body inside I need help with, too."

Another two men went into the bank and picked up the dead body and carried him to the undertaker's office."

***

Doctor Tim rushed into the bank. He immediately saw Hank sitting on the bank floor with the president of the bank wrapping a clean white cloth over his leg.

"Thank goodness you're here Doc," Hank said. "I know I'll be fine now," he said as he fell over in a deep faint.

"Hey fellows, give me a hand. I need to carry Hank to my office," he said laughing.

"Oh, Doctor Tim, do you think he will be all right. I hope this wasn't too much for his heart?" Claire said, still not recovered from Jeremiah's death.

"He's going to be fine. Hank has a very strong heart, but I want Albert to bring you over to my office so I can examine you."

"I was bringing Lucy into town so she could look over her new quarters and the classrooms. We need to take her to my house first."

"I have a suggestion, if Lucy will agree. She can spend the night at my office with Hank. He needs to stay overnight after I do surgery on his leg. Lucy, would you be willing to stay with him?'

"I will be pleased to stay with Mr. Hank. That's the least I can do for him. I am the one who shot him, but I didn't mean, too. He has been so good to me while I worked for Miss Hope."

"Good. Thank you. I will see you at the office in a little while," stated Doctor Tim.

Chapter 31

Hank sat on the front porch in Ollie's rocker and was enjoying the peace and quiet. Since he had been shot at the bank, Miss Ollie and Rae had babied him. He couldn't bear to sit in the house all day, so Rae helped him out to the porch. She propped up his hurt leg.

Hank could see the young colts prancing and jumping around in the corral. The cool air was making them frisky. Out of the blue, two boys came from the side of the house, spitting out nasty words, pushing and shoving on each other. Hank sat up, careful not to hurt his bad leg, and saw Jay and Boo begin to wrestle on the ground. Surprised and not believing what he was watching, he yelled at the two boys. "Hey, you two. Stop fighting this minute."

The boys didn't appear to hear him at all. Ollie came to the doorway and asked Hank what did he want? She thought he was calling to her or Rae.

"Look at them two. If I could get up, I would jerk a knot in their tails. Make them stop fighting this minute."

***

Ollie was shocked to see the two best friends tangled up on the ground and nasty words spewing from both of their mouths. "Jay Maxwell, you better behave yourself right this minute." Ollie hobbled down to the boys and tried to pull Jay away from Boo.

"What's got into you boys? Stop it!" Ollie yelled as Boo hit Jay in the stomach while she held Jay by his shirt. "Boo Downey, control yourself before I take a switch to your behind. Now, stop and stand still."

Both Rae and John came running to see Ollie who was holding Jay by the neck while fussing at Boo to behave himself.

"Jay Maxwell, you better start talking. You and Boo have

never had a fight before. What brought this on?" Neither boy spoke, only dared the other to tell. Rae waited for one of them to speak.

"So, it going to be that way, is it? Jay, you go and sit on the porch next to Hank and you, Boo, sit on the other side of him. You will sit there until you are ready to apologize to each other." Miss Ollie watched the two marched to the porch. They had dirt in their hair and were missing buttons on their shirts. Their noses were bleeding. She was sure they might have black eyes tomorrow.

John picked up his apples and went over to the corral to feed the ponies. It appeared that Miss Ollie and Rae had the situation under control.

***

The boys hung their heads as they positioned themselves on the porch. They were fuming bad and mumming under their breaths.

Rae went into the house and came out with a cold wet cloth for the boys to wipe their faces. Normally, she would have wrapped them in her arms and loved on them as she cleaned their faces. The boys took the wet rags and wiped at their noses and busted lips. Neither boy made a comment.

"You'd better not ever say that again, or I will beat you into a pup," Boo said softly.

Hank heard the statement but he pretended not too. Maybe, if the boys talked about the problem, they could resolve their anger with each other.

"Well, it's true and you know it. She's my sister and you ain't got any business watching her. She hollered for you to git."

***

My goodness, thought Hank. Boo was peeking at Willa while she was in the outhouse? Jay was only trying to make him stop. Attempting to sit still in his rocker, he hoped to hear Boo's excuse.

"I thought that big fat rabbit ran inside, but when I got there, the door was locked from inside. I didn't know that brat was inside. Besides, she only a gal, and I've seen girls naked before."

"You have! Who?" Jay appeared shocked at this new piece of news.

"I've seen my sister and that old Justice when they are bathing. Sure ain't a pretty site."

Hank nearly choked on his laughter, but he grabbed his hanky and wiped his nose and mouth.

Both of the boys turned around and looked at Hank. He pretended to be asleep.

"Well, if you're sure you was after that rabbit, then let's just forget it," Jay snorted. "Besides, Willa ain't got nothing different than us but ruffles on her pantaloons."

"Rosie always ties white rags around her chest. She looks like a small mummy. Ain't never figured out why she would want to wear those rags, but women ain't got too many brains. That's what Bud says anyway."

"You better not let Miss Ollie hear you say that. When talking about some men here, she will say *even a blind hog finds an acorn once in a while,*" Jay looked into the air, thinking and hoping he said that right.

"What does that mean? Is she calling men hogs?" Boo shook his head at what he had just heard.

"I think a man gets lucky sometimes, other than at the gambling tables." He paused for a moment and then declared, "Shoot, I don't know what she means, but it ain't nice. All the ladies laugh when she says something like that."

Rae walked out on the porch and stepped down onto the ground and looked at both boys. "Have you made up? She realized that the boys had been discussing their problem with only words instead of fists.

"Yes madam," both boys said in unison."

"All right, but Boo, I think you need to get on your pony and stay away from Jay for two days. After two days, you boys can play again if you have really settled your differences." Rae smiled at each boy.

Boo stood and walked over to Jay. "See you soon. Tell Willa I wasn't trying to see her naked. Bye," Boo turned to Hank, who pretended to be sleeping.

Jay stood, looked down at his dirty shirt and walked with Boo to the corral. Hank watched as the two boys put their heads together and finally laughed. They shoved on each other. Boo leaped on his pony and headed home.

Jay was walking back to the porch when Hank said, "Glad you boys made-up. You know I have never known you two to even say a crossword to each other, must less fight like two young bulls."

"Well, I started it, but it won't happen again. Boo is my pal and he's bigger than me. He could have beat the snot out of me."

"I don't know, buddy. You look like you were holding your own." Hank had seen enough of the fight to see that young Jay was giving as much as he was getting.

****

After the twins, and Jay had laid down for a long nap, Hank told Hope and Willa about the fight between the two friends.

"I know about that, but Boo didn't mean to peek at me." Willa said like a young grownup.

Hope raised her eyes and glanced at Hank, wondering what Willa meant.

"Now, you just take care of your cookie dough while I tell this story. After he completed his tale about the two boys, Hope said she had asked Jay how he got a bruise on his face but he didn't tell her."

Ollie laughed to herself.

"What's so funny, Miss Ollie?" Hope looked into the bedroom at her children who were fast asleep.

"I was just remembering when Will got into a fight at school with a young boy who has long been gone from this area. Mr. Jake had to ride into school that afternoon. Will and this boy were sitting on the front steps of the schoolhouse while their teacher was inside working on some papers while he waited for the parents to come.

Mr. Jake wasn't too upset after he saw that Will wasn't hurt, but the other boys' father was fit to be tied. He was so angry he was ready to hit anything, especially his son.

The teacher came outside and thanked the men for coming. He had put up enough with these two boys. Although, he had punished them before, but they seemed to still push and shove on each other. Well, today, the boys got into a fistfight, and he could hardly break them up.

"Will, what was this fight about today?" Mr. Jake looked at Will and he only hung his head down between his knees. "I'm not asking you again, son. Speak up."

'I'll tell you!" the other boy jumped up off the porch and pointed his finger at Will. "He won't leave my sister alone. She told him time after time to leave her alone, but he just kept trying to lure her behind the schoolhouse where he could kiss her.'

'That's a lie!" Will looked at his papa. "I like Mary, but I would never try to kiss her. She's a nice girl, not like her brute of a brother.'

'All right, son. No name calling. What were you doing with his sister that made him mad?'

'At lunch, I wanted to share mine with Mary. She had very little to eat. Miss Ollie packed me enough for three people. I didn't want her to be hungry.'

'My children have enough lunch. Mary don't need charity from your rich son.' The other boy's father yelled.

It seemed that neither the boy nor father could speak in a civil tone of voice. They pranced around in front of the porch steps while the teacher looked on.

'So, Will, are you telling us that you only wanted to share your lunch with Mary. Did you try to get her to go to the back of the schoolhouse?'

'No sir. On the side of the building is a big shade tree. Since we eat outside when the weather's nice, I like to sit over there. I guess *this fool* thought I was leading his sister to the back of the school, but Mary knew different.'

'Had you shared your lunch with Mary before?' Mr. Jake asked.

'No sir. Today we the first time I got the nerve to ask her. She was a little hesitant about eating my food, but she said she would sit with me. Out of nowhere, her brother showed up, grabbed me by the collar, and tossed my lunch pail onto the ground. He stomped my sandwiches and cake with the heel of his boot. And he never said anything about me attempting to kiss Mary.'

The teacher finally spoke. 'When I questioned the other students, they told the same story.' Looking at both of the parents, the teacher said, 'I don't care who's at fault. I just want this to stop. I am tired of trying to teach while the boys are ready to jump out of their desks and have at it. Do you understand what I am talking about?'

'Well, Mr. Teacher, you don't have to worry about my boy or girl any longer. We are pulling out tomorrow anyway."

"No Pa! I don't want to move—again. Please, "Mary cried.

'Shut your trap gal. I'm your father and I have to move where there's work. I am the one that feeds you and the rest of our family. Now go inside and get your things so we can get home.'

Mary and her brother walked up the steps into the schoolhouse. Will sat on the porch, trying hard not to say anything to the old mean man. No wonder his son was so bad, Will thought. He acted just like his old man.

'Will, apologize to the teacher and let's go. I am sorry that you had to put up with two angry boys. Next time, if Will is giving you trouble, no matter what the reason, I want to know. Please don't wait until it comes to blows.'

'Thank you, Mr. Maxwell. I will tell you that I have never had any problem with your son's behavior. He's a big help to me and he is a nice young man."

Ollie sighed real big. "That is the only time I can remember Mr. Jake having to go to the school because of Will's bad behavior. He liked school and he has always had a big heart. He told his pa after that day that many children didn't get enough to eat at lunch. Later, Mr. Jake had the owner of the dry goods store take fresh fruit to the school every morning. The children never knew that Will's papa had donated the treats. Sometimes in the winter, he would have the café take enough soup and cornbread to feed all the children. Mr. Jake was a good man, and I am sure that's where Jesse and Will got their ideas about caring for the less fortunate."

Chapter 32

As Ollie and Rae were cooking a big breakfast, Jess came walking in from the bedroom all dressed in fresh jeans with a new leather vest over a plaid shirt. "Well, don't you look grand this morning? Come over here and let me suck the sugar right off your cheeks, "Ollie said as she came around the kitchen counter.

"Oh Miss Ollie, you're something else." Jess held his hands over his head while Ollie smacked her lips on his face. "Thanks for the compliments," Jess said as he laughed and wiped his face, "I'm going to see Mary Beth for a few days."

"Well, Ollie is right son. You do look like one of those guys in the catalogs at the dry good store." Rae gave him a big hug. "What time is your train today?"

It's at 1:00 p.m. I'm all packed, so after I eat, I have got to go and talk to pa. I haven't asked him if I can go."

"You don't have to ask permission to go to see Mary Beth," Rae said.

"Well, pa is my boss and I know the men will be working with the new calves while I'm gone. I haven't planned very well, but the letter I got from Mary Beth --well, she really wants me to come."

"You just tell Jesse that you have to go. He will understand, and he can always hire Bud or Tater to come and lend a hand for a day or two."

"Thanks Mom, you give me courage," he said with a big smile. Jess walked out to the barn and stopped in from of his pa. Jesse looked at his son's expression and asked if he was going to stand there all day or get to work.

"I want to go see Mary Beth." Jess finally said

'Are you telling me or asking for my permission?"

"I'm telling you," Jess said, with a frog in his throat.

Jesse laughed and looked at his son. "Finally, boy, I'm glad you are making your own decisions. Thanks for telling me so I can hire an extra hand."

****

As Jesse ate breakfast, Hank helped Jess with his carpet bag. He tied it on the back of Jess's saddle and waved goodbye, then watched him ride down the road until he was out of sight. With a big sigh, he walked into the house. "Boy, something sure smells good," Hank said as he held his hat on the rack and slipped off his dirty boots.

"Did my boy get off all right?" Jesse asked Hank.

"Yep, he will arrive in town with time to spare. He's so excited to be on his way to see the love of his life."

Ollie glanced over her shoulder. "Did he say that?"

"Not to me in so many words, but I could tell." Jesse and Rae held hands and smiled at each other as Hank helped himself to the platter of eggs and biscuits.

***

Early the next morning, Jess arrived at Mary Beth's apartment. He knocked on the landlord's door and asked if he could board his horse and carriage in his barn while he visited his wife. The man didn't appear happy about being woke up so early but he said yes. He could always use the exact money that he charged.

Jess walked to Mary Beth's door and knocked. She stood on the other side of the door and asked, "Who is it?" May Beth quickly wiped her mouth with a cool rag and looked down at her gown. She had retched her guts only minutes before and she didn't want anything showing on her gown and robe.

"I'm not a stranger!" he said.

Mary Beth cracked the door and pushed it wide open. She screamed and leapt into her handsome husband's arms. "Oh Jess, I prayed you would come, but I never dreamed you would come so soon."

"In your letter, you said you wanted me to come and here I am."

"Oh, Jess, I am thrilled you're here. I have the most wonderful news, and I only wanted to share it with you first. It's been hard to keep my secret," she said, as she wrapped her arms around his waist.

192

"Do you want to sit on the sofa and tell me what has made you so happy?"

"First, you remember when you were here last time, I wasn't feeling on top of the world-- I was so tired."

"Yes, I worried that you were studying too hard and not getting enough rest."

That's right, I thought the same thing, but that wasn't my problem. Oh, Jess-- she scooted closer to him. "We're going to have a baby!"

"Oh, my goodness. Are you sure?"

"Jess, I'm living in a hospital filled with nurses and doctors. They would know what's wrong with me," she said laughing.

He pulled her in his arms and hugged her tight. Tears of joy fell from his eyes. "I'm so happy. Everyone will be thrilled. Doctor Tim and Hannah will be over the moon and mama and papa, too."

"Poor Miss Ollie, she'll be fussing around all our babies. With Hope's twins, Claire expecting already and now me--that will be one happy old woman."

"Have you been all right? Going to school has to be hard."

"Sometimes, but food doesn't agree with me at night. Most ladies have morning sickness, but I have night sickness," she said laughing. "Speaking of food, can I fix you something to eat?"

"I ate hours ago in the dining car but if you have the makings for a sandwich, I could eat a couple." He stood and removed his boots and hung his new vest on the back of a straight back chair.

"Come in the kitchen with me while I prepare you something."

After eating, washing up and putting on her nightclothes, Mary Beth invited Jess into bed with her. As they laid facing each other, Jess pushed her away from his body and looked her over. "You look a little pale but otherwise you look wonderful. Can I touch it once? Your stomach? I haven't never touched a pregnant woman before."

"Of course, you can. You can touch me all over until the last few weeks of my pregnancy."

His hands molded the sides of her stomach as if it were the most precious thing on this earth. "It so fragile. Oh, Mary Beth, you feel so good."

"So do you." She touched his thick hair and smelled his unmistakable individual scent. "I've missed this."

***

He closed his eyes. If he lived to be a thousand, he'd never get enough of the feeling of her hands in his hair. In a moment he opened his eyes and braced up on an elbow, stared at her and swallowed. He kissed her with gratitude, changing from a tender moment to a search with his tongue in her mouth. He pushed her softly against the pillow, let his fingers spread over her face. His body beckoned to join her, but suddenly, she pushed him away and jumped out of bed.

He rolled over on his side and listened to the loud retching sounds coming from the bathroom. He slipped on his pants and walked to the bathroom door.

"Can I help you, sweetheart?"

"No, it's that blasted . . . night sickness . . . that I told you about earlier."

"I know, but you didn't eat anything," he said wondering how she could be so sick on an empty stomach.

"It was the smell of your food, I guess. I'm better now. Just give me a few minutes, and I will be fine."

Jess went back and sat on the edge of the bed. His body was back to normal now. He laid back up against two pillows and waited for his lovely wife to return to him. He had never imagined happiness such as he knew this night. The girl to whom he had given his heart was now going to give him a child. He was so blessed.

Mary Beth slowly returned to the foot of the bed and looked at her husband who beckoned with his hand for her to come to him. "Are you better, sweetheart?"

"Much, thank you. I'm so sorry—she began, but Jess placed his fingers over her lips. "Never apologize for something like that."

***

"Mary Beth crawled into bed with him and rested her head on his chest. She was content and happy for the first time in a long time. Oh, she had almost forgotten the other news she had to share with Jess. "I have some more wonderful news to tell you. I know this will make you happy. I took a test and I passed it. Now, I am officially a nurse. No more schooling."

"What?" Jess wanted to leap out of bed and dance all around but he laid still as she continued with her school news.

"The school needs more space for new students, so they offered this test to some more advance student nurses. I hope you don't mine, but I used some of our money and paid for registration fee to take the test. I passed and now I can go home with you and start working for my papa."

"That's wonderful, babe. I am so proud of you. Having you home with me and your family is all I care about."

"But Jess, I am worried about the future. Working, I mean for papa after the baby comes. I want to be a good mother *and* a nurse."

"Well, we will have to make some plans and work it out, so you can do both. Maybe, you can keep the baby in the office. Remember Esther?" he asked Mary Beth.

"Of course, I do. She was always so good to me and John when we had to stay at Papa's office. Why do you ask about Ester?

"We could hire another lady like her. She can help your parents in the office while taking care of the baby while you are working. The baby will be with loved ones all the time."

"Oh, Jess, that's a great idea. Mama has said many times she wished she had hired another woman to stay in the office."

"Now, I would like to have an older woman, someone you could depend on each day." Jess said.

"Yes, I would like a nanny. Someone like Esther, who I wouldn't have to worry about caring for our child." Mary Beth agreed, as she looked at her husband. "It seems like you have given this a great amount of thought, and I just told you about it."

"Well, I have thought about you having a child . . . in the future, and I have always known how much you love nursing. I would never want you to give it up, unless it was your own idea." Jess took her face in his strong, rough hands. "We can make it work. Anything to make you happy."

Let's get some rest. I can't wait to get home and tell the family. Everyone is going to be just as happy as I am tonight."

The next morning, Jess hurried to the train station and purchased two tickets. He wanted a sleeping compartment so Mary Beth could stretch out and rest while traveling the long trip home.

***

The next morning, Jess hurried to the train station and purchased two tickets. He wanted a sleeping compartment so Mary

Beth could stretch out and rest while traveling the long trip home.

Once they arrived in Limason, Jess left Mary Beth on the train platform and rushed to the livery.

"Hey Jess," Jules, the livery owner called to him. "You're back mighty early. Wasn't expecting you until next week."

"Change of plans. Can I rent a horse and carriage to drive to my folk's ranch? I can tie my horse to the back. I have Mary Beth with me."

"Wonderful!" the older man replied. "It ain't too smart for young people to live apart. I will get the carriage if you hitch up the horse."

***

After the couple were on their way down the street, Mary Beth noticed that her papa's office still had lights on. "Oh Jess, let's stop and see if Mama is with Papa in the office. I would like to tell them first about the baby."

Jess stopped the horse and carriage in front of the office as Hannah walked onto the boardwalk with Doctor Tim. He was bending over locking the front door when he turned at Hannah call to Mary Beth.

"Mary Beth? What a surprise? Has something happened that you came home, in the middle of the night?"

"No Mama. Hello Papa. Can we go into your office for a few minutes? Jess and I need to get home. We have traveled all day on that rocky train."

Doctor Tim unlocked the door and hurried to help his daughter down from the carriage while Jess tied the horse's rein to the hitching post.

Once the four were inside the office, Mary Beth was almost giddy. She could hardly keep from smiling and jumping up and down.

Hannah and Tim looked at each other, with great worry.

"Papa, Mama, Jess and I are going to have a baby this spring."

"Oh, honey, I can't believe it, but I am thrilled." Hannah pulled Mary Beth into her arms, tears drifting down her cheeks. Doctor Tim shook Jess's hand, then gently moved his wife over, so he could hug her.

"I have more news," Mary Beth said. "I was able to take an advance nursing test, and I passed. So now, I am officially a nurse.

No more schooling, and I can begin working for you as soon as I rest. Isn't this wonderful news?"

"The best, other than the baby," her papa said, smiling. "We have always planned that you would be our nurse. This will take a load off your mama."

"Wouldn't you like to stay in your room at the house, instead of driving miles out to your place?" Hannah asked.

"We both want to be home, so first thing in the morning, we can share our wonderful news with my folks," Jess said.

"I certainly understand. Jesse and Rae, and Miss Ollie, are going to be as happy as we are. I will have a chat with Rae. Maybe we can have a celebration this coming Sunday at the ranch."

"Drive safely home. You know you have precious cargo in your carriage." Doctor Tim untied the horse while Jess helped Mary Beth in the carriage.

As Tim and Hannah watched the young couple drive away, Tim took Hannah into his arms. "I can't wait to tell John and his wife, Susie. They'll be so happy that they will be an aunt and uncle."

Chapter 33

The next afternoon, Will stopped by Bud and Rosie Downey's place to deliver them some homemade blueberry muffins. Rae and Ollie had put up so many berries that Rae declared they would never eat them all. They began making blueberry everything--homemade bread, muffins and pies.

While there, he told Bud that Jess and Mary Beth were going to have a baby, and Mary Beth was home for good. She will be working as a nurse with Doctor Tim.

"Gosh, that's great news. I can't wait to see that old man," laughed Bud. "I remember how Jess tease me when I came home with Rosie and her two boys."

***

After Will left, a rickety, flatbed wagon drove in the driveway. "Hello, Mr. and Mrs. Whit. How are you both today? You want to get down and have some refreshments?"

"No, Bud, but thank you. We're here today to do some bargaining with you. I am in need of some bales of hay, and if you can spare it, a bag of feed for my animals."

"I believe I can help you with that."

"The only things that I can trade are several containers of fresh peaches. My crop of hay should be in next week, but the bank won't help me out."

Bud walked to the back of the wagon and took a look at the ripe peaches, then returned to the couple. He looked into the face of Mrs. Whit, and her sad expression nearly broke his heart. "Sure looks like a fair trade to me. Hop down and I will show you where the hay and the bags of feed are stored. "Let me put these peaches on the porch."

As Mr. Whit carried the hay bales to his wagon, Bud tossed a fifty-pound bag of sugar and flour on the tailgate. He noted the surprised look on Mrs. Whit face. "You need this more than we do. It's an early Christmas gift."

Mrs. Whit wiped tears from her eyes and gave him the sweetest smile. It warmed his heart to be able to help his good neighbors and know how much they appreciated it.

"Now, Bud, I can't take these things," mumbled Mr. Whit, as he rubbed his big hand over the bag of sugar.

"Mrs. Whit and I have already had a discussion about these two things. Go home and take care of your animals. Let Mrs. Whit take care of your children." Bud watched the older couple drive down his lane. He saw his pa walking the dog toward his place. He waved at him as he lifted the container of peaches and carried them in the house.

Rosie was in the kitchen and gave him a surprised look. Justice was playing with their two little girls on the floor.

"I traded with the Whit's for these peaches. Believe I got the better deal because these peaches are really ripe and juicy." He bit into one and the juice ran down his chin. "Delicious!" As he turned to walk back outside, he remembered what Will had said about Mary Beth and Jess. "Hey, Will told me that Jess is going to be a papa. And Mary Beth is a nurse now. She doesn't have to return to school. That's one smart gal for sure."

"So, are you saying that I'm not smart?" Rosie's voice was sharp and questioning.

"Now, Rosie, that never came out of my mouth." He gave her a smile and began walking away.

"Not out of your mouth, but still on your mind. I saw the expression on your face as you said what a smart gal she is."

"Hold on right there. I can't help how this dumb face looks sometimes." He stood straight and pointed at his face. "Stop putting words in my mouth." Bud turned to walk out the door when a juicy ripe peach hit him in the back of the neck. Juice ran down the back of his shirt.

He turned to see Justice picked up the baby and taking the toddler by her hand to leave the house. Something was brewing inside the kitchen and the children didn't need to hear or see it.

"Why in the hades did you do that?" She responded by firing another at his head, but it hit her newly painted wall.

Juice dripped off the wall onto the floor. "Just look what you did to your new paint? Have you lost your senses?"

"It my wall. I'm the painter, a sully-maid that scrubbed this floor and painted it, and I am the slave that cooks three meals a day, but I'm not smart of enough to be a schoolteacher or *nurse*. No! I am only smart enough to do manual labor around here."

"Rosie, what are you talking about? You know you don't have time to be a nurse or schoolteacher. You've been busy raising your two brothers and now our two young girls. Damnit, you must be breeding again," he said matter-of-factly.

"So, I'm just a breed horse to you?" Another ripe peach hit him in the face before he could dodge it."

As he threw up his hand, the door opened, and he was jerked outside onto the porch. He stumbled and fell onto his knees. His pa was standing above him holding out a clean white hanky in his hand. "What the hell Pa? You trying to kill me, too?"

"I had to get you out of her firing line. She's madder than an old rooster. What did you do?"

"Pa, I promise you I didn't do anything," he said as he wiped peach juice from his face. "I told her about Jess going to be a papa and Mary Beth going to start working for her pa as a nurse. Suddenly, Rosie said that I said, she was dumb. I never say anything like that?"

"Son, I have been married for many years. Something is in her craw, and she is taking it out on you. The best way to handle this problem is to stay away from her the rest of the day. She will steam some more, but she will come looking for you. Just say you're sorry."

"But I didn't do or say anything wrong. Why must I be the sorry one?"

"Because she wants you to be. You want to end this problem that she is having. Just follow my advice. *Be sorry.*" Mr. Downey stepped down off the porch and called his dog. He walked away whistling.

Bud walked over to the pump and wet his pa's hanky and re-wiped the peach juice from his face and neck. He glanced over at Justice and the girls as they played in the new sand box he had built. Maybe Justice knew what was going on with Rosie, but decided against it. If it was something bad, she wouldn't confide in him.

After lunch, and time for the evening chores, Bud realized that he had not seen or heard anything from Boo. Many times, if he was playing with Jay, he ate lunch with them but Hank would send him on his way home way before dark.

He sat on the front porch and looked up the road. Rosie had not come out looking for him or Boo. Man, she was really mad about something, but Pa said to let her stew and she would come around.

***

As the sun was preparing to go down, Jay and Boo sat as still as two scared mice as they Willa talking to an Indian girl. "What do you think they are talking about?" Boo asked.

"I don't know, but look at Willa. She ain't acting afraid of the girl. Do you think she knows her?"

"How would she know an *Indian?*"

"Look, they are going somewhere on Willa's pony. We got to get home and tell your folks that Willa is in trouble. Let's run!"

****

Earlier in the day, Willa went for a ride around the pasture near the front of the house. She enjoyed riding her new pony and teaching him tricks. As she neared the far end of the field, she saw a young Indian girl. She was dressed in a brown, deerskin dress with beads sewn all over it. She looked like an Indian Princess that she had seen in her story books.

The young girl waved at Willa, so she dropped down off her saddle and eased over to the girl. "I---need ---help." The girl made hand signals and spoke with an accent.

"What kind of help?" Willa asked as the girl frowned at her words.

She folded her arms together and rocked them back and forth, as if holding a small child.

"You have a baby that is sick or something?" Willa tried to guess."

She shook her head no but made pushing motions down from her chest to the edge of her thighs. Quickly, she took her fingers and made tears coming from her eyes.

"Somebody is going to have a baby?"

"The girl's head bobbed up and down.

"You need help to bring the baby in the world," Willa said.

"Please, come." The Indian girl pulled on Willa's arm.

"Wait, I can't do that but I know a lady who can. Let's go get her!" Willa led her pony over to the fence, hopped on its back, and then reached for the young girl to sit behind her. "My friend lives real close, so we will go get her to come with us."

As Willa rode into Bud's yard, there was no one around. "Stay here. I will look for my friend." Willa knocked softly on the front door, and Justice answered.

"Child, are you alone?" she asked looking over Willa's shoulder and seeing nobody.

"Miss Justice, an Indian woman is having a baby and she needs help. Please come with me and her. She pointed to the young Indian girl sitting on her pony.

"Let me get a few things. Go wait with the girl and I will be right out." Justice was outside in a few minutes with a black bag. She called it her bag of small miracles.

"Willa, I will get my mule and bring him to the side of the corral. Then I will follow you two girls."

"Oh, Justice, I told my new friend that you were going to help us. Thank you so much."

As they traveled several miles into the forest, the sun had gone down and it was pretty dark. "Willa, do your folks know where you are?"

"No madam. Guess they will be pretty worried in a little bit. But, I didn't think about telling anyone. This girl was pretty upset, and I knew I had to get her some help. That's when I thought about you. You helped Mama bring me into the world."

"Oh Lord, the whole countryside will be swamped with men folks before daylight. I hope this labor won't take long."

The Indian girl signaled for Willa to guide her horse down into a small valley. There were many teepees and campfires. Many men and women greeted them with little children running up to the horse and mule. The people appeared to be friendly, but one woman jerked the young Indian girl off the horse. The upset woman spoke to her in their language, and Willa knew the girl was in big trouble—probably her mama. The woman dragged the girl into a teepee.

Willa was sure the girl received a tongue lashing. They could hear cries coming from a big teepee. Finally, the girl's mother waved at Justice and Willa to follow her. Both got off their animals and followed behind the Indian woman.

***

When the woman pulled back the door of the teepee, the heat nearly knocked Justice backward. The heat was horrible. Justice turned to the girl's mother and said, "Heat me two buckets of water and then put that fire out. It is too warm in here. The new mother and baby can't breathe in here.

"No," the woman said. "She can't get a chill."

"Do you want my help or not. Please," Justice turned to the Indian girl and said, "Tell this woman I am here to deliver a baby. I don't have time to fight." Justice nodded her head to the girl's mother. "Tell this Indian Princess to help me or get out."

Justice walked over to the Indian woman who was in labor. Piles of blankets covered her frail body. Sweat was pouring down her face. "Willa, get my bag and then you and that girl get out of here. This is women's work, not a place for children."

Justice wiped the young mother-to-be's forehead with cool water. She removed all but one blankets, then peeked under the last one to see how large the mother was. She was a very petite young girl, about twenty or so. She lifted the girl's legs and parted them to see if the baby was coming. So far, she was just having terrible pain.

Justice opened her bag and removed a few seeds. She pushed several of her miracle seeds under the girl's tongue. "Keep your mouth closed, like this. Justice demonstrated and the girl obeyed. In a short while, the young girl relaxed and fell asleep. The poor girl needed rest before the delivery began.

The witch doctor was dancing and chanting outside the teepee.

"Make him go away. He is scaring me," Justice said, then her eyes landed on Willa. "Maybe, I can get one of these Indian braves to take you home before a posse comes storming out here."

"Those boys scare me. All they want to do is pull on my long hair. One of them said I was pretty. I don't want to be an Indian brave's woman."

"Willa, you are too old for your young age," Justice shook her head as she chuckled. Later, Justice motioned to the Indian woman. "She needed to go to an outhouse. Her bladder was about to burst. Finally, after making her understand what she needed, she guided her to a big patch of bushes. When Justice had completed her private business, she felt that she was being followed.

Two older men were standing close enough to touch her.

"I remember you two," Justice said as one of them tried to touch her hair covering. It was pretty, with all different colored stripes and a large bow tied at the front.

"Pretty. I—want--!" The old Indian man wore a beaded braid wrapped around his head, with a feather sticking up from the back.

"No," Justice slapped at his hand as he attempted to touch it."

"I . . . scalp you," he mumbled and reached for his bowie knife.

"Get away from me, you old fool! I will put a spell on you and you will soon be a toad, hopping around."

"What did she say?" the old man asked his Indian partner.

"Not catch all, but I think she called you a toad. Let's go and get the little Princess to help us talk to her."

Justice watched as the two old men walked away, then she walked by six young braves who were tossing knives in a circle. She heard one say in perfect English that he was going to get the big black mule.

After returning inside the teepee, Justice wasn't too sure how safe she and Willa were. "Where's my little girl?" She asked the older woman.

"Girls . . . in my teepee with my mama. They are safe. No harm . . . will come to your girl. "

Justice peeked at her patient's belly and felt strong kicks coming from the child. "A good sign. The child is moving around. She will be ready in a couple hours."

"Why no screams . . . with pain? What. . . you do?"

"I gave her a few herbs that helps all my new mamas. She doesn't need to be in too much pain. The baby is turned to come feet first." Justice yawned really big and smiled at the older woman. "I need to rest. Where can I lie down while we wait?"

"You can sleep in my teepee. I . . . will stand watch."

"No, I don't want to leave her. May I sleep on the floor next to her?"

Chapter 34

Will came storming down the hillside into his brother's front yard. He stood looking all around and went inside the house. "I'm looking for Willa. Is she here with you?" he asked, as Ollie rocked and knitted.

"No, I saw her riding her pony in the pasture out front this afternoon. You know she has trained that horse to do all kinds of tricks."

"Willa has not come home, and she is nowhere around. Let me go and see if her pony is in the corral." He rushed out the door.

"Hank," Will called inside the barn.

"Here I am. What's wrong?" Hank saw panic on Will's face.

"Willa is not home. Her pony is not in the corral. When did you see her last?"

"She was riding her pony out in the pasture. Let me saddle up and I will ride around out there. She could have fallen or something." Hank rushed to the stall.

Will rushed back inside the house. "Did Willa say anything to any of you about going somewhere? It's not like her to stay out after dark."

Jesse and Rae rush

"Let all get a lantern and walk around calling to her. She could be nearby. I will go to Jess's house and see if she is there."

As everyone walked around the house, the spring house, barn and the two outhouses, Bud came riding into the yard. Will rushed over to him. He saw all the lanterns waving in the dark. Will rushed over to him. "Do you have Willa?" Immediately, Will knew the answer when he didn't see his baby girl behind Bud.

"No, is Willa missing too?"

"What do you mean too? Who else is missing?"

"Justice didn't come inside and help with supper. She is nowhere on our place, but Rosie noticed her black miracle bag missing. And so is her mule."

"Oh Lordy," Ollie yelled from the porch. "Justice must be caring for someone. I don't know of any woman going to have a baby this soon. But something is wrong." Ollie rung her hands together.

"Just maybe Willa is with her." Will said, silently praying she was with the old Black woman.

"I haven't seen Willa near our place since Sunday when you stopped to pick up Boo to go to church services," Bud commented.

"We've got to form a search party. I will ride over and get John and Tater. I know Pa will want to help, too. We will meet you at the curve in the road. Bring some torches!" Bud rode off.

"Pa!" Jay and Boo were wet from sweat and out of breath as they raced up to Will.

"Listen boys, Willa is missing. Have you seen her?" Will asked.

"Yes sir," Jay said. "We saw her in the back pasture talking to an Indian girl. They rode off. We came running."

"What did the girl look like?" Will was near panic.

"She looked little, not big. She got on the back of Willa's pony."

"You don't think she forced Willa to go with her."

"No, they made hand signals at each other, and then they took off into the woods."

****

Hours later, Justice bent over the small Indian woman. "The babe is coming. Get some clean, soft rags and help me hold her legs wide. There is going to be pain because the child is turned wrong, but I will try to turn it." Justice placed her small hand inside the young body and began smiling. She been successful. The baby's crown was showing with a head of dark hair. "It's coming—one more push and it will be over."

The young mother bit her bottom lip and pushed as sweat popped out over her face.

"It's here. A beautiful baby girl. She's small but just fine." Justice turned the baby over in her hand and wiped the mucus out of her mouth. A weak mew sound like a small kitten came first and then a wail like a tiger. All the other Indian women smiled and rushed over to look down at the new baby.

Justice passed the baby to her grandmother and watched as she splashed warm water over its body. She immediately wrapped it in a nappy and soft blankets. Justice stacked some blankets behind the girl's shoulders and lifted her to sit up. Her mother gave her the baby and she smiled down as tears flowed.

From nowhere, a tall, black-haired young brave appeared and stood next to the new mother. He looked down at his wife. You brave woman. No screaming came from this teepee." The young father looked down at the babe. "My baby is a girl?"

"Yes, Brave One. I'm sorry I didn't have you a son. Maybe next time."

Justice looked from the girl to the brave. "He needs to wait awhile for another child. You're very weak and needs to stay in bed for seven nights. No work for you."

"No, she will be up tomorrow. She has many chores. She's not lazy woman."

"No, she will not. This child is very weak, and she needs rest to get her strength back. As her mother—," Justice turned to the lady that helped her deliver the child, "you must see that your daughter stays in bed."

"I say no. She's my wife and will obey."

Justice stood slowly and turned her back to the brave. She began shaking her head cover side to side. With her arms high, she began swaying her small frame and chanted a Creole song. Reaching into her bag, she slid a long sharp, fingernail onto her pointed finger. Justice had probably scared the young brave, but he didn't move away or show fear. He had no idea what was happening to the old Black woman.

Suddenly, she whirled around, then lunged at the feet of the young brave. She pointed her long, red painted fingernail at him.

As he stared at the funny object, Justice did a "z" design on the front of his loincloth. He yelled in Indian language and jumped backward.

"If she gets out of that bed before seven nights, your manhood—may—fall--off."

He looked down and covered his loincloth. He wasn't sure if he was cut with one more glance at Justice, he raced out of the teepee. Justice stood and heard many of the older women giggling.

."I believe you scared my man, "she said smiling. "I'm sure he will be good to me. He was just showing that he's head of his teepee."

"You are a young woman, and he can give you many sons if you take care of yourself. All white women stay in bed for two weeks, but I knew that your ways are different. I was pushing for seven nights but I think it worked." As Justice removed her dangerous fingernail and placed it in her black bag, she heard Willa calling to her papa. She rushed to the front of the teepee and stepped out into the cool night air.

Hank rushed to Justice. "Are you all right?"

Jesse, John, Bud, and Jess were standing together circled by the entire small village of braves, women and children. Several braves guarded Mr. Downey as he held the men's horses.

The chief and his daughter, the Princess of the tribe, stood at the front of the largest teepee. The daughter motioned for Jesse to come forward.

"Welcome friend," the old chief said. "It has been many moons since we have smoked together. Get your little brother and come inside my teepee."

Jesse waved for Will to put Willa down and join him to share the peace pipe with the chief. Will pushed Willa into Jess's arm and said, "Don't let her out of your sight."

After the Princess told the story about her granddaughter going for help—without telling anyone—they understood how Willa and Justice came to be at the village.

"My daughter didn't tell anyone either. That's the reason we were so worried. Thank you for taking good care of her. She likes your granddaughter. They are now blood sisters," Will smiled.

After the men smoked the peace-pipe of friendship, Jesse shook the old chief's hand. "If you allow three of your young braves to follow us to my ranch, I will have my men cut out a dozen steer and one fat milk cow for your people. They can sleep in my barn tonight and should be home before dark tomorrow."

The old chief grinned, showing his tobacco-stained teeth. He gestured with a few hand signals and three braves rushed and jumped on the back of their ponies.

***

As Bud rode into his barn, Rosie met him there. She rushed into his arms, and he held her tight, whirling her around. The shared a passionate kiss before he stood her on the ground.

"Oh, Bud, I'm so sorry. I saw Justice. She said she's fine. What about little Willa?"

"She just fine, too. Justice will tell you all about their adventure. Willa came for Justice to go to the Indian village that is located in the valley. A young Indian maiden was having a baby."

"I was so afraid for both of them, but I felt that they were together all this time. I knew Justice wouldn't let anybody harm that child." Rosie said as she watched Bud unsaddle his horse.

After he fed his horse and bedded him down for the night, he looked at Rosie. "Do you want to tell me what I said to make you so mad at me? That peach juice nearly ruined your new paint job?"

"Oh, I said I was sorry." She fingered a button on his shirt. "You didn't say or do anything. I just thought I was in the –you know—family way again. I am ashamed of myself for being angry. I'm not ready for another child, but if God wants me to have one, I should be happy."

"Hey, pretty girl. I certainly understand. We just have to be more careful. Our baby girl is only eight months old," Bud said, as he nuzzled her neck. "Take me inside and feed me woman," he patted her backside and led her to the house.

****

Will rode passed his folks house and went straight to his place on the hill. Willa slept in his arms. He stopped his horse in front of the house. Hope rushed down the steps asking, "Is she all right?"

"More than all right. She is now blood sister to an Indian girl," Will said, with a big grin. He carried her to bed, then Hope removed her riding boots.

"Let her sleep in her clothes. She looks exhausted." Hope pulled a blanket up around her baby girl and smiled. "You have to tell me what happened."

"I'm starved. Do you have something to make me a sandwich or two? I will tell you how she came to be with Justice while I eat."

****

Jess rode his big bay horse into his small stall behind his house. He saw Mary Beth peeking from the kitchen window. Gosh, it felt good to be home, he thought, and to have his lovely, wife waiting for him. He sat on his horse and said a short prayer of thanks to the good Lord.

Chapter 35

On a beautiful fall afternoon, Tater Downey was working on the edge of the pond on the flower farm. He was excited about being able to build a new house for his lovely wife and child. Jeremiah had left five acres of ground next door to Missy's parent's house. Tomorrow, he and Missy would be riding into town and meeting with a builder to choose a design for the structure.

He whistled as he filled pail after pail of water and placed them on the flatbed wagon to carry to the plants. Texas had been having a drought all summer so the workers had to haul water from the pond to the small trees and bushes. Katie took care of the three green houses where she grew lovely flowers all year long.

As he bent over to snatch a pail of water, a strange creature lunged at him. Tater knew it was an alligator like he had seen while living in the swamps of Louisiana. His massive jaws opened wide, and he clamped down on Taters leg. He screamed for help as he kicked and scooted around on the muddy ground. The monster pulled Tater toward the water, but he kept hanging on and digging into the mud, slipping and sliding. The gator thrashed his large tail wildly and kept hold of his dinner.

Tater struggled to find solid ground to hold onto. He managed to grab a root with both hands, twisted around and kicked at the snout of the gator with his good leg. One last kick made the gator relax its hold enough for Tater to reach the pitchfork lying near him. He hurled it toward the gator's head, which caught him in the eye and buried it deep into his skull.

Even as the gator knew death was close, he kept thrashing, but let go of his leg, then he floated out into the center of the pond. He continued to flail his large tail until he couldn't lift it again.

Tater lay on the wet, muddy ground near the bank. Blood was everywhere. He crawled over to the wagon and climbed onto the floor under the bench. Somehow, He found the reins and snapped them hard making the mule walked to the front of the garden.

***

Missy was walking her son outside. When she saw Tater, she called to him to wave at the baby. When Tater didn't answer, she walked over to the wagon.

She couldn't believe what she was seeing. Tater lay perfectly still on the wagon floor covered in blood. Was he dead? "John, Katie, help!" she screamed. "Tater, what happen?" Missy asked, but he was unconscious. Her husband had caked mud mixed with blood on his body. His leg looked like part of it was missing. She willed herself not to faint at the gruesome scene.

Two young Mexicans men hurried to Missy's side and then to Tater's. One said, "He needs doctor. I get big carriage and we take him to town. Tie a tourniquet around his leg to help stop the blood.' The young man raced to the barn.

***

Katie came running from the house, along with John, after the young boy came for them. "Mr. Tater hurt badly!" he told them.

"Missy stood over Tater, white as a sheet. The baby was pushing to get down from her arms, but she didn't seem to notice.

Katie took little Johnny from her. "Grab that blanket and cover his body. Keep him warm—he may go into shock."

Three of the Mexican workers placed Tater in the carriage. Missy climbed into the seat next to her husband. The other young Mexican man sat on the other side, balancing Tater in their lap, holding him tight.

"Go, Pedro and don't spare the rod! We need to get to town as fast as we can." Katie quickly packed a bag for the baby and rode straight to Jesse and Rae's ranch. Rae was in the front yard cutting the last of her summer roses when she saw Katie.

A chill rushed down her spine. She knew something bad had happened. "What's wrong?" Rae asked, while Ollie and Hank watched from the front porch.

"It's Tater. He was filling buckets with water at the pond, and he was attacked by something. Whatever it was nearly took off his leg. He's in a bad way."

"An alligator most likely," Hank stated. "The boys were talking about seeing one the other day. One boy said it was a 'log' but the other said, if it was, it was a long black log with eyes."

"I've got to be with Missy. Tater has lost a lot of blood and he's unconscious. It's really bad. I would appreciate it if you would take care of Johnny."

"Go and don't fret about this baby. There are many hands here that will help with him. Send word if you need any of us. We will pray for Tater."

****

Tater began to shake uncontrollable. Missy held him tight around the waist while the man kept the blanket up around his neck. Tears streamed down Missy face as she watched the young man sitting next to her make the sign of the cross across his body.

Once they arrived in to town, the driver stopped in front of Doctor Tim's office. Luckily, he was standing outside talking with one of his patients.

"What's happened?" he asked while helping Missy to the ground.

"Tater . . . was attacked by something."

"Tim looked to the young man who was holding Tater close. "I think gator bit him. He was working in the pond water."

Tim lifted the blanket and blinked hard. "Hurry, we have got to get him inside. "You," he said to Missy. "Tell Hannah to get the operating room ready while we carry him inside."

"Hannah!" Missy screamed, rushing in the doctor's office.

"Here I am. Mary Beth, come, something bad has happened." Hannah said as she grabbed Missy's shoulders and gave her a shake. "Get a hold of yourself. What's wrong?"

"Tater needs the operating room," she struggled to say.

"Mary Beth, get the table ready while I scald Tim's instruments. Hurry!"

***

Tim and one of the men carried Tater into the operating room. Then the doctor immediately went to the medicine cabinet and unlocked it. He took down some morphine and gave Tater a shot in his bad leg.

We need a lot of hot water to rinse his leg where the animal bit him." He looked up at Hannah as she carried his clean instruments and placed them at his elbow. "What happen?" she whispered.

"Not really sure. One of the boys said he thinks it was an alligator attack while he was in the pond."

"I never heard of any gators being in the waters around the ranches."

"Neither have I, but you never know what creatures live below free-flowing waters," Doctor Tim replied.

After the water was ready, Tim cleaned Tater's wound. The bone wasn't broken but a large piece of skin with meaty flesh attached needs to be sewn back to the leg. "I can put his leg back together, but I think his muscle will be damaged. He may limp, but he'll still have his leg. God was merciful this time."

After many hours in surgery, Tater was still alive, even though he had lost a lot of blood. Doctor Tim was pleased with the surgery. He was thankful that he had the helpful hands of his sweet wife and his daughter's knowledge. Mary Beth had suggested that he use large clamps to help hold the many stitches together.

He covered Tater with several blankets and said a silent pray over his young patient. He turned to Hannah and Mary Beth. "If infection doesn't set in, he should recover very well. The pond water was very muddy, but I believe we got it good and clean. He needs to remain here with us until we know he's out of the woods."

Missy had been waiting for the operation to end. She had taken patients' names of those who came in to see the doctor and told them he and the ladies were all in surgery. He would call upon them later or if they could, come back tomorrow. She was thankful that she didn't have to turn many people away. Propping herself on the small sofa, she rested her head on a pillow. She was so exhausted, she fell asleep.

When Tim saw Missy asleep, he picked her up and carried her into the sickroom and laid her on the small bed. He covered her with a light blanket and closed the door. He told Hannah that he knew she would want to stay with Tater, but she needed to rest too. "She had a big shock today."

****

Katie rode back to the Maxwell's with John. They went inside and told them about Tater. "Missy will be staying with Tater a few days at the office. Hannah said that they have to watch him closely to make sure infection doesn't set in on the wound. He should be fine, if that doesn't happen."

Miss Ollie set extra plates on the dinner table for them to eat. Hope and Will came walking in with the children. Will carried little Jerry while Hope held Olivia. Willa and Jay rushed to their Aunt Katie and hugged her tight.

"Johnny is getting so big," Willa declared as she took his hand and shook it.

"Yes, he is." Aunt Katie said, "He can say a few words now, too,"

"Hank was telling us about Tater outside. Sure happy that they were able to save his leg." Will said.

"Hush Will. The children don't need to hear about the accident," Hope said, looking around the room.

"I don't agree with you, Hope," Ollie said. "They need to be very careful around water. I remember when I was very little, about six or seven I never got to go outside and play with the field hands' children. I could never get dirty."

"How come you couldn't get dirty?" Jay asked.

"If the Master needed something, I usually had to take it to him and I couldn't be a dirty little helper. He would have put me outside to work with the other field hands in the heat and cold." She looked around at all her children and their babies.

"Well, one week, the master was gone away, so the old cook that gave me orders, told me I could go play outside with the children. Oh, I was so happy I changed my clothes and hurried and joined the young'uns. The boys were going fishing. A few girls were tagging along, and they asked me to go with them. While the boys fished, the girls and I played with a little brown and white puppy. We took turns tossing a stick in the water, and he would jump in and bring it back."

"How could the boys catch anything if you girls kept making a lot of noise?" Jay asked.

"Jay, be quiet and let Miss Ollie tell her story. Stop interrupting," Will said, firmly.

"The little dog leaped into the water and suddenly, he howled really loud. We couldn't believe what we were seeing. A large scaly black creature rose out of the water with it long jaws wide open. He swallowed up the pup. Screaming, we all raced back from the water. The boys heard us and came running. We all watched as the creature rose from the water, opened his big jaws, showing large sharp teeth. He closed his big eyes and made a strange loud sound, then he burped really big. The puppy came flying out of the creature's mouth and landed about three feet in front of the monster. The little puppy swam as fast as his little legs would carry him to the bank. Willy scooped up his dog. The little thing was bleeding on his back and stomach, but otherwise he was fine."

Not a word was muttered as they all sat staring at Miss Ollie. "Mercy," she heard someone say. The room went quiet. Finally, she asked. "Don't ya' believe me?"

"Miss Ollie, in all my life, I have never heard anything so *unbelievable* come out of your mouth," Jesse said. Will and Jess muttered as they glanced around at the others. Hope laughed along with Rae, and Katie.

"I haven't ever seen an alligator before," said Hope, "but if Miss Ollie said this happened, I believe her."

"Come, my *believers,* and help me serve the dinner meal to all these men who can't appreciate the truth when they hear it." Ollie stood and looked around the room and smiled. She loved her family.

Chapter 36

The town was all abuzz about Tater's accident with a strange creature. The church prayed for him, and several ladies volunteered to sit with him while Missy rode home to check on her baby. Doctor Tim and Hannah appreciated the help.

Claire and Lucy came into town after visiting with Tater and Missy. They went to the schoolhouse to get ready to register the children for school.

Lucy had gone to the dry goods store, and she overheard several ladies talking about not being able to send their children to school. She pretended to be shopping, hopping the ladies would give their reasons for not sending their children. One of the ladies said, very sadly, that her son had outgrown his pants and he refused to wear knee knicker knockers and have the boys make fun of him. Another lady said that she had three girls, and their dresses were almost in rags.

Lucy had been poor all of her life but her grandmother had managed to keep her in decent clothes to wear to school. She did understand how the boys and girls felt about being teased. Once Lucy got back to the classroom where Claire was cleaning the black board, she sat down and bowed her head and start praying silently.

"Lucy, what's wrong? Why are you praying?"

Oh, Miss Claire, I overheard some of the mothers talking about not sending their children to school because they didn't have decent clothes. We must do something to help them. One lady said her son didn't want to grow up ignorant."

"Oh my, you're right. We must do something and do it quick. With school beginning in two days, we don't have much time."

***

"Much time for what, girls?" Jesse and Rae walked into the classroom. They had come to town to get supplies and see for themselves how Tater was doing.

"You are two of the people we must talk to since you're on the school board," Claire said.

What's going on?" Jesse asked. "I did make that bad teacher leave," he said as Rae rolled her eyes.

"Pa, so many of our students don't have clothes to wear to school, their mother's said, and they aren't coming. We must find a way to help these children. My heart breaks when I know we have so many that are in need."

"Tell them to go to the dry goods store and get what they need. I will pay for it."

"That's wonderful, but that is charity, and people are too proud to take it."

"Maybe, we could tell our students that they will be wearing uniforms. I lived near a big city one time, and all the rich kids went to a nice school where everyone was dressed alike," Lucy said.

"How many children are we talking about?" Rae asked.

"I believe we had twenty-eight last year. Should be about the same give or take one or two."

"Rae, go and ask Homer to come here and let's discuss this problem."

Jesse and the girls' watched Rae hurry down the street. "Now, what kind of uniform would the boys and girls wear?" Jesse asked.

"Something simple. Boys could wear dungarees, plaid shirts and boots. Girls could wear simple jumper-dresses with a long pinafore over them with sturdy shoes."

"Mrs. Goodyear carries all that in her store. Every student could go to the store, try on their clothes and be fitted for shoes or boots. They would not have to pay for anything. The community would understand that a special donation had been made for our students to wear uniforms and they would be supplied by the school. Problem solved." Jesse squeezed into one of the larger desks and took a seat.

"Sounds wonderful, but who would be the donor?" Claire asked

"You leave that up to Homer, your mama and me. No one has to know who the donor is."

After a long discussion with Homer, the school superintendent, the uniform situation was all set. Jesse and Hannah spoke with Mr. and Mrs. Goodyear about having the clothes all ready. Everyone was excited about the new school year to begin.

****

Jay put on his new dungaree and an older blue and green plaid western shirt. He strutted around in his brown cowboy boots. This would be his first day and he could hardly contain his excitement. Aunt Claire was going to be his new teacher and he wasn't sure what he should call her. His mama had told him to call her Mrs. Underwood, and the other students will do likewise.

"Sound funny calling her that. I ain't never heard her called nothing but Aunt Claire." Jay said laughing.

"Lordy me boy, its time you went and got some learning. You never say *ain't* and *nothing*. Mercy, here comes your papa to take you and Willa to school.

It wasn't long, while on the playground, one of the bigger boys grabbed Jay up by the collar. "Why are you wearing that plaid shirt with western snaps on the pockets? It doesn't look like ours." He pointed to the circle of boys standing around him. "And those boots. They are cowboy boots, not work boots like these." He picked up his boot and showed Jay the difference.

"I already had these things at home. My folks didn't buy me anything new. My clothes are old; yours are new."

"Maybe so, but they look better than mine." He shoved Jay on the ground and threw a handful of dark brown dirt on his shirt. "Now they don't look so good," he said, laughing. "Come on boys, let's get out of this new kid's way so he can run and tell the teacher. He's her pet."

Willa raced over to Jay. "What happened? Did that big bully hurt you?"

"Yes, but I will get him back. He said my shirt and boots were different."

Willa raced away from Jay and jumped on the big bully's back and bit his ear before he knew what had hit him. He bent over and tossed her over his shoulder onto the ground.

Claire had just came out onto the school porch when she saw Willa in a struggle with a big boy. "Stop it, right now, Charlie,

Willa! What in the world? Both of you go inside this minute. Wait for me in the coat closet."

Lucy hurried outside and took the bell from Claire. "I will get the students inside while you take care of this problem."

Willa walked in the schoolhouse and entered the coatroom, Jay stood in front of her like her protector. Even as small as he was, he dared Charlie to touch his sister again. Both Willa and Jay stood quietly waiting for Claire to show up when they heard boots stomping up the stairs.

Boo popped his head in the room. "I just got here. Who's been picking on you Jay? I'll beat him into the ground."

"Oh, you will, will you? Well, I'm the one who shoved him to the dirt, and I will shove your face in it too."

Boo turned and slowly looked at the tall boy. He grinned and slammed his small fist into the boy's belly before he knew what hit him. The boy doubled over in pain just as Claire entered.

She must have figured out what happened when she saw Boo. "All right. Jay, do you want to tell me what happened on the playground?"

Glancing at Willa, he just hung his head and looked at the floor.

"Willa, what's your story?"

Willa just looked straight ahead. She wanted to scream that Charlie started it, but she wasn't going to tell.

"Well, Charlie, if you don't want to be expelled on the first day of school, you better start talking."

"Why does that little squirt get to wear a nicer shirt and cowboy boots, and we all have to wear these duds, plain as day?"

"You are wearing brand new clothes. You don't know this, but Jay is wearing hand-me-downs. Those boots and his shirt belonged to some other little boy once. His mama took good care of them so she passed them down to Jay. They look just like your uniform. His mama didn't want the school board to have to spend extra money on clothes for him. Besides, all of you children should be proud of your new clothes. Many of the children didn't have pants or shirts that fit them, and now they do. A wonderful man donated his money to purchase all the uniforms because he said that when he was a little boy, he couldn't attend school because he had nothing decent to wear."

The teacher bent down and locked her eyes on Charlie. "Are you going to be mean to Jay because of his choice of clothes? If so, you can turn in your uniform and go home. Now that is all I am going to say on this matter."

Claire walked out of the coat room and left the children alone. Charlie mumbled to Jay that he was sorry, and all of them filed into their classroom.

When school let out, Rae was waiting for Boo, Jay and Willa. "How was your first day?" Before they could answer, Rae looked down at Jay. "How in the world did you get so dirty?"

The three raced to the carriage as Jay called back. "Just having fun."

****

At dinner that evening, everyone wanted to hear about Jay's first day. Willa didn't give Jay a chance to tell about the fight he had on the playground before school. "Well, Charlie shoved Jay down, so I jumped on him and bit his ear. Later Boo punched him below the belt. He doubled over just as Aunt Claire came into the coat room."

Everyone was stunned and didn't say a word. They just looked from Willa to Jay. Finally Hope spoke up. "Rae, did you know that this had happened to my baby when you picked them up at school?"

Oh, mama, I ain't no baby. I didn't cry when he pushed me down and threw dirt on my clean shirt."

"My goodness," mumbled Ollie as she looked to Will.

"Let's eat our meal and we will talk about this later. Willa, not another word, please." Will glanced at both of his children giving them a stern look. Both of them knew that they better keep quiet.

"Well, Miss Ollie," Hope said. "Do you have a childhood story about Will and Jesse getting into fights when they were boys?"

Ollie laughed and smiled at Jesse and Will. "To be honest, there was a lot of fussing, but not fist fights. There were too many years in-between them. Jesse was eight years older than Will. Wouldn't have been a fair fight."

"No, I guess not."

"We wouldn't have fussed very much if Jesse wouldn't have tried to be my papa after Pa passed. He wanted to boss me around." Will grinned at Jesse.

"And he did, if I recall," Hank spoke up and everyone laughed.

Chapter 37

After all the dishes were put away and the twins were fed and changed, Jesse brought up the subject of a big fall picnic for the family and nearby neighbors.

"Let's roast a big, fat pig in the ground and have a lot of delicious desserts to eat. I'm just kidding. The ladies can take care of the food. We should have a small band and set up the dance floor. Might as well do it up big and have a grand time. It will be our last until Thanksgiving." Jesse looked at everyone at the table.

"Sounds like a good idea. This way everyone can meet Lucy. I believe we can move Tater over here in a padded wagon. His leg is heeling very well," Hope said. "And I can show off our twins. I will soon be taking them to church."

"Can I invite some of my new friends from school," Jay asked.

"The more the merrier," Jesse responded.

"When do you want to do this? This coming Saturday or the following week?" Rae asked.

"This Saturday. We have everything already except spreading the word to our guests. Hank, you ask Jules if he can get the men to play their music. I heard tell that his thirteen-year-old niece can belt out a great song or two. Maybe he can get her to sing for us."

"I can sing, Uncle Jesse," Willa said.

"Now, that will be a special treat for all of us." He smiled at Willa.

"Will, please oversee the digging of the fire pit. The Mexican boys can help you because they know how to roast a pig."

"I'll be glad to do that."

"When I drive the children to school in the morning, I'll spread the word to our friends and tell them to bring a covered dish and wear their dancing shoes."

"Jesse, have you been drinking?" Rae asked him, knowing fully well that he hadn't. "You are so giddy about this party?" Everyone laughed as Jesse stood.

"No, sweetheart. I am so happy to have my family here and mostly in full bloom," he said, meaning that Claire and Mary Beth were going to have a babies come this spring.

When Saturday arrived, the men had put up a huge white circus tent away from the house and placed many tables and chairs inside. The men rolled up the sides of the tent to allow fresh air to flow across the large room. Each time the men put up the big tent, Jesse congratulated John on the great trade he did for the tent.

The dance floor had been placed down and Jules's small band set up their instruments on the edge of the platform. Many couples danced and Jules's niece sang several lively songs. After hearing her sing, Willa decided not to sing. She would sing when she got a little older.

The men gathered at the punch bowl, some adding liquor to their cups, talking about their summer crops and many calves that had been dropped. Jesse was pleased to hear that his neighbors had a great year and would be prepared for a hard winter.

***

Hope was thrilled to show her twins to the neighbors and planned a special Sunday with the minister to baptize her babies. Mary Beth and Jess, along with Albert and Claire were happy to announce that both of them were going to have a baby in the spring.

One man said to his wife, "Mable, for gosh sake, don't drink any of the water on this ranch. We don't need another little one!" Everyone laughed.

Once the party was over and all the dishes washed and many of the tables and chairs put away, Mrs. Downey needed a ride home. Her family had gone home earlier because Rosie's little girls were tired and cranky.

Rae walked Mrs. Downey to the corral, and they saw that all the men were busy doing the afternoon chores. "Come Mrs. Downey, Hope and I can drive you home. Olivia and Willa will enjoy the ride."

***

After the girls climbed in Rae's big carriage, they drove away

224

from the ranch. Will stood in front of the barn with Jay and his baby son, Jerry waving them goodbye.

Jerry fretted from being wet and hungry again. "Jay, I've got to go and take care of this little runt. Stay in the barn and help Hank feed the pigs. The cow needs to be milked, too," Will said.

As soon as Will went inside, Ollie met him and took the baby. She changed him and fixed a bottle. After getting him settled, she sat in her rocker. "Sure feels good to get off these old feet."

Albert, Claire, Jess, Mary Beth, Tater and Missy were in the big sitting room laughing and talking. Will was pleased to see these young couples getting along with each other and sharing news. Will left his baby son with Ollie and went outside to check on Jesse, Hank and Jay. John and Katie were taking a short walk around the outside of the big house, looking at Rae's roses and other plants.

Hank stood on the path that led into the house. "Jesse, Will, look at the sky." The wind had picked up and dark clouds were rolling. Lightning flashed in the distance. "Look at that dark cloud."

Suddenly, Jesse yelled, "It's a tornado! We've got to get everyone down in the cellar, "Jesse yelled. Hank, turn the horses' loose into the pastures. Push the cattle out of the barn, but leave the pigs. They'll be fine."

Jesse held open the cellar door while Jess and Albert helped Ollie down the ladder. John and Katie helped Tater and Missy, trying hard not to hurt Tater's damaged leg. Large hail beat down with large sheets of rain. After several candles were lit, Will remembered that Jay was in the barn with Hank. He stared up the ladder but felt Jesse pulled him back to the floor. "Hank will take care of him," Jesse yelled. "I pray that the girls made it to the Downey's farm."

Hank stood in the doorway of the barn. The black funnel cloud was close to the ranch. The wind was blowing strong, and he knew that he couldn't get himself and Jay to the cellar safely. He grabbed Jay and tossed him to the floor and lay his old, crippled body on top of him. Jay squirmed, but Hank yelled at him to lie still.

****

Rae and Hope saw the black funnel cloud hitting the ground

and going back up again and again. The noise coming toward them was deafening.

"We've got to get into a ravine." Rae told Hope to hang onto to Olivia while she held tight to Willa. "Look, there's a big ditch there."

The girls dashed to the large ditch and Rae lifted Willa into her arms and slid down into it. She took the baby while Hope joined them.

"Lean into the dirt wall," Rae said, as she removed her long floral skirt. She took it and covered all of their heads as best as she could. The material helped keep the hail from hitting them on top of their heads.

"A train's coming," Willa screamed and placed her face into Rae's middle.

"It's only the wind! Be still baby. We're safe as long as we stay quiet and still." Rae tried to comfort Willa as she saw skinny pine trees and twigs flying overhead.

As fast as the tornado came, it was over. Heavy sheets of rain fell for a few more minutes, but the rain soon faded to only a sprinkle. The sky was bright again. Rae unwrapped the girls and smiled big. "Well, that was something. Thank goodness we're safe."

Hope looked down at Olivia who had slept through the storm. Grabbing Rae, Hope hugged her sister and thanked her for saving them with her quick thinking. "I would probably have tried to outrun the storm."

"Don't think about any of that. Let's get out of this ditch and see if my horse and carriage are still somewhere near." As they stood on the high ground, their luck had run out. The horse was long gone. Rae prayed he was not harmed by the debris and hail.

"We are going to have to start walking. The men will come looking for us soon." Rae was trying to be positive, but she was scared that the storm may have hit their ranch house.

"I feel sure that Will has taken care of Jay," Hope said.

****

Everyone climbed out of the cellar. "Thank the Lord," someone said as they all stood looking around at the little damage to the property. The house and barn were still standing, with only a few shutters and shingles missing. The outhouse was down, and the frame built around the spring house was gone.

Will raced to the barn and met Hank and Jay wiping hay and dirt off their clothes. "Jay, my boy, I was scared to death when I realized you weren't in the cellar. Jesse said that Hank would take care of you."

"He did Pa. He laid on top of me in the barn. I might have flown away, if not for him. He saved my life." Will laughed and hugged Jay again before sitting him back on the ground.

Will, Jay and Hank stood looking toward Will's and Jess's houses and were happy that both of them looked fine. As they turned to go inside with all the others, Jay noticed Rae's horse walking slowing up the lane. "Look, there's Rae's horse. He's dragging something!"

"Jay, go get Jesse," he yelled as he raced to the horse. Hank limped slowly behind him.

The horse looked fine, but Rae's nice carriage was turned over on its side with two busted wheels. When Jesse got to the carriage and team, he said for Will to round up the horses. They have to find the girls."

Hank tossed hay into the corral and the horses rushed inside the open gate and began eating. Will and Jesse saddled the animals and told Hank that they would follow the carriage's trail. "The horse most likely got off the road and went into the woods. The wagon ruts will be deep so we should be able to find them without too much trouble."

In a matter of minutes, John, Jess, and Albert were following Will and Jesse. Between all the men, the girls would soon be found.

***

Katie and Missy came outside of the house and watched Will and Jesse ride down the road. Katie was looking at Rae's roses that had been stripped of all the flowers and leaves when she noticed the carriage. Hank had already removed the horse and was checking him over for damage.

"My goodness, look at Rae's carriage," Katie said, as Ollie came out of the house.

When she saw Rae's carriage lying over on its side, she fell to her knees and began to pray and cry. "Oh Lord, please hear me. I know that I have asked for many blessings, but I am begging you now. Please allow my children to be found safe and without harm. I know you don't make deals, but I'm telling you right this minute, I will be a better, faithful servant to you. There won't be anything I won't do to please you. Oh, merciful God, please hear my prayer." When Ollie covered her face and cried, Katie and Missy said "Amen."

"Come back inside with me," Claire said as she helped Ollie to stand. "Jesse will find them."

****

What seemed like hours, with Rae and Hope taking turns carrying Jerry, Rae saw her handsome husband riding toward them. She dropped Willa's hand and raced forward, waving and calling to Jesse.

Jesse leaped from his horse and ran to Rae. He grabbed her up in his arms and swung her around and around. "I'm so happy and look at you. Just prancing around in your underclothes. Where's your skirt?"

"Never mind how I'm dressed. Just help get the children and take us home. We're wet, hungry and exhausted, in that order."

"Yes ma'am, Will has Hope and the baby. One of the others will take Willa home." Jesse helped Rae on the front of his horse and looked at the others. "Let's get this cargo home, fellow."

"Cargo? My word," Rae shook her head and leaned back into Jesse's chest.

Chapter 38

After everyone was settled back at the ranch house, Will and Hope took their babies into the bedroom to feed and change them into their night clothes. Willa and Jay were so excited about what they found outside.

"You know, mama, the wind turned over the outhouse, but the catalog that we use, and the bags of lime are still in the same place," Jay said.

Willa wanted to tell what she had seen, too. "The spring house's roof and door are gone, but there are clean milk jars and buckets still standing on the small table. Just like always. Isn't that funny?"

"Yes, that is funny how the strong wind can blow some things away and not touch others. Just like the old windmill. It's still turning slowly like it does all the time. It was untouched." Hope hugged both of her children. "We must thank God for watching over us, our homes, and animals. We were very fortunate today."

"Why don't you two go and see if you can help Miss Ollie put some dinner on the table for everyone. She has a lot to feed," Will said. "Your mama and I are going to try to get the babies to sleep."

Willa and Jay saw Hank bringing in bowls of food from outside. "We came to help Miss Ollie, but it looks like you need more help than she does. What can we do?" Will said.

"Great! The big tent wasn't touched and inside is all the leftover food we had from the barbeque. I need help bringing it in the house. Come, Jess and Albert. Help us bring in the bowls of food and pies and cakes."

Ollie and Katie immediately started making room on the kitchen counter to place the welcome food. Rae and Missy set the large dining room table and set up two smaller tables near the front room for everyone to have a place to sit.

Miss Ollie and Rae stood at the stove and warmed many of the dishes while the others stacked plates and silverware at the end of the counter. Rae had suggested that everyone serve themselves before taking their place at the table. Everyone readily agreed because they were all very hungry.

Once the dishes were washed and put away, everyone moved to the front room to sit together. Will sat on the floor leaning up against the stone fireplace. He was holding his baby son, Jerry. Jay sat beside him playing with the baby's toes. Albert and Claire were cuddled together in a big soft armchair, while John, Katie, and Missy sat together on the sofa. Hope, Olivia and Mary Beth were sitting at a small table close to the big room.

Ollie wiggled her way through the family members to her rocking chair and took her seat, a queen preparing to rule over her family. Ollie smiled at everyone as she took up her knitting needles. "You know," she said to the group, "we have been very fortunate today. I think somebody should lead us . . . *bump, bump, bump* . . . in a prayer." *Bump, bump, bump.* "What in the world is that noise?" Ollie said.

Suddenly Missy jumped off the sofa and looked in the front bedroom. It was empty, so she rushed to several other rooms and looked inside. She stood in the big room and declared loudly, "Tater is not in the house. That must be him . . . in the cellar!"

Jesse had been standing in the kitchen with his arms wrapped around his lovely wife, Rae. He rushed out the back door with Jess, John and Albert on his heels. Jesse lifted the big wide door. John and Jess slid down the ladder. Jess fumbled around until he found the candle with matches. The room became brighter, and the men stood looking at Tater. He was sitting up on the long table.

"Hey fellows," he said. "Is the storm over?"

Jess and John laughed. "Yep, it's over. Have you been lying there all this time?"

"I guess. My leg was killing me after I got carried down here so Missy gave me some of my medicine. It knocked me out. I don't know how long I slept but when I woke, I was alone. I could hear someone walking above me so I used my crutch to pound on the ceiling. Thank goodness you heard me because I've got to pee something awful."

"Jesse cupped his hands. "Jesse tell Claire we are bringing Tater up. He needs to use the outhouse first."

"There ain't no outhouse! The wind turned it over," Jay yelled down. "I guess he can use the bushes like I did earlier."

The boys carried Tater to the bushes and afterwards, he was carried into the house. They carried him to the kitchen table and Missy used her hand to comb his hair back from his eyes. Rae prepared him a big plate of hot food.

Missy told him that after he ate, she would change the bandage on his bad leg. "It's bleeding, but since you aren't in great pain, it's all right."

"It does hurt some, but I'm too hungry to worry about it right now," he said between bites. Missy laughed and sat down beside him.

"I'm so sorry that we left in you the cellar. Once the storm was over, we all climbed up the ladder to see what damage had occurred. Thank goodness we only have a little. John rode over to our place and one of the green houses was blown over, but everything else was fine. I'm sure some of the plants were damaged but we were lucky."

With his mouth full, Tater nodded his head. "More than lucky, I would say."

Jesse and Rae left the two young people at the table and walked in the big room. Rae sat down in a chair while Jesse sat at her feet.

"Well, Miss Ollie, it would seem that you will have another great 'story' to tell. It will be a funny tale about Tater being left in the cellar for hours."

"Rae, my stories as you called them, aren't just stories. The things I have told Hope, and some to you, are my life memories. Everything that I said did happen in my life, my world, from the time I was three."

Everyone looked at Hope and Rae, not saying a word. Rae hung her face down and said, "I didn't mean that your stories weren't true. I'm sorry."

"Oh, please don't be, but Hope asked me to share my life with her, so I started from the time I was little."

"Miss Ollie, please tell something about your life now. Some of the family members here haven't heard about your life before you came here," Mary Beth pleaded.

***

"If you all are sure you want to me, too," Ollie glanced around the room and saw the family smiling and waiting for her to begin. "Well, from the time I was about three, maybe four, I was a servant to a little girl named Patricia. She was the master's daughter at the Wavering plantation. We were the same age but I watched after her until she was about seven and she went away. But I got to work in the big house where I learned to cook and clean. I had three meals a day, clean clothes and a place to sleep.

When I was a big girl, about fourteen, I fell in love with one of the boys' on the plantation and being two dumb kids, we had a baby boy. He died along with my folks from typhoid fever.

When I was sixteen, the master gave all his slaves freedom papers and told us to leave. I had lived on the plantation all my life, but I watched many of them as they raced down the long rode to a new life, so I decided to go too. I walked barefooted down the hot sandy road, with only the clothes on my back. I sat on a log to rest when Jesse and Will's grandfather and young son came by. Mr. Jacob needed someone to help care for his ten-year-old son, Jake. I went home with them, and I have been here ever since. Once Jake grew to be a man, he married, and the couple had these two wonderful boys." Ollie glanced down at Will and across the room at Jesse.

"Years later, their mama passed and several years later, their pa died too. These rascals were left to me. Hank had come to the farm to help build the addition to the house, and he just stayed. So, he and I raised the boys.

My greatest joy was the evening Jesse brought Rae and Hope to live with us for a few weeks. Hope was the most beautiful white child I had ever seen. My prayers were answered when Jesse and Rae married.

One of my saddest days, while living here in Limason, was when I lost my best friend Esther. She worked for Doctor Tim, but we were as close as sisters."

"Miss Ollie, may I tell something here?" Jess didn't wait for permission. "When I returned home, after being gone for two years, I rode my horse by the cemetery as I crossed the pasture. I stopped when I saw a fresh grave. My heart stopped. I rode closer but I couldn't read the name painted on the small cross. So I got down on one knee and saw the name Esther. And I cried. I was so happy to know that the grave wasn't yours, Miss Ollie. Then I was ashamed. I really was very fond of Esther. She was always good to me."

Mary Beth pulled Jess closer to her. She whispered something sweet to him and he nodded. The memory was so fresh in his mind, he wanted to cry again.

Ollie smiled at Jess and continued with her memories. "I always knew that Will was waiting until Hope grew up before he asked her to marry him. Lordy, those two fought like cats and dogs. Will disliked her boyfriends and Hope couldn't abide the girls that he brought to the ranch."

"Miss Ollie, since Jess interrupted you, I would like to tell about an adventure Jeremiah and I had with my precious young wife."

"Do you have a story about mama," Jay said. "Tell it papa!"

"Go ahead, Uncle Will. I'm sure we'll all enjoying hearing these memories," Missy said.

"Well, I was building my house and I wanted to take a trip to Dallas to get some modern items for the kitchen and water closets. I needed to take two wagons, so Jeremiah volunteered to drive one for me. Hope heard about my plans to go to Dallas, and she pleaded and begged to go, but Rae said no, she couldn't travel with two men. So, we planned our trip, but we had no idea that little Sweetheart was making plans, too. Once we stopped after a long, hot day on the first leg of our trip, up popped Hope, who had been hiding under a large heavy tarp stored on the back of Jeremiah's wagon. She slid out and raced to the woods to relieve herself, but Jeremiah discovered her. Boy, was I mad. I wanted to paddle her hide but Jeremiah told me to stop it. I was really mad, but she said she had left Rae a note telling her where she was.

Later, after we got to Dallas, it turned out that she was a big help in picking out my supplies and Christmas shopping for you, Miss Ollie and Rae. After that trip, we became very close and married soon after that."

"Yes, they had a beautiful wedding and I know some of you were young, but old enough to remember that wonderful day." Ollie smiled at everyone.

"Speaking of wonderful days, I've got a memory that I will

always remember, and I know you do too, Miss Ollie," Hank said, laughing.

"Tell it, Hankie," Willa cried. "Is it about Mama?"

"Well, my child, it is. When Rae and Hope came to live with us, I loved that little gal. She had me wrapped around her little finger. Will was too, but he probably won't admit it. Anyway, it was getting close to Thanksgiving, and I went to one of our neighbors and chose the biggest turkey I could find. Without me knowing it, I discovered Sweetheart, your mama Willa and Jay, feeding the bird out of her hand. She had made a pet out of that turkey. I told her that the turkey was going to be on the Thanksgiving table.

When it got time for me to prepare the bird to cook, she flew into a hissy fit. She screamed and carried on something awful. Finally, Jesse told me to go and get another bird and leave Hope's new pet alone. Believe it or not, I had to go the butchers' shop in town and get one already prepared. So, Thanksgiving Day our many guests arrived. Rae had dressed Hope in a new dress with a big bow in the back, new shoes and socks. She was the prettiest little thing strutting all around and winning every ones heart. When it came time to eat, Hope wanted to feed her pet turkey. She looked all over the ranch, stomped in puddle holes, lost a shoe, untied her lovely bow on her dress and her pretty hair was a mess. When she couldn't find her pet, she saw a big turkey with his legs pointed toward the sky in the center of the table. Man, she went wild. She raced to the table and started screaming that I was a murderer, and all our guests were monsters for eating her pet.

"Well, you all can guess how our guests felt. They mummied under their breaths that she was one bad brat who needed to be spanked," Ollie said, chuckling.

"Did you kill her pet, Uncle Hank," Jay asked with big eyes.

"No, I found it and came running, carrying the wild bird around the food table. I had one boot on, my dress shirt was pulled out of my pants, and I had mud all over me. I looked a sight for sure. I screamed to Sweetheart that I had her pet as I stumbled and fell down in front of everyone. Sweetheart came over and sat down beside me and said she loved me, as she petted her turkey."

"I'm sure many of our neighbors still tell that story every year at their Thanksgiving tables," Ollie said, as everyone laughed.

"Good gracious," Albert said, "I have lived a very dull life."

"Well, I know Miss Ollie, you were telling us your memories, but I have one that touched me, and I will always remember it. So, I am going to tell it," Jesse said.

He sat up on his knees and smiled at Miss Ollie. "You had fallen sick with a bad cold one winter. You didn't listen to Doctor Tim and rest so it wasn't long before your cold turned in to pneumonia. You were so sick we thought for sure you were going to leave us."

"Where was she going?" Willa asked, biting her fingernail.

"What I meant, Willa, was we were afraid Miss Ollie might die. Doctor Tim had done everything he knew to do. As nighttime came, we heard singing coming from outside. We went to the door and our front lawn was filled with people holding candles and singing led by Miss Ollie's minister. After the song ended, the minister prayed loud enough for the good Lord to hear. We all went outside and kneeled down with Ollie's friends and our neighbors.

Doctor Tim was in the house with Miss Ollie, but he was exhausted so he fell asleep in the big chair beside her. Justice prepared some special tea and woke Ollie and made her sip a whole cup of it. She told Miss Ollie that she wasn't going to die. God wasn't ready for her, and she had best start breathing better. It wasn't long before Doctor Tim awakened and found Miss Ollie recovering. Her lungs were stronger, and her heartbeat was much better. He came outside and told everyone that their prayers had been answered and to go home before they all caught pneumonia. Everyone shook my hand and blessed our household. It's a night that I felt God's presence and we were blessed with so many white and black friends."

"I am so pleased that you boys have special memories living here in this home. I never had a home until your grandfather brought me here. As I got older, I didn't wanted you to move away and I always prayed that you would stay here on this ranch. But, this house is just a place made out of stone and boards. It's who lived here with love, kindness and Jesus in their hearts that has made it a home. When your grandfather brought me here, it was the luckiest day of my life."

No one said anything. They all sat staring at each other.

Miss Ollie looked out the front window and said, "I believe it is safe enough for all of you to return to your homes. God has protected us this day and we are all thankful. I will see most of you tomorrow." Ollie said, as she stood and wiped her eyes and nose.

Chapter 39

As Thanksgiving drew near, the men were very busy working with the two hundred new calves that had finally arrived on the train from Fort Worth. With Jess living at home, Jesse didn't have to hire another cowboy to help. The work was hard and hours long once the fire and branding irons were hot. The calves were pushed through a small chute and held until it was time for them to be branded. Will turned them loose, one at a time, grabbed the animal by the neck, tossed it on the ground and tied its legs. The hot branding iron was placed on its rump and a perfect M was stamped in the hide. After thirty calves a day were wrestled to the ground, Will could hardly move at the end of each day. He had to admit he wasn't as young as he used to be.

Jess's shoulder muscles were not the same since he had been shot, and with John and Jesse being older men, the branding went slower than expected. Jay and Boo sat on the fence and watched the men. Both of them carried cool water to the workers. The boys begged to chase the calves, but were told to stay out of the corral while the branding was going on.

Jesse and Rae had decided to only have family members and closest friends for Thanksgiving dinner. The branding was a lot of work and they needed to get the calves out into the pastures as soon

After Thanksgiving, the men continue to work from daylight till dark with the cattle. Once all the calves were in the fields, it was time to start preparing for Christmas. One evening, Jesse, Will, Ollie and Rae sat at the dining room table discussing Christmas Eve. It was going to be different without Jeremiah.

Several days before Christmas, Jeremiah had always visited many families and carried hams, turkeys and plenty of flour and sugar. He left the food with the wives with instructions not to tell where the items came from. Many of the mothers with many children would cry and praise his goodness.

"I'm only the delivery man," he would say, but they all knew different.

On Christmas Eve, Jeremiah placed bag of toys on front porches for the smaller children. He always included peppermint sticks and fresh fruit. There would be clothes, boots, and sometimes a .22 rifle with shells for a teenage boy. Jeremiah always seemed to know what was needed and wanted in most of the households. He was the perfect Santa.

"Christmas Eve will be here before we know it. What are we going to do for out needy friends and neighbors? So many have depended on Santa to bring their children's toys," Miss Ollie said. "We can't just let Jeremiah's tradition die with him."

"We don't get around and visit people like Jeremiah did. How will we know what to leave each family, besides food, of course?" Jesse brows furrowed.

"I have an idea. Why don't we get Claire and Lucy to ask their pupils to write down what they would like for Santa to bring them," Rae suggested.

"That's a great idea. I'm going to need some material to make cloth dolls for many of the little girls. Rae, can you go to the dry goods store and get some for me?"

"Yes, and I will ask Mrs. Goodyear to watch some of the ladies shop while purchasing the things they need. Some of the wives like to look at pretty things, but never have the extra pennies to spend on themselves."

"Will, I'll get Jess to help me Christmas Eve with the deliveries. You will be needed at home, but Jess can open presents Christmas morning with Mary Beth."

"Now, you all listen to me," Ollie said firmly. "I want to use some of my money that Jeremiah left me to purchase all the extra food, toys, whatever is needed to make our community happy. It will be like he's still playing Santa," Ollie said, wiping the tears from her eyes.

****

Rae had visited Claire and Lucy a week earlier and asked them to get the children to write down what they would like for

Christmas. After completing her shopping, she stopped at the school to pick up the children's list. The ladies sat down in school desks and began reading the lists. Rae wiped her eyes and said to the girls. "Listen to this list."

"I *won't ask for anything for myself because my folks try so hard to give me all I need. I would love for you to bring my mama a new store-bought dress with a few undies. Mrs. Clause will know what I mean. My sister has never had a new doll to call her own. She plays with mine. Pa could use a fresh can of tobacco. He keeps dumping his old ashes back into the can and tries to reuse them. God Bless you dear Santa. Lily"*

"My goodness, this is so sweet. Claire, how old is Lily?"

'She eight." Claire said, shaking her head.

"Here's another one," Lucy said, holding the paper out to read to the others.

"*All I want is enough food to eat. Mommy serves us a good portion, but I go to bed every night hungry. Santa, you can bring my brother a ball and bat and my sister a new doll. She will love it. Love Mary.*"

"What wonderful children you have in your classes," Rae said.

"Now I know why Willa sets with Mary at lunch. She shares all of her extra food with her," Claire said. "Tell Hope to keep packing enough food for two."

"Some of these are very helpful. They write what someone else in their family needs, but this also gives me an idea what to get them, too." Rae picked the papers up and placed them in her tote bag.

Claire waddled over to the door to hug her mama bye. "Gosh, Claire, I believe you are further along than you suspected." Rae couldn't believe how much larger Claire had gotten in just a week.

"I see Doctor Tim tomorrow. I'm going to ask him. The baby sure moves a lot and keeps his foot under my ribs all the time," laughing, she rubbed her side.

****

Rae, Jesse and Jess nearly bought out the dry goods store and many items from the leather and gun shop. They placed all the items in the storeroom in the back of the barn. When Hank realized what the three of them were planning, he wanted to help. "I'll drive a wagon. I did help Jeremiah several times and I caught him one night placing a big bag on the Walkers' porch. When I asked what he was doing, he swore me to secrecy."

"We will be happy for you to help us. Tomorrow, we will drive to the back of the dry goods store and pick up the food. The Goodyear's have divided the food and fruit for each family. Miss Ollie has her sugar-cured hams all wrapped in cheese cloth. The turkeys have been dressed out at the butchers. He was thrilled with the big order. Anyway, we will deliver the food tomorrow after most of the men are out in the fields," Jesse said. "Rae and I will deliver to the church and many families, too."

"Why are you taking food to the church?" Hank asked.

"Sometimes, travelers stop by and ask for a handout. It is nice when the minister can give them something." Jesse said.

****

"Are you sure, Doctor Tim?" Claire couldn't believe that she could have her baby in January, if not sooner.

"You and Mary Beth might have your babies within weeks or days of each other. Your children will grow up together." Doctor Tim smiled broadly.

"Albert is going to be so surprised. His parents planned to come this spring in time for our baby's birth. With all the snow on the tracks up north, I'm afraid they will not be able to travel by train."

"I wouldn't tell them about your date changing. I could be wrong, and they might have to stay here months."

"Are you ever wrong -- when it comes to when a baby might come?" Claire asked, with great concern.

"No, not yet," he laughed, "but there's always a first time. Get dress and come in the kitchen with Hannah and me. We're about to have a noon snack."

After sharing a cup of tea and half a sandwich with Doctor Tim and Hannah, Claire rushed out of the office. Albert always took his lunch hour at home, and she wanted to be there when he arrived. What a surprise, she was going to have for him.

Chapter 40

Christmas was a wonderful time of year for the Maxwell's. With Willa and Jay big enough to enjoy Santa's gifts, it was fun to watch the surprised expressions on their faces. Next year the twins would be toddlers, most likely trying to destroy the Christmas tree.

Will gave Hope a beautiful gold necklace with a locket that opened up. He would take the family to Dallas this spring and have pictures made to fit inside it. He lifted her hair and placed it around her neck. He nuzzled her neck as she told him she loved him with all her heart. Will told her that he never got tired of hearing her say that.

Hope gave him a brand-new Mexican style saddle with his initials carved into the leather. It was a perfect saddle for the shiny, black stallion that he rode. He was very pleased and couldn't wait to saddle his horse, but he would wait until after all the presents were opened at Jesse's house.

****

It seemed forever that the tensing pains had been flowing through Mary Beth's body all night. Her back hurt so bad she could hardly sit down. She couldn't get comfortable anywhere. She walked the floor, a spasm made her grab her belly. She needed to go to the water closet because her bladder felt like she might burst. As she took a step, water flowed from her body onto the floor. She cried out to Jess, but she remembered he wasn't home yet. Being Christmas Eve, Jess had left earlier with his pa to carry special gifts and toys to the needed neighbors and friends.

Mary Beth was afraid because she didn't want to have her baby alone. As she attempted to change her gown, the front door banged. One look at her face was all it took. Jess assured her he would be right back with his mama, and he would get his pa to go get Doctor Tim and her mama.

Hours later, Mary Beth was comforted by all the women in her room. Rae and Ollie prepared Mary Beth's bed with layers of several oil cloths and put Mary Beth in it. Ollie asked Hank to go and get Justice. In a matter of two hours, Mary Beth saw the reassuring familiar faces of her papa and mama. She sighed with relief and lay back on her pillow.

Hannah stroked her hair, calming her wild-eyed fear with a soothing voice. "Don't worry, baby, we are here for you, and it won't be long now."

"Is Justice here?" Mary Beth asked, nearly in a panic when she didn't see her.

"Here I am child." Justice said, as she eased over to the side of the bed.

Mary Beth pulled Justice closer and asked in a whisper, "Did you bring me some of your special powders?"

"Yes," she said softly." Be still and open your mouth now," she said, as Hannah watched. "Lift your tongue and close your mouth. Just relax now." Justice smoothed her patient's long hair and smiled at her.

***

Once Mary Beth was relaxed and calm, Hannah asked Justice. "What did you give her?"

"Something I give all my special friends while they're in labor. It's a few magic seeds that I heard about from a mid-wife while living in New Orleans. They won't hurt her or the babe, but please," she said, "don't tell . . . him," she nodded toward Doctor Tim as he was preparing his instruments.

"Is that the reason Mary Beth wanted you to be here?"

"Yes. Hope told her that I helped with both of her babies. She had promised me that she wouldn't tell, but I guess she did anyway."

"I won't say anything. Even though she's a nurse, Mary Beth, has been very afraid of childbirth, but she is being very brave now. Thank you," Hannah said.

It wasn't long until the contractions built and swelled, leaving no rest between each one. Her pa said that the baby was coming. Someone placed her hands on the cold bedstead above her head and she grasped it.

In a matter of minutes, her mama said, "I see the crown. It's coming baby, just one more big push."

Mary Beth screamed and pushed. Sweating with tears flowing, she fell back on the pillow.

She wasn't aware of calling out to Jess. In the next second, the baby was out in her papa's large hands. Through tears, she watched as he wiped mucus out of her baby's mouth.

"You have a girl, Mary Beth. Just like you!" Doctor Tim wiped his eyes on his sleeve.

***

Justice and Ollie walked out of the room smiling at each other. "Another successful birth," Ollie said to her friend.

"Yes, and on Christmas Day, too."

Ollie noticed Jess leaning over with his hands on his knees. He was shaking his head, trying hard to stay awake. All night, he had helped his pa play Santa for many of the neighbors. He felt good about what he had done, but now he was exhausted and scared.

"Jess, you have a girl," Ollie said.

He jumped from his chair and hesitated. "Can I go to her now? Are they fine?"

"Fit as a fiddle, both of them. Hannah will come and get you in just a few minutes." Ollie smiled and sat down.

"Hank, will you take Justice home?"

"Be happy to as soon as I get to see the new baby," he said.

In the following hours, as Mary Beth slept, Rae and Ollie left to go home. They needed to get the ham in the oven and prepare all the other dishes for dinner. They would gather around the tree with Will, Hope and the children and open Christmas gifts from Jesse, Rae, Ollie and Hank. Around lunch time, Katie and her family would arrive.

Rae looked out the kitchen window and saw Albert and Claire driving into the front yard. "Hurry, Jesse, our daughter is here!" Rae laughed and rushed to the porch.

Albert slowly helped Claire down from the carriage. She doubled over as she placed her feet on the ground. "Are you all

243

right," Rae asked as she saw the very pale face of her daughter.

"No, something wrong, but I need to go to the water closet," she responded.

"Hank, go to Jess's and get Tim. Tell him that something is wrong with Claire. Tell him to hurry," Rae said, as she stood at the water closet door listening.

****

Back at Jess's home, Hannah asked him if he would go to their carriage and bring in the two large bags of Christmas gifts. While her husband was in the bedroom watching his daughter and his new grandchild sleep, Hannah was placing the gifts under the tree. She smiled thinking that this was going to be a wonderful first Christmas for Jess and Mary Beth.

As Jess was unhitching the horse from the carriage, he heard Hank calling to him. "Jess, tell Doctor Tim to come to Jesse's. Claire is in pain, or something."

Jess dropped the reins and rushed into the house. "Papa Tim, you're needed down at Jesse's. Something is wrong with Claire."

Tim tossed back his head and laughed. "Hannah, come with me. I'm sure its Claire's time. I told her last week she might deliver really soon."

Claire's labor was long and painful. She slept off and on during the day. Jesse's family opened their Christmas gifts and had a midmorning snack while waiting on the birth.

Katie and her family came for Christmas Eve dinner. As the ladies were placing the food on the table, a sharp scream came from the bedroom. Hannah rushed into the bedroom with Justice on her heels.

"Justice, help me," Claire cried, reaching her arms out to her.

Doctor Tim looked at Justice and then turned to Hannah. "Why does she want Justice?"

"Never mind. Go and get some coffee and allow Justice to visit with Claire. She'll calm her down."

"How?" He gave his wife a hard stare. "What is she going to do, that I can't?"

"Please, darling. Give us girls a few minutes—alone," Hannah said as she walked him to the bedroom door.

In a short while, Claire laid back on the bed and closed her eyes. She was beginning to relax. "Thank you, God, for Justice's

244

magic," she mumbled.

The Christmas dinner dishes were washed and put away. Everyone was sitting around in the front room waiting for another Maxwell grandchild to be born. Albert was a nervous wreck, but Jess, who had walked down to see how his sister was doing, placed his arm across Albert's shoulders and said, "Doctor Tim will take good care of her. He took wonderful care of Mary Beth and she is doing great—considering she just had our little girl."

"Thanks, Jess, but I wish it was me. She's in so much pain."

'Believe me, Albert, you don't want it to be you," he laughed. "God made women to have babies, not men, thank goodness."

"Albert!" Doctor Tim called. "If you want to hold Claire's hand you'd better come now. The babe is coming."

In a matter of minutes, Claire delivered a beautiful little girl. Albert fainted dead away. Hannah leaned down to make sure he was all right, while Ollie laughed so hard she nearly peed on herself.

Once the baby was cleaned and dressed, Rae carried the baby out to the front room so the family could see another wonderful Christmas Day miracle.

****

After breakfast the next day, Ollie wrapped a warm shawl around her shoulders. She picked up her bag of yarn and knitting needles and walked out the back door. Being careful with her footing, she walked up the hill to the Maxwell cemetery. The small yard inside the fence needed to be raked, but she would get the boys to clean it later. She walked over to the pretty wooden bench that Jess had built for her. He had even built a small wooden stool for her to put her feet upon. Doctor Tim had told her whenever she sat for a long period of time, to always lift her legs, if possible.

Jess had carved Jeremiah's name into the back of the bench which always gave her great comfort to lean her back against. As she looked around at the graves, she got settled on the bench.

"Good morning, my love," Ollie said, like she did each time she addressed Jeremiah. "Lord, I miss you so much." She sighed as sat still for a few minutes.

"We had a wonderful Christmas. Jesse and Jess took your place and delivered food and gifts to all your friends and needy neighbors. We knew that you would want us to do this for you,"

Ollie said as she laid her knitting down and wiped the tears that flowed. "One day I'm going to talk to you without crying, but I guess today is not the day," she laughed.

"I wish you could be here and see the most beautiful babies. Mary Beth and Claire both had little girls yesterday. Can you believe that? Both born on Christmas Day. Our Tim had his hands full, but what a blessing. The little ones will grow up and probably be best friends."

She clicked the needles together and smiled over at the grave. "Maybe tomorrow they will have named the little miracles. Oh, you should see how Willa wants to mother the little ones."

Click, click, the needles flew together, bringing the lovely yarn together. "You know, my love, my birthday is tomorrow. Do you remember driving me to Waverly Plantation to place flowers on Patricia Waverly's grave? We both had the same birthday. I will always remember how sweet you were to me on that trip."

Ollie placed her needles down and stared off into space. "I am trying to be happy, but it's so hard not being able to touch your hand or bring you another cup of hot coffee. Believe me, I have enough to keep my mind off you, but when something special happens, I want to share it with you like Hope's twins sitting up and eating at the table now. Willa is such a good mother to her little brother and sister. She is so much like our precious Hope.

"Oh, I want to tell you about Justice. Doctor Tim almost caught her giving her magic seeds to Claire," she laughed. "That's a story for another time."

"Well, my love, I best go back to the house. Those clouds look bad, but I'll be back very soon," she said, gathering her knitting. Ollie came as often as the weather permitted to visit with her husband, best friend and confidant. She kept him informed about the daily lives of the Maxwell's, Katie's family and their close friends. Just sitting on the new bench, in memory of Jeremiah, brought her great joy. She needed to get back to the house and warm all the leftovers and feed her wonderful Maxwell family lunch. Caring for her family is what she did best.

****

Late that night after the terrible rainstorm, Jesse and Rae laid in each other's arms. "You know,' Rae said softly, "I never appreciated this big, lovely bedroom before. After learning from

Miss Ollie that your father had it built just for your mama makes it very special. With each board and nail, he only had thoughts of making her happy. It is a shame that she didn't want to share it with him."

"I know that I never spoke to you about my mama. It's because she wasn't happy, and I never understood why she wasn't. I watched my Pa try to love her, but she would only run to this room and slam the door. I know now that she really was sick," he turned over to face his lovely wife. "I guess we all learned something from Ollie while she recited her tall tales." Grinning, he pulled Rae closer, "How do you feel love? Are you too tired tonight?"

"You should know by now I can never say no to you."

He chuckled ruefully, "I do have my charm."

Epilogue

The following Sunday after church, everyone met at
Jesse's ranch to celebrate Miss Ollie's eighty birthday. Rae
wouldn't allow Ollie to cook breakfast or prepare lunch. "Today is
your day. Why don't you go and visit Jeremiah for a while like you
do each Sunday."

While Ollie was at the cemetery, all the family arrived. The
girls all brought a covered dish while Hank and Will fried fish they
had caught the day before. Mr. Downey and Bud joked and
laughed with the men as they battered and fried the fish. Once in a
while, Bud would pretend to catch one of the children as the
played tag near the barn.

Willa was a great babysitter. She made Boo and Jay help play
with Rosie's girls until dinner was served.

After the delicious meal and before the cake was cut, Hope said
she had an announcement. Every head turned to see Will's face go
pale, but he pretended to look happy.

Hope burst out laughing. "No, I am not going to have another
child, yet," she added playfully. "Our precious daughter is going to
sing a song she wrote for Miss Ollie. So everyone please give
Willa your undivided attention."

After Willa belted out her song, she ran to Miss Ollie's open
arms. "Thank you, my precious child," she said, wrapping Willa in
her big white apron."

Claire and Mary Beth sat on the sofa with their new babies on
their laps. Both infants slept while the men gathered outside to
look over the new stock. Jesse had received new horses that he had
purchased to train. His dream one day was to have a horse ranch
and it looked as if it was coming true.

Ollie began to clean the table when Rae and Hope jumped in.

Let's go and sit in the big room and leave these things for later.

Ollie sat in her rocker while Hannah and Rae rested at her feet. Hannah laid her head over in Ollie's lap and said, "Miss Ollie, remember when we were sitting, just like this, on your birthday, years ago. You were rubbing my long hair and you asked me when I was going to let Tim catch me?" She lifted her face and smiled up at Ollie. "I told you that I had told him Christmas Eve that I loved him."

"Child, I remember that day very well. I knew my boy was starry-eyed over you from the first time he brought you to meet us. He couldn't visit with us for watching your ever move"

Ollie looked down at Rae. "Just like Jesse and you, Rae. You both fought with each other all the time until I locked you together in the cellar. Man, you two destroyed the cellar, but it wasn't long after that you and Jesse had a beautiful wedding. My prayers were answered because I loved you and Hope so much.

For years, I prayed that my baby boy, Will, would realize that he was only waiting for Hope to grow up and marry her. Those two had always fought like cats and dogs but I knew they loved each other."

Ollie leaned back in her rocker and smiled. "I remember many wonderful things about each of you and I will carry all my cherish memories to my grave. **Each of you, and the others, have been my world.**"

The End

For Get Me Not – Winged Publication, Where Stories take Flight

Proudly Announces

Story Untitled

Linda Sealy Knowles

Coming Spring, 2023

The following is a preview of my new book . . .

Prologue

"Please, Papa, don't ask me to honor your wish. I don't love him, and I can hardly bare to be in the same room with him. Please, I will do anything you want, but not that," Jocelyn buried her face into the mattress of her dying father's bed.

'My daughter, I'm so sorry,' his words were barely spoken above a whisper. 'If you do this one thing for me, I can go to my maker, a happy man. I'll know you will be well-taken care of. You will live in the lifestyle that I have always given you,' Mr. James Norwood mummied, struggling to breathe.

'Please Papa, tell me what you have done? 'The last time we spoke about my future, you never said anything about not having money for my dowry.' Jocelyn wiped tears from her face and held her papa's hand close.

'I gambled it all away. I had a full house, but Luke beat me with four aces. I kept betting money that I didn't have, so I had to sign an IOU. Now, the banker wants his money, but all I have is this house and land.'

'Why do I have to marry the banker's son?' What does that have to do with your gambling?'

'Mr. Sullivan, the banker, says he will pay my debt off if you marry his son. I told him you would agree.'

'Oh, Papa, how could you use me like this. I want to please you, but I don't believe I can this time." Jocelyn glanced around at her lovely surroundings. This house was a mansion. The governor had even asked to purchase this home place.

"Come closer, child. I don't have long on this earth. You must tell me now that you will obey me."

'I can't Papa, I can't. Please don't make me do this . . . Papa? Papa! 'Get the doctor quick. 'Oh, Papa, I will, I will marry.'

'I love you. . . . Josh.'

Jocelyn's pleads not to marry fell on deaf ears. She was in mourning for her papa, and it was customary to wait a year. Since Willard Sullivan was a well-known businessman in the town, she felt he would allow her time to get over her papa's death.

Mr. Sullivan had no patience and demanded that she marry his son in two weeks, or he would toss her out on the street, penniless.

While Marie, her personal maid, dressed her in her lovely wedding dress, she cried.

"Please Miss Jocelyn. Don't cry. You'll ruin your beautiful face."

"Oh, Marie, I can't help it. I had rather care for myself than let that creep put his hands on me." Slamming her hand over her mouth, "I'm going to throw up," she raced to the bathroom.

Someone knocked on the bedroom door and Marie opened it. Mr. Sullivan stood in the doorway and asked if the bride was ready. Marie begged for just one more minute.

Marie knocked on the bathroom door and when she didn't receive an answer, she eased open the door. A beautiful wedding dress covered the floor and the bathroom window stood wide open. Jocelyn had fled. Marie smiled and strolled slowly to the bedroom door to give the groom's father the unpleasant news.

Chapter 1

In the town of Midland, about fifty miles north of Perryville, Texas, Jocelyn stood in front of a bulletin board. She pulled her bonnet closer to her face as she viewed a poster which read, *"Brides wanted in Amarillo, Texas. The bridegroom will pay for a contract. Sign up on the 2nd floor of the Freedom Hotel on Main Street. George Campbell."*

Jocelyn eased away from the notice and sauntered down the old wooden boardwalk. She tried to remember how much money she had at the hem of her shift. While waiting to marry the banker's son, Marie, her maid, had helped her sell her mother's treasured items. They sold over two hundred dollars' worth of paintings and small figurines. This fund helped her to escape Perryville without being seen. While plotting her escape, she had hidden a carpet bag with small items that she might need. Careful not to remove anything from the house that would be noticeable, she packed some of Marie's dresses and a few pieces of her mother's jewelry to have as keep sakes. She dressed in Marie's clothes and purchased a ticket on the Pacific Railroad to Midland, Texas. She didn't dare use all her money, so Midland was a reasonable distance away.

Being careful, she strolled to the café on the corner to get some dinner. Posters about her disappearance were nailed on many posts. She felt like a criminal, and she would be treated like one, if caught. On the other hand, a reward was offered for any information as to her whereabouts.

Sitting at a table in the corner of the café, three young women were discussing the wagon train that would carry the brides to Amarillo. They were three beauties who didn't need to marry someone sight unseen, but listening to their conversations, they wanted to get away--just like her.

"We'll sleep in a covered wagon or on the ground and have to cook our own meals," one girl said.

"I can't cook! My ma did all the cooking, but I had to do everything else. I'll never go back home. My Pa has hit me his last time," another girl swore.

"I can't wait to get going," the last girl finally spoke. "I'm sure my brothers are looking for me now. And I don't want to be discovered, so I'd better return to our room."

All three of the young ladies left the café. Jocelyn looked around the place and noticed that she was the last customer. A large, robust woman walked up to her table. "What'll you have, honey?"

"A bowl of soup and a ham sandwich, please."

"Have you signed up to be a bride on the wagon train that's leaving in the morning?" She asked when she returned from the kitchen with Jocelyn's order.

"No, but I must admit that I was thinking about it."

"Me, too. I want to get out of that hot kitchen and find a nice man to take care of me," the woman said. Jocelyn didn't think this woman needed a man to care for her. She stood nearly six feet tall and was as round as a barrel. Her hair was her best feature. She wore it braided on top of her head like a crown.

"I would love to go, but I don't intend to be a bride. I don't want to be tied to a stranger for the rest of my life I can take care of a home and cook for a rancher and his hands."

"What happens when the man finds out that you don't intend to honor the contract?"

"I'll like to think he would understand," she chuckled.

The large woman sat down in the chair across from Jocelyn. "How would you like for me to travel with you to Amarillo? We can look out for each other. It's gonna be a hard rugged trip, but I can drive a team of mules and I have cooked over a fire many times. I don't believe a pretty gal like you has ever done any hard labor, am I right?"

Well, I'm not as fragile as I look. My mama taught me to take care of our home, working beside our hired help. She insisted that our cook teach me. Mostly, she wanted me to stand on my own feet and never depend on a man to survive. As a result, I am educated, a good cook, I can care for livestock, sew, and make my own clothes. So you see, I'm not helpless just because I have a pretty face."

"Mercy, I admit I was wrong about you, but I know it's' not safe to travel alone. Myself, I will feel better having you as a traveling companion. My pa never allowed me to go to school, so I can't read. You'll be able to help me understand what I'm getting myself into," Sadie laughed. "I'm like you, somewhat. I don't want to marry any yahoo, just because he paid for a bride."

Jocelyn wiped her mouth and placed the napkin down on the table. "Well, I believe if you and I get accepted to travel on the bride's train, we'll make a good team. If you're sure you want to go, we better find the hotel, and hope that George fellow will let us travel with the others.

"That a girl! I need to tell Henry that I have to run an errand. By the way, my name is Sadie Rowe."

"My name is . . . . 'J'," she smiled at Sadie and both of them laughed.

****

The girls knocked on the George Campbell's hotel door. As they entered, Mr. Campbell was sitting behind a large wooden desk. He surveyed the two girls from their heads to their toes before offering them a seat.

"What can I do for you ladies? Do you want to travel on my bridal train and marry up with a cowboy in Amarillo," he said shifting his cigar from one side of his mouth to the other. 'Well, speak up. I ain't got all day."

My name is Sadie Rowe. I do want to sign up to go with you. I'm a cook over at the City Café and I'm ready for a change."

"Yes. . . . I've seen you there. Food is good, but you look too old to snag a husband."

"Mr. Campbell, I don't appreciate you speaking to my friend in that manner. Sadie is not an old woman. She's just tired of working twelve hours every day. Older men will appreciate a woman who can cook and take care of their home."

"I'm sorry, Miss Rowe. I didn't mean to be rude, please forgive me." Mr. Campbell really liked the young woman who was with the older woman. She would be a prize for any man in Amarillo and he didn't want her to change her mind about signing on his train.

"What about you, young lady? Are you ready to travel on my bridal train? I can assure you that I have many men willing to pay your passage, that is, if you can make the long, hard trip."

"I assure you, Mr. Campbell, I am stronger than I look. But,

254

there is one thing that you have to understand before I sign your contract."

"What can that be? It's a straightforward contract that states you will agree to marry the man that I choose for you. The gentleman will pay me your passage before you marry."

"That is just it. I don't intend to be a bride. I want to travel with you, but not as a bride-to-be."

"Look lady, I ain't giving no free ride to Amarillo. I'm only taking willing women who intend to marry. I furnish each wagon with plenty of beans, potatoes, flour, lard and sugar. Barrels of water will be tied on the sides of the wagons. So, I can't afford freeloaders," he stood and gave them a mean look. "Besides, I have many men who have waited months for a wife. If you don't want to marry, then go and catch the train or the stagecoach to take you wherever."

Jocelyn sighed and turned to Sadie. "Don't let my decision keep you from traveling with Mr. Campbell. I'm sure some man will be looking for a nice lady who can cook and is a hard worker. I was hoping to get a good job as a cook on maybe a farm or ranch, but it looks like I will have to get a job as a hotel maid—for now."

"I don't want to go without you," Sadie said. "Please Mr. Campbell, you said my friend is a beauty. You can see she's an innocent, decent lady. Any man would love to have her working for them—whether she'll marry or not."

***

Mr. Campbell stood and walked to his window. He looked down on the street and watched the people rushing from one side to the other. He remembered his conversation with Matt Colburn and how he only wanted a woman to cook on his ranch. Finally, he looked at Jocelyn and declared. "Well, there's one man who said he didn't care what his bride looked like if only she can cook. He has a ranch, and he has needed a good cook for months. I don't think he wanted to get married. But Amarillo has very few women so he hired a man to cook and the ranch hands nearly lynched him for burning the food all the time. This man I am thinking about is a tough young man. He has a fierce temper and I found him hard to deal with."

Mr. Campbell thought for a minute. "Look, if the rancher doesn't like you, maybe you can work on his ranch until you pay off your passage. He would have a new cook for a few months and get his money back, too."

Mr. Campbell chuckled. "Once Matt gets a good look at you, he will most likely want to marry. He would be crazy not to. He's a strange fellow, so who knows what he might do." He sized Jocelyn up again and finally leaned back in his chair.

"On the wagon train, you must pull your weight. There will only be a few men and they are traveling to protect the train from bandits, rustlers, and drunken, rowdy men who want to rob, steal, and have fun with the women. They will hunt for fresh meat and share it with the women. The men don't drive the wagons or care for the livestock. The women do everything. What do you think about these rules?"

***

"I agree with your rules as long as it's in my contract, that I will not be a bride." Jocelyn turned to Sadie, "What do you think?"

"I feel the same about marrying," Sadie gave Mr. Campbell a hard stare.

"Fine! I will have your contracts ready to sign in the morning, but you must keep your traps shuts about the conditions that I am granting you both."

Jocelyn and Sadie smiled and hurried out of the office on to the boardwalk. "You got any money, Jocelyn?"

"Yes, I have some. Why?"

"We need to go and purchase a few personal supplies for the trip. We need some men britches to wear under our skirts. They will make moving around on the trail so much easier. We need to get some medical supplies in case we get scratched, cut or bit by a critter."

"Goodness, Sadie, how do you know so much about what is needed?"

"My folks traveled a lot before my pa decided to settle down. My ma wore my older brother's pants and shirts, and she always had bandages to care for wounds. So, let's learn from her and take care of ourselves."

"Let's go, and I need to purchase a few undies because I left home so fast I didn't take time to pack," Jocelyn remarked as they headed to the dry goods store."

"So, like some other girls, you're a runaway from home?"

Sadie asked.

"Let's just say I had to leave, but I will tell you about my life while on the trail. I'm not wanted by the law, so don't fret about my personal life—for now."

Chapter 2

The following morning, Mr. Campbell had his clerk assign the ladies their wagons. They were told to go to the corral and get four mules and hitch them to their wagon. Sadie smiled and reached for Jocelyn's arm. "Come on gal, let's show these men that we can take care of ourselves. We'll choose four strong mules and lead them to our wagon. You hold their heads while I hitch them. I haven't had to do this in a long time, but I haven't forgotten."

Once the big mules were hitched, Sadie and Jocelyn carried water to each mule and gave them a apple treat. "Now, I know why you purchased a bushel of apples," Jocelyn laughed.

If you treat your animals well, they will gladly follow your instructions," Sadie said. I learned this from my pa.

Sadie watched a man herd about ten milk cows by their wagon. "I can milk cows, too. Maybe, we can get a reduced price for a pint of milk each day, if I help with the milking. What do you think?"

When Jocelyn didn't response, she noticed the scare look on Jocelyn's face. She was as pale as a ghost. "What's wrong, gal? Are you sick?"

"No, I have to hide," she whispered. "See those men? I believe they are looking for me." She began to shake.

Sadie saw the three men looking around and then glanced their way. Sadie recognized the sheriff of Midland, but the other two men were strangers. "Come quick, get in the wagon."

"That's the first place they will look," Jocelyn pulled away from Sadie.

"Come on now and get inside. They'll never find you as she pulled the front and back curtains closed. Sadie lifted boards from the floor. There was a hidden crawl space between the bottom and top floors. "Get in and lay on your stomach. You'll be able to breath. I am going to sit boxes on top of you."

Jocelyn lay down into the bottom of the wagon. She could hear the men talking to the sheriff about looking in their wagon.

"What are you fellows looking for?" Sadie asked, as the sheriff pulled back the curtain at the end."

'We're searching for a young lady that ran away from home.'
'Where'd she run from?' Sadie pretended to be interested.
'Perryville, Texas. Ever heard of it?'
"Sure, I lived in that small town when I was a young'un. Who is the girl you looking for—maybe I know her folks."
'Her people are dead. She's a runaway bride, you might say," chuckled one of the young men.
'Mark, keep your remarks about our client to yourself. It's no one's business who we are searching for."
'Sorry,' he said, as he moved closer to Sadie. 'I just found it funny that the gal ran away from a rich fiancé," he whispered.
"All right sheriff, we're burning daylight," Mr. Campbell said. "Besides, I don't remember signing on a gal with the description that you gave me. So, we will be pulling out in ten minutes."

***

Sadie climbed on the wagon bench and clicked to the lead mule to move out. The team followed the wagon in front. Mr. Campbell rode up beside Sadie and said, "Miss Rowe, take care of my valuable cargo." He gave her a wink and rode away.

Once the three men had ridden away from the wagon train, Sadie gave the lead mule its head, and quickly remove the boards and helped Jocelyn from the crawl space. "You all right honey?"

"Yes, thanks for your help." She brushed the dust from her clothes. "Do you have spices stored in here? I could smell garlic, or something like that?"

"Yep, when I told Henry I was leaving, he fixed me a box of things I could use on the trail. He gave me twenty pounds of dried beans, and a small basket of eggs, a container of sugar, jars of jam, and white lard for baking. And look, he even gave me this big black skillet."

"It looks like we will be set for a while. Let's go and being our new live."

***

The first day was long and hard for two women who had not worked outside in years. Jocelyn worked outside when she chose to in her mother's flower garden. She wore a big bonnet to keep the sun from touching her soft white skin.

Sadie worked in Henry Jerkins' café for five years. She walked to work before sunrise and home in the moonlight. The hardest work she did was to help the Chinese man wash dishes or mop the kitchen floor.

Both ladies took turns driving the wagon. Once they stopped for the mid-day meal, Sadie watered the mule, while Jocelyn built a fire and put on the coffee. Sadie set up a small table that she tossed in with her supplies and whipped up griddle cakes to eat with strawberry jam.

The three ladies that they had seen in the café two days ago, walked over to Sadie and watched her cook. "Those flapjacks sure smell good. Do you think you can share a couple for use?"

"First of all, these are called griddle cakes. Ain't much in them but flour, sugar, eggs and milk. You gals can cook them without any trouble."

"Wish that was true, but I can only cook soup. You know where you toss everything in a big pot and let it stew of the fire for hours," Janet, the younger girl said.

"That's more than I ever cooked. My ma made me work outside with my pa. Oh, I cleaned and mopped the house, but she never let me work in the Kitchen," Martha spoke, sadly.

"To tell you the truth, Miss Sadie, out of the three of us, Janet is the only one that knows anything about cooking," Tony said, as she walked over and sat on a stump.

"What did you plan on telling your new man about cooking for him?" Sadie asked.

"Surprise?" All three girls said in unity and laughed.

Said looked at the girls and shook her head in disbelief. "All right, if Jocelyn doesn't mine, I will cook for all of us, and you can take turns in helping me. That way I can teach each of you to cook before we get to Amarillo." Mattie gave each gal a plate, but she quickly said, "I'll need your supplies to help with the food."

"Of course. Just let us know when you need something and one of us will bring it over.

"After we eat, we clean our dishes, put things back in the wagon, and secure the fire. We'll work as a team." Sadie looked at each girl.

The girls wanted to help Sadie clean up, but she told them that Jocelyn would help today. I'm going to soak some dried beans while we travel the rest of the day and tomorrow night, I will cook them. I ain't a gourmet cook, but you won't go hungry."

"Did you water your mules?" Sadie asked.

"Yes, Janet did that as soon as we stopped," Tonya replied.

Jocelyn, these girls want to share our meals and fire while we are traveling. They can't cook, so I'm going to try and give them a few lessons so their new man won't starve. Do you mind if they join us?"

"No, I don't mind." Jocelyn looked at the girls. "While in the café, I believe I overheard one of you say that you were running away from home. Will we need to hide you," she looked at each girl, "if we get another search party like we had this morning?"

"Me." Martha said. "My brothers are probably looking for me. But, I am not going back. I'm tired of being tossed in the cellar for days, just because I smiled at a man in town. My pa is mean, but my brothers follows his orders."

"You don't have to be afraid." Sadie said, putting her arms around the sad girl. "We will all protect you."

Linda Sealy Knowles is originally from Saraland/Satsuma, Alabama. Linda wrote her first novel in 2013, and since then she has written fifteen books. Who would have ever thought that she would write so many love stories? After completing a story, she is joyful and sad at the same time. Her characters are like family and wonderful friends, and it's sad to write, The End. God has blessed Linda, and she enjoys sharing her stories with her readers.

Made in the USA
Middletown, DE
30 January 2023

22657318R00156